SOUTH BAY

A James Gardiner Mystery

Michael Wolf

Published by Famous Shamus Books

ISBN: 9798218821685
LCCN: 2025922273

Edited by: Heidi Stangeland
Cover Art and Design by: Guy Vasilovich

For Jungja
-and her unwavering support

Acknowledgements

The first book is supposed to be the hardest. It's the one where you learn from your mistakes. It's the one where you learn how to write, not just in putting words down on paper, but in disciplining yourself to push through the droughts of inspiration. I found this, my second literary adventure, to be more difficult, but in different ways. I now had a goal to surpass, a time to beat, a benchmark to measure my next attempt against. I'm happy with this book. I hope you will be, too.

Again, a special thanks to Guy Vasilovich for another excellent cover design. And a big thank you to Heidi Stangeland for her help in getting this book out on the market. And, finally, an extra special thanks to Detective Greg Gomez for his fine expertise in steering me straight on the ins and outs of the world of law enforcement in Los Angeles.

OTHER TITLES BY MICHAEL WOLF

The James Gardiner Series

SOL CANYON

Memory is the mother of all wisdom - Aeschylus

PROLOGUE

It's funny how the mind works sometimes. Important things - events in your life that you would expect to be seared into your memory banks for all eternity – often struggle to come into focus when you try to recall them. Meanwhile, trivial things rise unbidden into your conscious mind at the oddest times. I sometimes thought of my brain as just an attic full of these mostly useless bits of memories and information, dimly lit and covered in dust and cobwebs. Well, maybe not an attic; perhaps a junkyard would be a more accurate description, or maybe still, a pawn shop, or a curio shop of exotic and interesting, but still largely inconsequential things. But hey, I'm not yet even thirty. God only knows what little shop of horrors will be crammed into my brain when I am old.

I would probably be great at Trivial Pursuit. If I had any friends who would play with me, that is. Though I considered myself more of a *Jeopardy!* guy. I didn't need friends to battle the nightly TV contestants. I loved *Jeopardy!* Alex was great, but I was still partial to Art Fleming and the original episodes. I always got a kick out of seeing the board with the prize money starting at only $10, $20 in *Double Jeopardy!* Back then, one could easily take the round with less than $1,000 in winnings.

As I sat in my office, well past midnight, digging into my second pint of Cherry Garcia, I listened to the sounds of Hollywood Boulevard drifting up through the open window. A warm spring breeze riffled the crime scene photos scattered on top of my desk – pictures of blood-streaked knives and bone saws, luminol-spattered bathtubs and dark fuzzy stills of a large man in a hoodie tossing black trash bags filled with who knows what into a dumpster, and a pretty blonde in a polka dot dress and straw hat standing on the beach.

I looked up at the bookshelf across the room, lined with detective novels that I'd moved to the office months back, not to reread in my copious free time, but to remember. The *Big Sleep, The Maltese Falcon,* hundreds more. What would Marlow do in this case, or Spade for that matter? They would not be pinning pictures on a board and connecting them with colored string, that's for sure.

Fortunately, it wasn't too hot and I didn't need my unreliable window unit. While poring over police reports and court transcripts of an old murder case, *Jeopardy!* kept me company. I had it playing on my laptop in the background. I wasn't really paying attention, but occasionally a clue would break through into my conscious mind and I would reflexively spout out the answer, framed as a question, of course.

"What is a McGuffin?" I'd say without looking up.

"That is correct." Art would reply. And the contestant would continue, "I'll take Hitchcock for fifty, Art."

The old case I was reading up on was a grisly murder trial down in the Beach Cities. Someone I once knew from my high school days had contacted me and asked me to look into it, re-investigate it, if you will. But as I looked at the photos and read the notes and details of the original investigation, my mind would wander back to that summer. The summer twelve years ago, between my junior and senior year in high school – the best summer ever.

The beach cities of South Bay – Manhattan, Hermosa, and Redondo – were an Eden unlike any other. Just south of the LAX airport and north of the Palos Verdes Peninsula, these three quaint little towns were an island paradise hidden in a big city. They sported wide, empty beaches that stretched for miles, mostly empty due to the city's planned scarcity of public parking, which meant that they were almost exclusive to the locals.

At the southern end, Redondo was the more touristy of the three due to its big commercial pier and marina. Manhattan, to the north, was more of a rich man's bedroom community and home to various sports celebrities. Hermosa in the middle was the funkiest of the three. Not that long ago, it used to be a beach hangout for bikers and hippies. It's been mostly cleaned up now, gentrified, and priced accordingly. But that's still where most of the fun bars were and where more of the older kids hung out back then. Being too young to get served in the bars, my peers and I mostly partied in private houses up and down the Strand.

We partied hard, too. Surfing at the break of dawn, which builds up an appetite, followed by a big breakfast, then getting high and lying on the beach till noon. Lunch was burgers and beer, or tacos and beer, or pizza and beer. After lunch, it was beach volleyball, paddle tennis (a variation of tennis and precursor to pickleball), or biking and roller-blading up and down the Strand. The Strand was a wide bike path and walkway that separated the beach from the beachfront houses. It was the Times Square of beach life. After sports came Happy Hour.

That's when the serious drinking started and the serious socializing. The athletics were mostly a guy thing. The girls would sit around in their barely-there bikinis, oiled up and smelling like coconut. They would lounge around and watch, making lewd or snarky remarks about the boys and giggling to one another. Once the drinking started and the parties moved indoors, the girls got off their blankets and joined in the fun. There would be poker games, backgammon and darts, or pics as the snootier players would call them, billiards and ping-pong if tables were to be had. The music would be cranked up and some would dance. There was also a lot of flirting and lots of stoned, pseudo-serious, deep conversations. I flashed on a memory of a cute blond girl in a white cotton crochet dress reading my Tarot cards, surrounded by candles. The partying would go on past sundown and late into the night, until we passed out.

Next morning, a quick dip in the Pacific would clear up all but the worst of hangovers, and the fun would start all over again. It seemed like an endless summer. Nowadays, my summers seem to flash by in the blink of an eye.

I brushed those memories aside, pushed back in my chair and looked again across the room at the bookcase. I wasn't much for decorating, but over the years it had accumulated enough stuff to fill all the empty spaces between my books: a couple of German ceramic steins, my replica Maltese Falcon, a golf trophy, various paddle tennis and table tennis paddles, a chess set with the men set up in their starting positions, and a backgammon set, folded up in its case and squeezed into a corner of the shelf. Those were probably my only mementos of that summer at the beach. I wasn't much for taking pictures. Live in the moment was my motto then.

Pictures would be nice now, though. But these days I collect other things, like a hundred or more crime novels and detective stories. In my first few years in business here, I found I had a lot of free time to read.

I glanced down again at the folders, files, and papers strewn across my desktop. I slapped my hand down on a few that had started to blow away in the evening breeze. Curious crime scene photos, but with no victim outline in chalk on the floor; dark, blurry pictures from a too-distant, cheap, closed-circuit TV camera, and a general lack of evidence left me bewildered. There was something in this mess that I wasn't seeing, a clue that I was overlooking. My gut told me it was there, if only I could concentrate long enough to find it. My other gut told me that maybe I didn't want to find it. A queasiness that maybe was related to something personal that happened that summer that I can't quite remember or don't want to remember, but that still nags at me after all these years.

As I re-read through the notes again, my mind kept drifting back to that hedonistic summer after my high school junior year, goofing off, drinking, smoking, and chasing girls, or rather chasing one girl in particular.

CHAPTER

ONE

My name is James Gardiner. I'm a private investigator and all of thirty years old. My first real case garnered me my Andy Warhol five minutes of fame when it exploded across the front pages last summer. Since then, it has been a lot less glamorous as I busied myself with the more mundane insurance and fraud cases that pay the bills. But heck, it sure beats working for a living.

Rachel and I had been in this on-again, off-again relationship for the past year. She thought I was funny but not serious about life, or at least not serious enough for her to get serious about me. And I was okay with that. I tried to oblige the funny part with my never-ending repertoire of corny jokes, though one could easily misconstrue my cringey attempt at humor as a misguided attempt to be endearing or maybe even auditioning to be a husband and dad. I had the 'Dad Jokes and Painful Puns Book' down pat.

Rachel was a blind date my mother had arranged after properly screening her for good genes, the right family background, and otherwise promising prospects as a wife. As far as mother was concerned, she checked all the boxes – a fellow Stanford alum, Law school, passed the bar with a top one percent score, and now works at one of those fancy Dewey, Cheetham and Howe firms in Century City. She was tall, maybe five ten, slender and fit, with shoulder-length brown hair. She was pretty, with a bit of a regal, princess air. I got more disapproving looks than smiles from her, it seemed. A few weeks earlier, I had taken her to a chili festival. I did try to mix it up on our date nights. Dinner at a fancy tasting menu restaurant can get tedious, no matter how many Michelin stars they have.

It was late morning and the marine layer was just starting to burn off. Soon, there would not be a cloud in the sky and it would be just another warm, sunny California day. We were driving down to Manhattan Beach with my other gal, Lola, my shiny two-toned, turquoise and cream, '57 Mercury Marquis convertible; she was topless today, with a matching vinyl interior, glistening white wall tires, and chrome in all the right places. I took the Marina Freeway and got off on Culver Boulevard. I could immediately taste the salt in the air as we neared the ocean. I cut through the Ballona Wetlands to the beach. In Northern California, the shore is pretty rugged. The ocean crashes ashore against a wall of tumbled boulders beneath towering cliffs. In southern California, the shoreline is mostly one long, wide sandy beach from Santa Barbara to San Diego. Past the wetlands, we cruised down Vista Del Mar, the beach road. It skirted past the airport, a water treatment plant, and an oil refinery before popping out into multi-million-dollar neighborhoods. The ocean today was a glistening blue, just a shade different from the sky. A steady stream of white crested waves fell upon the sand and then retreated. You could smell the salt in the air. On the horizon, a parade of container ships and tankers headed toward the harbor in Long Beach. Manhattan Beach was generally considered the sleepiest of the three beach towns down here in the South Bay, with fewer tourists and fewer bars, but more boutiques and fancy restaurants. Once a year, though, those bars got together to put on an amazing chili cook-off.

The taste testing and voting were to be staged at Fire House #1. The trucks were moved out of the Apparatus Bay, and tables and signs filled the empty space. We were running late; the event started at noon, and I feared that all the best chili would be gone before we arrived. Maybe running late paid off for us though, as we found a parking spot that someone had just vacated right across the street from the Fire House.

The place was still packed as we made our way in. With the bay doors wide open, the aroma of beef, cumin, and chili peppers greeted you like the warm embrace of a favorite but crazy relative. I glanced at Rachel to gauge her reaction. She still looked skeptical, glancing warily around the room.

"I thought you said you liked chili."

"I've been known to warm up a can when I didn't feel like cooking." She replied with a side-long glance.

"This is not hamburger and kidney beans with a cup of tomato sauce thrown in like your mother used to make."

"My mother didn't cook."

"Okay, fine. But that's not chili. Here is chili. Brown chili, red chili, green chili, white chili, even black chocolate chili. You've got your chicken chili, beef, pork, lamb, maybe even some buffalo or venison if we're lucky. You're going to taste chili like you've never tasted before. About the only thing missing is the heat."

"I do like a little kick to my food where appropriate."

"They tend to leave it mild for the general public. You know, people bring their kids to these things."

The girl at the admission table took our entrance fee and handed us each a bottle of water, a golf pencil, and a paper ballot that listed all the competing entries. The tables, each covered with a red and white checkered paper tablecloth and a poster board sign displaying the name of the bar or restaurant, were arranged in a serpentine pattern that led you past every contestant, although you could jump around if you had a mind to.

"I've been to a lot of chili festivals, cook-offs, what have you," I explained. "They are mostly bland concoctions of beans, tomatoes, and chili powder with a little hamburger thrown in to keep Kosher. This - this is the best in So-Cal. You will be impressed. I guarantee it."

The first table featured a burnt ends chili with lots of smoky sweet flavor, whipped up by a bar from the north end of town. The gal behind the pot ladled a good-sized tasting into a paper cup and stuck in one of those little wooden tasting spoons you see at ice cream shops.

"What do you think?" I asked after a first bite.

Rachel savored a bit for a minute, licking her lips when she was done. "It's kind of half barbecue and half chili. I like it." She admitted.

"Yeah, it's not bad. Reminds me of this kick ass chili place that used to be down in Hermosa, called Chili Queen. They had all kinds of chilis, ten different ones every day. They ranked them from one to ten, from mild to smoke coming out of your ears. They had all kinds of toppings and sides to go with, too. Too bad it's closed now."

"If it was that good, why did it close?"

"I heard the owner died. No one else had her passion to keep it going."

We moved on. Most tables offered chips or oyster crackers to munch on and cleanse the palate between samples. Others had grated cheese or scallion toppings to dress up their offerings. I grabbed a handful of crackers as we made our way to the next table.

"I usually try to rate them as I go. Like a one-to-five scale with a note to remember what was what. At the end, we get to vote our top three favorites and stuff our ballot in the box."

"Sounds simple enough."

"Oh, I think you'll find it will be a tough choice to make."

Rachel wiped her mouth again with a napkin. "I don't think my lipstick will make it past the next table."

As there was a bit of a line backed up at the next chili station, I took a moment to gaze around the facility. The high ceiling and big windows gave the room a bright, outdoorsy feel. Through the rear bay doors, I could see they had moved the trucks to the rear parking lot. Firemen dressed in full gear were posing for pictures and helping little kids climb onto their tiller-truck, the one with the rear-wheel driver cab. On another pumper, a kid manned the water cannon and pretended to spray the buildings.

"Did you know that a fire engine and a fire truck are two different things?" The trivia expert in me tossed out to my date. "People think they're interchangeable, but they're not."

"Do tell." She replied with less than bated breath.

"Well, a fire engine carries or pumps water from a hydrant. A fire truck carries ladders and other equipment." I smiled to her deadpanned expression.

As I continued to look around, I made eye contact with a middle-aged gentleman eating his chili, standing at the far side of the room, against the sliding glass doors to the Bay. At first, I thought he was staring at me, then decided he could be looking at just about anyone in my general direction. But then he gave me a small wave of his hand. At least that's what it looked like. I glanced around. No one else nearby seemed to be looking in that direction but me, so I looked up and gave him a weak wave back. It was awkward.

Our turn was next at the table and the guy there handed us each a Styrofoam cup of white bean chicken chili, which was surprisingly flavorful for a bowl of white chili.

"Mmm. What is this, a basil pesto?" Rachel asked. "Am I tasting a little coriander, too?"

"It's cilantro, essentially coriander leaves, plus a little oregano." Said the server.

"And what's this on top?"

"Toasted pumpkin seeds, I think."

"Whatever it is, it's delicious. I can see what you mean about making tough choices, James. I'm already conflicted after only two samplings."

"Jimmy? Jim Gardiner?" An unknown voice called out to me.

I looked around and saw the older gentleman from across the room approaching me. He held a cup of chili in one hand and reached out for a handshake with the other.

I felt a little apprehensive, but I shook his hand nonetheless. "Do I know you?"

"Dan LeBeau. Professor Dan, you kids called me. I have a house on the Strand. You and your friends used to hang out there in the summer. It was across from the volleyball nets. Gee, I guess it must have been ten or twelve years ago or more. I'm not surprised you don't remember." He rattled on, gradually shifting his gaze to Rachel and giving her a not-too-discreet once-over.

"Yeah, I guess I kind of remember. At least the hanging out at a house on the Strand. That was you, huh? Oh. This is my friend, Rachel." I quickly added, remembering my manners. "We're just down for the Chili Festival."

"Pleased to meet you, Rachel."

"Are you really a professor?" She asked, arching an eyebrow suspiciously.

Dan was not an easy guy to miss and didn't really look the professor type, if there is such a thing. He appeared to be fifty, but could easily be sixty or more, totally bald with a shiny pate, clean shaven with John Lennon-style rimless glasses perched on his round Buddha-like face with a beach goer's deep tan. He was tall, taller than me, maybe six-four, and at least three hundred pounds. He cut a ghostly figure in a faded grey Hawaiian shirt, with a barely visible pink hibiscus print. This over equally faded and wrinkled grey linen pants and cheap black flip flops. If he were standing by a wall, you could have mistaken him for somebody's shadow. Hanging around his neck and resting on his white chest hair was a black enameled Swastika pendant on a gold chain.

"No, not at all." He laughed. "The kids called me that because I was always going on and on about some arcane bit of trivia just to hear myself talk."

"And you wear a Buddhist good luck charm so you can explain to them at length that it wasn't always a Nazi icon."

"You're pretty smart yourself."

"I have friends like you." She said as she looked at me and discreetly rolled her eyes.

"Well, I'm glad they're your friends and not people you avoid." Dan laughed again, then turned back to me as Rachel gave him the stink eye.

"Well, I must confess, James, I probably wouldn't have remembered you either if I hadn't seen your picture on the internet a few months back. You solved that case with the Korean girl who tried to blow up a city councilman."

"Oh, that. Yeah, that was tragic for all concerned."

"So now you're a famous detective."

"I guess I've had my Andy Warhol five minutes of fame. And, yes, I am trying to make a go at it, being a detective."

"Then you're probably suspicious by now that I didn't come over to rehash old times. I wondered if I could see you professionally. Not today, of course, you're enjoying an outing at the chili festival with your lovely friend here. But if you had a card or email address, some way I could get in touch with you later this week or next about some business."

"Sure," I said, fishing out my wallet. "I do have cards. You'd think by now everyone had a cell phone or access to the internet, but they don't." I handed him my card. Rachel grabbed me by the elbow and started to pull me away and steer me towards the next table. "Korean Kalbi chili, James. Ko-Mex, they're calling it. Sounds delicious."

"Give me a call and we'll set something up," I called back to Professor Dan as I allowed Rachel to drag me down the aisle.

He stood there and watched us and grinned like a Cheshire cat as he faded back into the crowd.

CHAPTER

TWO

After eating our fill of chili samples and dutifully voting for our favorites, Rachel and I decided not to wait for the polling results and wandered a few blocks over to the center of town, where we found ourselves a quiet table at a rooftop bar with a splendid view of the ocean. As the first round of Habanero Margaritas arrived, Rachel brought up our chance encounter with Professor Dan.

"How do you know that creep?" She asked, taking the moment to reapply her lipstick. "I get such a weird vibe from him."

"Oh, Professor Dan? He's alright, really. He just comes off strange sometimes."

"You're a guy. You wouldn't pick up on that."

"It's a long story."

"Two margaritas worth or three?" She asked, taking her first sip.

"Should we order something to eat?"

"Are you kidding? I must have eaten a gallon of chili back there. That should last me at least until Monday."

I waved the waiter away. "In high school, I was on the golf team." I began, settling back in my chair. I licked a bit of the salt off the rim of my glass and took a sip. It needed more habanero.

"I was pretty good, number one on our team, my senior year. Our top rival was Loyola. They had this guy on their team; his name was Ike. Actually, his name was Dwight, Dwight Davison, but he hated that name, so he went by Ike."

"Like the President."

"Yeah. Anyway, I was matched up against him my sophomore year, and he beat me pretty badly. But I had improved a lot by my junior year and was hoping to get a rematch. I was usually slotted in the number two position in our matches that season, but I had asked the coach to pair me against Ike, who was now their number one. The coach liked the idea of a grudge match, so he agreed. We were playing them that year on our home course at Lakeside, which is in Toluca Lake."

"Yes, I know where Lakeside is," Rachel interjected.

"Lakeside's a beautiful course, designed by the same guy who did Augusta National. No golf carts allowed; they still have caddies, though not for high school matches. From the tee box, it looks like an easy layout, pretty flat, no water hazards, that, despite being called Lakeside. But it is deceptive. Being in high school, we played from the blues, not the tips.

"I started off pretty solid, parred the first few holes, then a birdie on the short par five. The two of us were even through six holes. That's when I noticed this hot girl who seemed to be following our match. Now, in high school golf, we don't usually have galleys, maybe a parent or two, and the coaches, but because we get out of school early for the match, there are never any other students there to cheer us on. Well, even if we played after school, I doubt there'd be anyone who'd come out and watch. It's not a popular spectator sport like football or anything.

"So, I'm noticing this girl, and she's super cute, and she appears to be watching me. She seems much older than a high school girl, maybe in her twenties."

"I heard you used to have a thing for older women." Rachel teased.

"Don't believe everything you hear from my mother. Anyway, she's wearing a tight t-shirt with no bra and really short shorts."

"You noticed that, of course," Rachel interjected with a smirk.

I ignored her and continued. "We make eye contact, and she smiles. Then, I start losing my focus. I start swinging harder, taking riskier shots. I guess I'm showing off, trying to impress her. Well, it backfires. I start screwing up, bogeying holes, falling behind after being ahead. Soon, I'm totally off my game. I'm trying to make up strokes, shoot for pins, and force birdie looks. It ends badly. I lost by three or four strokes. By the eighteenth hole, the girl is not around. I figured she was not impressed with my game and left.

"I was really disappointed in myself after that match, but I used the experience to learn how to better focus. Next time we met, at the State Sectionals, I beat him."

"You won the tournament?"

"No, I came in fifth, I think, but I beat Ike."

"Well, there's that, I guess."

"Later, I come to find out this girl is Ike's older sister, her name was Heather, and she's known for messing with her brother's opponents. I mean, we're only high school boys. It's not hard to get into our heads. I'd never had a real girlfriend at that time. I was six feet tall, a hundred and forty pounds. I looked like Ichabod Crane for Christ's sake!"

Rachel laughed and shook her head in a knowing way.

"So where does the Professor fit into all this?"

"That's part two. That summer, I came down to Hermosa Beach one day with my buddy, Jack. I don't think you've met him. Hermosa's the next town south of here. I think there was a professional beach volleyball tournament there that day or something.

Anyway, we're sitting in the sand, watching the women play, checking out other girls walking by, smoking a joint, and just chilling. Then, I see her."

"Heather."

"Right. She's the next court over where the men are playing, standing on the sidelines, flirting with some of the players. So, I'm glancing over there now and then, watching her, and after a while, she happens to look over and I give her a little wave. I can see that it takes her a minute to recognize me, but she does, and she walks over."

"I offer her a toke and she sits down. We talk about that ill-fated match at Lakeside, and we have a good laugh about it. Turns out she comes down to this beach almost every weekend. Then she invites Jack, my buddy, and me to a party at a house on the Strand. That's the Professor's place."

"Okay."

"Professor Dan, or "Dan the Man" as we kids call him…"

"Dan the who?"

"Like "Stan the Man Lee.""

"Who's that?"

"The Marvel Comics guy. Surely, you've heard of him."

"You called him that to his face?'

"Sure. He loved it. It was a play on his name, LeBeau, the Man. Get it? Didn't you read comics as a kid?"

"No, I was more of a book reader, "Moby Dick, War and Peace, Ulysses.""

"Mmm, hmm." I grinned knowingly. "I guess if you have to explain a joke, it's not funny. Anyway, Dan had this fabulous pad right on the beach. The whole first floor is one big room, kitchen, dining, and living room that spills out through sliding glass doors onto a patio. The second floor is all bedrooms, but the front bedroom is furnished more like a second living room since it has a big balcony. It has deep cushioned couches and coffee tables. He had a foosball table up there and an old pinball machine, like a game room.

"There must be dozens of kids here, mostly older, college age, smoking weed and drinking beers and margaritas. A few of the kids were underage, like I was, still in high school, but no one seemed to mind. Most of us were cautious enough to do our drinking and smoking inside and not out on the balcony or the patio where the bicycle cops were patrolling. Hermosa was a lot more laid back in those days."

"Ha." Rachel snorted. "You say those days like you're a grandpa or something."

I took a big sip of my margarita. "As I was saying, Professor Dan's place was pretty big, three stories, maybe three thousand square feet, but there were sometimes twenty or thirty kids there. The girls would mostly lounge around, showing off their tans and bikinis. Guys would hang out on the balcony and hoot and holler at passersby. Backgammon was a big thing; people played that a lot. Played for money. It's all about the betting cube, you know. There were always several boards lying around. Sometimes there was a poker game in one of the back bedrooms. And there was a lot of hooking up in the other bedrooms.

"And a lot of drinking and dope smoking, you said," Rachel added in mock disapproval.

"And coke. That's where I was first introduced to those little lines of white powdered magic."

"You had quite the ill-spent youth, James." She teased. "And Professor Dan did this all out of the goodness of his heart?"

"Well, it was all free. Some dudes did bring their own, especially beers and weed, but, yeah, drinks, food, all on the house."

"So, you of course didn't say no."

"I confess, I tried it out. But where he really got me hooked was the single malt scotch. He taught me all I know about the glories of Scottish whiskey. It took me a while to figure out his angle, but eventually I realized he was bedding the girls."

"Wait. You were all high school age or thereabouts. He was old enough to be your father."

"Right. A guy like him isn't going to pick up a twenty-year-old in a bar. He was a spider drawing in the young flies to his web."

"That sounds pretty sick."

"It's the beach scene. A lot of older guys with money were trawling for young girls looking for fun. Dan certainly wasn't the only one."

"I don't see it. That guy is pretty gross-looking."

"Well, I have to say, he has let himself go. As I remember, he wasn't so bad looking then, ten, twelve years ago. He was more fit, dressed stylishly. You know a lot of hot movie actors today are in their fifties."

"Still." Rachel sipped her drink, mulling over the scene I had laid out for her. "So, where did this guy get his money? What did he do for a living, deal drugs?"

"No," I laughed. "He was in the real estate biz. He was a broker; had his own agency in town, I heard, and made millions in commissions, I guess."

"No doubt he brought some special clients over to hang with the kids on the weekends."

"I think he probably did. Maybe he wrote it all off as a business expense. Evenings were a lot more subdued. It was kind of just known that the party was over at sundown unless you were invited to stay.
That's when some of Dan's older friends showed up. We'd usually scrounge up a few six-packs and move up the beach to Dockweiler. You can build a campfire on the beach there, so we could hang out all night, knocking back beers around the fire."

"So, who got invited to stay at Dan's? The youngest and prettiest girls, of course."

"Of course." I agreed.

"So, Dan was pimping out these teenage girls to his real estate clients."

"I don't think it was quite like that. You paint him like some sort of modern-day Humbert Humbert."

"Did you ever get the invite to hang out for the evening?"

"Sometimes. My buddy, Jack, was seriously into poker, and the poker games would really get going in the evening, so I would hang around with him since we always came down together."

"But you were really going down there to chase Heather, right?" "I had a steady girlfriend from high school at that time, but she wasn't the partying type, not to mention she was a year behind me, so only sixteen. I couldn't really bring her down to this scene even if she wanted to come. Our relationship was pretty strait-laced, chaste as you might guess."

"So then, did you ever get lucky with Heather?"

"I tried. You're right, that became my main motivation for coming down to Hermosa every weekend. But the parties were loud and crowded. It was hard to have a conversation and get to know anyone. Heather wouldn't give me her phone number; she'd just say, 'See you next weekend, maybe.' And leave me hanging. But, to answer your question, we did finally hook up, the last weekend before school started back."

"Right there in Dan's back room?"

"I had stayed because Jack was playing poker, Texas Hold-em. There weren't a lot of players that night, so I sat in for a few hands. I didn't even know that Heather was still around until she came into the room. She didn't sit at the table, but lounged behind the card players on the couch. She sat there and eyed me just like she did on the golf course.

"I'm not a very good poker player, and I wasn't winning that night, but on the next hand I drew pocket spades, ace high, and there were three spades on the flop. I had a sure win. Maybe my lack of a poker face gave it away, but I tried my best to stay cool.

"So, I'm waiting for my turn as the betting starts, and I look up at Heather, and she just stares back with a knowing look. She gives me a little smirk of a smile, like she knows what I'm holding. Then she stands up and walks around the table to stand behind me. I show her my hole cards as discreetly as possible. She gives me a long look, then walks away, slyly taking off her top as she walks out of the room and into the next bedroom.

No one else seemed to notice, and I'm just staring at the open bedroom doorway when Dan says, "It's a hundred to you, James. You in?"

"I folded and followed Heather."

"Wow. That turned out to be a pretty expensive roll in the hay for you, didn't it?"

"I never saw her again. Actually, never went back to Dan's again."

"Why would you? Mission accomplished, right? Was the sex worth it?"

"I don't really remember. I was seventeen and that was my first time. Maybe not the most mature seventeen-year-old. But that was certainly the most memorable summer I've ever had."

"Most memorable, so far."

Fresh drinks appeared before us, and we toasted.

CHAPTER

THREE

Monday was another day at the office. I had two small offices with a pass-through door that created an inner/outer office suite in the old Cahuenga Building on Hollywood Boulevard. The office was styled in the classic film noir décor, dark wood, opaque pebbled glass, Venetian blinds, and ceiling fans. I guess I'm a sucker for the old school look. As I headed there, I first made a quick drive through at Starbucks for my usual order, then a short walk from the parking lot up Cahuenga, where I grabbed my morning papers. Am I the last guy in Los Angeles who still reads a paper newspaper? I had a brief jaw with my sidewalk neighbor and namesake buddy, Jimmy. I still brought him a morning coffee, even though he no longer had any goldfish in a baggie in exchange for me. He had finally given up on the goldfish racket when he realized that most of the tourists had no way of getting a goldfish in a bag back home to Indiana or wherever they came from. Jimmy now sold "Murder Maps", sort of like the old "Maps to the Stars," except these showed one where all the most notorious crime spots in Los Angeles were.

"How's business, Jimmy?" I asked.

"Could be better." He replied. "This town needs more scandalous crime. Not that I would wish that upon anyone. But I haven't added any new locations since your little headline-grabbing escapade last year."

He was, of course, referring to the exploding house in Solano Canyon where I almost died.

"And that's now just a patch of weeds. Nothing to see." He moaned.

"Yeah. I don't know if Mr. Lachlan is ever going to rebuild. Last I heard, he's still fighting with his insurance company."

"A fire is a fire, right? Should be covered."

"Well, in the insurance adjuster's view, his daughter started the fire, and she's family. Self-inflicted arson is not covered."

"There's always a catch." Jimmy shook his head in dismay. "I just need a couple of sites where there is something for my tourists to see and take pictures. The Manson ranch is long gone, as is the Tate house. The Labianca house isn't visible from the street, just a gate across the driveway. The Ambassador Hotel is a high school now. Your empty lot fits right in."

"What about O.J.'s house?" I queried.

"Demolished. I have Nichole's house on the map, but it has been completely remodeled, with new privacy landscaping, a new street number, the works. L.A. just has no appreciation for its history."

"How about the Menendez Mansion? It's still standing."

"That's about the only one, and that's been thirty-plus years."

"Well, I can't say having fewer gruesome murders is a bad thing," I commented as Jimmy handed me one of his maps. I already had several stuffed in a drawer in the office somewhere. "You take care that you don't end up on a map someday yourself."

I crossed the street to my building, then it was up the noisy old elevator with the sliding cage door that always stuck, then down the hall to my office, a cheery hello and a Frappuccino for my secretary and all-around girl Friday, Yana; and finally, a toss of the old fedora onto the hat tree. I checked in on my goldfish family and my Chinese Moor, whom I had named Puyi, all purchased in trade from Jimmy. I finally wandered into my inner office and settled down with a resigned plop into my chair.

My attention to the morning headlines lasted to the bottom of my cup, about fifteen minutes. Then both hit the waste bin. I passed the rest of the morning typing up notes on a few ongoing cases that stubbornly refused to get resolved. In between looking over old files, I was also filling out those tedious time and expense reports for my biggest client, Commercial Casualty. I grouse, but they pay the bills. And on the plus side, I hadn't been shot at in almost nine months now. Business was picking up. I had given up the divorce work and the candid photography that went along with it. There was plenty of workers' comp and other insurance fraud to investigate to keep me busy. I had been trying to get my friend Jack to come in and work with me full-time. He was going to need a steady paycheck now that his parents were moving away. He had still been living with them, but they'd pulled up stakes and moved to Las Vegas. And, though Jack loved Vegas, he opted to stay in L.A. and get an apartment of his own. So, for the time being, he worked for me part-time and continues with a variety of side hustles to pay the rent.

I was also going to be interviewing for a new secretary /receptionist. Yana had given me notice that she couldn't continue. It seems that her law school workload was more than she could handle if she was also putting in twenty hours a week here babysitting me. So, she asked me to find someone else as soon as possible. I will miss her. She was smart, organized, and didn't put up with any of my nonsense.

As if sensing my despair, Yana stuck her head in and gave me a smile. She handed me a folder and announced my ten o'clock – my interview with one Vera Keppler.

Vera was a surprise at first glance. She looked to be six feet tall, in flats. I checked. Her blonde hair was pulled back in a ponytail so tight it gave her eyes a slight Asian slant and looked like she'd Botoxed her forehead, not that she would need that; she was too young. She had a Nordic look, good cheekbones, and a squarish jawline. She wore navy slacks and a white buttoned-up, short-sleeved blouse with the sleeves rolled up slightly, showing off a pair of toned biceps. She looked like she'd skipped out of class from a nearby Catholic high school. I was somewhat taken aback and completely forgot the usual flirty spiel that I impose on all my female clients – not that Vera was a client.

Instead, I rose and gestured to a chair for Vera to sit. "Nice to meet you, Vera. That's an old-fashioned name. Were you named after Vera Miles?"

"I was actually." She replied with a tight little smile and a firm handshake. "My mother was a big Hitchcock fan."

"Psycho. One of my favorites." I settled myself, leaning back in my chair with a cursory glance over her single-page CV in the folder.

"Are you twenty-one or older?" I asked. "It looks here like you're still in school."

"I'm just twenty. And, no, I am not in school. I completed two years of community college and have obtained an associate's degree."

"Why are you interested in this job in particular? Do you have any career plans?" I continued.

"I plan to join the police force, but I have another year to wait before I'm old enough to apply for the Academy, so I thought I would gain some relevant job experience in the meantime. Then I saw your ad and thought working for a detective agency would be informative." She smiled slightly. It looked like it took some effort.

"Informative. That's a good word." I mused. "So, what makes you want to be a police officer? Is your dad a cop?"

"No. My father is a lawyer, a public defender to be specific. No immediate family on the force."

"Public Defender, eh. That must make for some interesting dinner conversations."

"We have our debates, sure. My grandfather, though, on my mother's side, was a captain with the Santa Monica Police Department."

That caught my interest. "When was that, in the 40s, 50s?"

Vera gave me a look, a disbelieving frown. "He's not that old. In the 70s and 80s."

"Oh, yeah, I guess the 40s was a long time ago."

Vera glanced curiously around the room. My office does look a bit like an overly decorated movie set.

"So, you a big Dashiell Hammet fan or something?" she said, noting my falcon statuette.

For the first time, I felt awkward about that. "I'm more of a Philip Marlowe buff, I guess," I replied.

"I'm more into Bosch myself." She continued, still perusing the stuff in my room.

"Oh." I felt somewhat less embarrassed now. "I've watched that show."

"You should read the books." She admonished before continuing. "What kind of detective work do you do? I hope not just cheating spouse surveillance."

"Not anymore. I started out with those types of jobs, but now it's mostly insurance fraud, missing persons, cases like that. I do most of the legwork, but this job isn't all answering the phones; I need help digging around in public records and such. Are you good with the computer, internet research, social media and all that?"

"Sure. I have some programming skills. I can code a little. I could hack into your phone if I wanted, not that I have ever done that."

"I wouldn't ever ask you to do anything illegal," I interjected with a smile.

"I'm sure you wouldn't."

"Have you ever worked before? I mean, in a paying job. You don't have anything listed here. I was wondering if you had any references."

"No, this would be my first job. There are references on the back. My Forensics instructor and my Criminal Investigations instructor."

"So, you majored in Criminal Justice?" I said, looking now at the back of her one-pager.

"It's only an Associate's Degree. As I said, I am hoping to get into the L.A.P.D. Police Academy at Elysian Fields."

"You're only looking for a short period of work, then?"

"Well, if I get in on my first try, that won't be for another year. But that's my goal. Sure."

"I notice here that you live in Simi Valley. Lot of nice golf courses out that way."

"I wouldn't know. I see them from the freeway, but I don't play."

"Sure. Still, that's a long commute to here."

"Closer than downtown and the Academy."

"True. So, this would be a weekly salaried position, but the hours could be irregular. I'm looking for someone who can be available at all hours."

"Not a problem for me. I'm a bit of a night owl myself."

"Okay." I stood up and offered my hand. "I'll get back to you by the end of the week. It was a pleasure meeting you, Vera. Your Mom didn't like Janet, huh?"

Vera shook my hand again. "No, Janet was the not-so-bright, criminal one. Thank you for meeting with me, Mr. Gardiner."

As I walked Vera to the door, Yana stood waiting with a phone message.

"A Mr. LeBeau called, wants to meet with you. Offered to buy you lunch at Musso's today if you're available. He said he would be in the area."

"Okay, sure. Do I have any other appointments?"

Yana smiled and pretended to consult the calendar. "Looks like you're free for the rest of the day, and tomorrow and..."

"Don't need to rub it in."

I went back into my office feeling slighted. I was going to miss Yana's ribbing.

CHAPTER

FOUR

Musso and Frank was one of my favorite hangouts. The restaurant was over a hundred years old and had a long history of catering to the most famous names in Hollywood. The red leather booths and red-jacketed waiters immediately transported you back to the good old days. And it was only three blocks from my office.

Of course, since it was so close, I was five minutes late. Professor Dan was already seated toward the back, wearing a light grey sports jacket and a dark grey T-shirt underneath. He waved his arm as I entered.

"Sorry, I'm late. Things, you know." I apologized as I sat down.

"Not a problem. What are you drinking? I'm having a martini? They don't skimp on the olives here."

"I'm more of a whiskey drinker thanks to you," I answered, just as the waiter brought Dan his drink, the classic martini glass with three big olives speared and perched on the rim. He set the glass down and poured the drink from a small carafe, filling it nearly to the rim. The remaining gin he left in the carafe on the table.

"I'll have the Macallan 18, neat," I ordered.

The waiter nodded and went away.

"Don't wait for me." I encouraged.

Dan took a good, long sip and let out a satisfied sigh. "Now that's the way to start lunch. Don't you think?"

"Well, for some, that is lunch." I joked.

Dan set his drink down and bit off one of the olives. He leaned forward, elbows on the table. "So, you're a big shot detective now, huh?"

"As I said, I've had my five minutes of fame. It kept the phone ringing for a few months, mostly reporters, not clients. Now, not so much."

"I remember seeing you on TV. I recognized you, though you've changed, grown up. You're taller now."

"That happens," I replied, keeping up my end of the small talk until Dan decided to discuss what he really came to see me about. "To be honest, I didn't recognize you at first. But, then, I was only down at your place for a few weekends that one summer."

"I guess I've changed, too, lost some hair, gained a few pounds. Those were good times, though, huh? Backgammon, volleyball on the beach, beers and babes all day and all night. Poker games after dark or sitting around campfires on the sand. Didn't get any better than that."

"Well, I certainly enjoyed myself."

"But you didn't come back the next summer?"

"I was working on my golf game, trying to make the team at Stanford. Every day, hitting balls, either on the course or on the range or both."

"How'd that work out?"

"Didn't make the cut."

"Too bad." Dan chewed on another olive. The waiter brought me my drink and took our order. I had the pastrami sandwich, and Dan ordered the lamb.

"Don't remember what year you were down there, but those wild parties only lasted a couple of summers. I got serious myself with a girlfriend later; she moved in, so we tamped down the crazy a bit, moved away from the underage crowd, and partied more with people my own age. You may have met her. She was around for a couple of years before we started keeping house. Anyway, I couldn't keep up with you kids anymore, so it was all good."

"Yeah, well, times change, people change. You can't keep repeating your good years, no matter how much you want to."

"In my case, things changed for the worse, much worse."

I took a sip of my drink and waited for him to continue.

"As I said, I settled down with a girlfriend. This wasn't a falling madly in love and going to get married relationship. She was young, not robbing the cradle young but maybe only a few years older than you. She moved in, and we played house. I was happy. Sure, we had our little fights. She was "a wild and crazy girl," to paraphrase Steve Martin, but we were a good fit most days.

"Then one day she disappeared. At first, I wasn't alarmed, more irritated. She'd done this before, gone back to an old boyfriend for a night, or gone to see her folks for a weekend. She was kind of flaky that way, but she'd call in a day or two and cry and apologize and explain it all away. I'd forgive her, and we'd be back to normal. But not this time.

"After a few days, I began to get worried. People were showing up for appointments that she hadn't bothered to cancel. She read palms and tarot cards, did astrology charts, all that fortune-telling shit. So, I began to worry maybe she'd been in an accident. I discovered she hadn't taken her purse, so she had no phone, no ID with her, and if she was unconscious, in a hospital or something... So, I filed a missing person's report with the Hermosa Police."

"What's her name, your girlfriend?"

"Skye, with an 'e'. Typical hippie name. Her parents are tree huggers, live up north of Santa Barbara in a commune. I have some pictures. Let me send them to you."

I pulled what he texted over up on my phone. I remembered Skye, vaguely. She was a cute, blonde girl, older than me. She looked a lot like that girl, Heather, that I had been pursuing. She could have been her older sister. She was prettier than I remembered. One picture in particular was alluring – her standing on the Strand, the wind gently blowing her hair and her red and white polka-dotted sundress, she held a big straw hat down on her head with one hand, tilting her head and smiling bewitchingly at the camera. I was captivated.

"Anyway," Dan continued, "After a couple of days, the police show up at my door with a search warrant. Seems they had tracked down her old boyfriend, and he claimed that the last time he saw Skye, she looked like she had been beaten up. Claimed that Skye accused me of hitting her. Total bullshit. I never, ever struck her. I don't do that shit.

"I let them search away. I had nothing to hide. All her stuff was right where she left it a week before, including her purse, cell phone, I.D., wallet full of cash and credit cards. The cops tossed the place for a few hours and then left. I probably didn't do a good job of hiding my annoyance. If she ran away because I was hitting her, you'd think she would have taken her purse at least. And what girl today can part with her phone for more than a few hours?"

"The first rule of investigating is you don't rule anything out until all the evidence is in." I opined professionally.

"A couple of days later, the police were back with another warrant to search my units." Dan continued. "I own a couple of apartment buildings. Most of the places are always rented, but there's always one or two empty at any given time. I usually spruce them up with paint and new carpets if necessary.

"I told them to go ahead. They could pick up keys from my office."

"They thought maybe Skye was hiding out in one of your empty apartments?" I asked.

"Who knows what they were thinking. It's what they found that turned everything upside down.":

"Such as?" I prodded gently.

"Blood spatter in the bathroom, evidence of a hasty clean-up with bleach in the bathtub. Later, they found CCTV footage of someone who looked like me dragging black plastic trash bags to the dumpster behind the building. A lot of evidence that all pointed to me.

"I was arrested and charged with murder, if you can believe that. It was pretty sensational for a quiet little beach town, front page on the Daily Breeze for a week, on all the TV news channels, though it probably didn't make page three in the Times."

"I must have been up at school. Didn't hear anything about it." I added.

"Anyway, I got the best lawyers I could find. They weren't cheap. It cost me most of what I had. I sold my agency, not that I would be able to keep the doors open with all this bad publicity. Sold most of my rentals. I was able to keep my place on the Strand. I was determined to exonerate myself. I wasn't going to be run out of town on some phony frame job."

"You're here talking to me now; I'm guessing you won."

"Their case had one huge hole in it. They never found her body. They tried to hang me on circumstantial evidence. Well, the jury didn't buy it." Dan filled his glass from the carafe and drained it, then signaled for another.

"My old life was over, though. I kept to myself, kept the blinds down on the first floor to thwart the curious and mostly sat on my deck and read. Later, I tried my hand at writing some young adult, fantasy-type stuff. I guess you could say I was running away mentally."

"Stuff like Harry Potter?"

"More, Lord of the Rings or Game of Thrones."

Our lunches arrived and we stopped talking and focused on eating for a few minutes.

"They have the best pastrami," I said with my mouth full. "Which brings us to why we are sharing lunch here today."

Dan finished his bite of lamb and began his story. "A couple of weeks ago, I was at Trader Joe's up on P.C.H. That's where I always do my shopping. I walk. I need the steps. Anyway, I had a couple of bags of groceries and I was waiting at the light at Pier to cross and go home. And I see her."

"Skye?"

"Yes, Skye. She pulls up to the light in an old red MGB with the top down, she had a scarf on her head and those big Hollywood sunglasses, trying to look like an old-time movie star, Jayne Mansfield or somebody.

"She looked at me and I could tell she knew I recognized her. The light was still red, but she zipped through it like a frightened rabbit."

"Did you go to the police?"

"No. They think I got away with murder. The last thing they want to see is me peddling stories about how Skye is driving around Hermosa in a red sports car."

"Was that her car?"

"No, I've never seen that car before. She had one of those old VW bugs with the flower decals all over it. I had bought it for her, but she didn't like to drive it. It was a standard transmission, and she said she could never get a handle on using the clutch. I tried to teach her, but she was too nervous."

"Where's that car now?"

"I don't know, I think I sold it. You can imagine my surprise not only at seeing Skye, but seeing her behind the wheel of a sports car. I've been trying to decide what to do. I did tell my lawyer. He suggested I hire a private detective to find her. A few days later, I saw you at the chili festival. And, here we are."

"Wow," I said with a big exhale. "That's some story."

"Now you can write the next chapter. I want you to find her. She framed me for murder. I need to know why."

***

Later that afternoon, back at the office, Jack was loading some new databases onto my computers. I started to recount my remarkable lunch conversation while he worked. Jack was more intrigued that I had reconnected with Professor Dan than he was with a murder victim who rose from the dead.

"I was in the area. You should have given me a jingle. I would have loved to join you guys for lunch and catch up on old times."

"It was his lunch invite. I couldn't very well bring you along."

"Ah, he would have loved to see me and talk poker."

"I think he had other things to talk about."

"Does he still have that place on the Strand?"

"Yeah, but the party days are over. See, if you were listening, I was telling you how he had this little run-in with the law, and how it's kind of put a bit of a damper on our old friend's glory days." I briefly continued the story of his arrest and trial for murder and the recent reappearance of the victim.

"I remember Skye. She was hot, if you're into older hippie chicks in those embroidered peasant dresses. I think she read my cards once, or maybe it was my palm. She was quite the flirt. But, wow, what a frame-up." Jack whistled. "Why would she want to do that to him? That's kind of harsh. I mean, he could be a jerk sometimes, but I can't see the old Professor ever doing anything that would warrant that."

I pulled up a couple of pictures on my phone that Dan had given me of Skye, both her alone and the two of them in happier days. I pushed the phone across the desk for Jack to see.

"Oh, yeah, that's her all right." He remarked with a lecherous eyebrow twitch.

"I can't say that I know Dan all that well. He was a great host, threw terrific parties, but I'd have to swear, today's lunch was the longest conversation I ever had with him."

"You can tell a lot about a person by watching how they play cards. Dan was not a greedy guy; he rarely bluffed. He would never let the size of the pot change the way he played, no stupid bets. He always stayed within himself. He had a lot of self-control."

"I wouldn't know. You're a much better card player than

I."

"You think he still has card games at his place?"

"No, I'd say his old card buddies probably cross the street when they see him coming."

"Hmmm. That's a shame." Jack nodded his head, thinking it over. "So, what's your next move?"

"Dan gave me the name of his lawyer. I gave him a call, and he offered to send over a copy of the trial transcripts to read. I'll familiarize myself with the case first. I'm going to meet with him in the morning to see what insight he might share with me as well."

"While you're there, I can try out some of these databases and give the program a shake-down." Jack offered as he continued installing the software.

"I hope so. They cost enough." I leaned back and put my feet up on the desk. "When you're through downloading, you can try them out on our mysterious back-from-the-dead girl. Maybe we'll get lucky and find her right off the bat. Oh, I interviewed a new girl this morning. You know, to take over for Yana. She seems pretty smart, competent, and wants to be a policeman when she's old enough."

Jack looked up from the computer and arched an eyebrow. "You like her best so far? Head and shoulders above the rest?"

"Well, she is tall, and she is the only one who's applied so far."

CHAPTER

FIVE

Dan's high-priced lawyer, Jon, had an office in one of those tall buildings in Century City, one with a nice view of the Los Angeles Country Club golf course, which went unappreciated by Jon, as he was an avid tennis player. I could only imagine what his hourly billing rate was. Jon Pulliam was everything James had expected in a criminal justice attorney – fit, impeccably dressed, manicured and coiffed, with a voice like butter. It didn't hurt that he had the hint of a southern drawl and the countenance of a young James Mason.

He talked freely about the case and, per Dan's request, had arranged for the case files to be pulled from storage and sent over to my office.

"Dan says that he was framed." I began.

"Yes, that is the line of defense that we went with, and the jury was convinced. The evidence presented against Mr. Lebeau was entirely too convenient."

"What was the prosecution's answer to that?"

"They argued that criminals are usually not smart. Masterminds are the stuff of fiction. Murders are rarely well planned but rather spur of the moment, and covering them up is done while the killer is most emotional and least rational. They almost always mess up and leave evidence behind."

"But this killing would seem reckless even by those loose standards."

"They briefly toyed with suggesting that Mr. Lebeau had framed himself, but so clumsily to throw off any suspicion."

"So, a criminal mastermind after all." I chuckled. "That seems like a risky gambit."

"Mr. Lebeau is a smart man. He would know that the police would see through any such clumsy attempt on his part."

"Unless Dan knew the police knew he was too smart for that and would be expecting then, a more professional diversion."

"Ad nauseam. Yes, I am familiar with the abductive fallacy of Vizzini in The Princess Bride. Ultimately, the State presented the evidence as sufficient in and of itself. They were not going to confuse the jury with conspiracies."

"What kind of evidence did they present? Dan mentioned there was blood in one of his rental units and some bleach."

"There was blood. The Luminol detected lots of it. It was matched to the deceased's DNA."

"Why would they have her DNA on record?"

"It appears that in her younger years, she sold a lot of blood to local blood banks. When you're broke, that's an easy fifty bucks. The police didn't do the best job in investigating. That actually worked against us. A better investigation would have proved Dan's innocence long before the trial."

"What, they messed up?"

"Just not thorough. Can't blame them too much. It was a three-ring circus down there with the reporters clamoring for updates every hour. Hermosa P.D. didn't have the manpower to deal with this case, the media, and their everyday workload. They had to bring in the Sheriff's department to help out. No prints found at the apartment whatsoever. Totally wiped down. Who would do a sloppy clean-up but a professional wipe down if not pros trying to frame someone? Bloody knives, saws, and rags were recovered at the county landfill, but not the body parts. The tools were then plausibly traced back to the apartment dumpster. But even though the implements were obviously new, they couldn't trace a purchase to anywhere in Southern California. Closed-circuit TV of the back of a man throwing bags into that dumpster while wearing a sweatshirt hoodie with a slogan on it that Dan admitted was his, but he could no longer account for it. Police never found that either. And a few other slightly less damning items. It's all in the files."

"And no body."

"That was what swung the jury to our favor. They couldn't bring themselves to convict without more evidence that a murder had been committed."

"Especially a solid citizen like Dan."

"There was plenty of character assassination at the trial. They painted Dan as a wild man, a partier, underage kids at his house at all hours, pushing drugs on friends, friends of friends, sex trafficking underage girls, that sort of stuff. Dan had as many enemies as friends. But no police record, no files of complaints to point to. It didn't stick."

"Yeah, I was at some of those bashes one summer. Pretty innocent fun except for the underage part."

"I don't judge my clients. I'm paid to provide them with the best defense available and let the justice system pass judgment. Dan was found not guilty. I did my job, but I'm not going to be meeting him for drinks after work."

"Oh." My eyebrows must have shot up at that remark. "Well, I'm not saying we were best buds, either. But if Skye is alive, I'll do my best to find her. Is she in legal jeopardy if I do?"

"She didn't file a false police report herself, but conspiracy to commit fraud is one possibility."

While I let that sink in, I gazed past the attorney and out his window to the golf course below.

"You golf?" He asked, catching my wandering eye.

"Not as much as I'd like," I replied, wondering how many weeks it had been since I played last. "You?"

"No, I'm more of a tennis guy, myself. It's better cardio. A fit body keeps the mind sharp." He advised.

Just beyond the sixth hole, I could sort of make out the roof of my house, or rather my mother's house. And right on cue, my phone vibrates. I glance down. It's mother.

"You need to take that?" Jon asked.

"No, I'll call back," I replied. "But I've taken up enough of your time. I appreciate the information. I'll try to get your files back as soon as I can."

"No rush. They've been collecting dust for ten years. I really should have had them digitized by now, but, oh well."

I don't know how my mother knows I'm in the neighborhood, but she always does. Seriously, I've checked my phone for tracking devices and locator apps, and it's always clean. Maybe it's just a mother's intuition.

As I left Jon's office, I gave her a call.

"Hi, James." She twittered.

"Morning, mother."

"Are you free for lunch today?"

"Sure. I just happen to be on the West Side today. Where would you like to meet?"

"Oh, just come over to the house. No sense spending money on lunch if you don't have to. You waste enough of yours on those fancy course tasting dinners you always go to. I'll make you a nice, healthy salad."

Fifteen minutes later, I pulled into the drive of the old family abode, if you can call a five-thousand-square-foot Wallace Neff Spanish Revival in Holmby Hills that. Mother was in the kitchen preparing lunch. I guess the housekeeper had the day off. Mother was in her Liz Taylor phase, gaudy flower print or Asian print caftans every day, with matching turbans and big hoop earrings. We had lunch on the patio, caprese salad and bruschetta with a bottle of pinot grigio to share. It was good, but I had moved on from my salad days. I was going to need to grab a cheeseburger and fries on the way back to the office. So far, the red meat and carbs had not shown up on my waistline.

"So, how's Rachel these days?" She wasted no time in grilling me about the latest developments in my dating relationships, especially the ones she'd arranged.

"Fine," I said, trying to talk and not choke on the toast and tomatoes. "We were down in Manhattan Beach for the chili festival last weekend. Very creative stuff. Michelin should have a rating guide for chili these days."

"That's nice, but I asked about Rachel."

"She's good. She likes chili now, but otherwise not much different than the last time I reported in."

"Don't be smart. You should really start thinking about settling down. You can't do better than a girl like her, you know. It's a shame things never worked out with you and Stacy. I really liked her."

"I'm not even thirty yet. People my generation don't settle down as early as you did."

"You exaggerate. I'm sure many of your classmates are married."

"Yeah, and they're all fat with three or four rugrats running around the house."

"Must you be so contrary? I know why you're always running around with older women. It's to avoid family and responsibility. Well, mark my words, one of these days you'll wake up and it will be too late."

"I picked up a new client while I was down there," I said, changing the subject.

"Where?"

"At the chili festival," I replied, somewhat annoyed at Mother's flightiness. "Remember the summer before my senior year in high school when Jack and I would go down to Hermosa every weekend?"

Mother thought for a moment. "That was the year I stopped talking to your father, as I recall." Then she took a long pull on her pinot.

"Yeah. That's probably why I was at the beach every day." I said, matching her drink for drink.

I then told her about my encounter with Professor Dan and a cleaned-up version of my trip down memory lane that summer. Mother's only memories of that summer were the constant fights with father and the turmoil that led up to their separation and eventual divorce. She barely recalled knowing what I was doing half the time. I didn't recall the fights so much. Maybe I blocked them out of my mind.

A few hours later, I strolled into my office clutching a greasy bag of chili-cheeseburger and fries. Jack was still there, searching away on the new programs for our mystery girl. I had completely forgotten he might be here.

"Jack! Breaktime. I brought you some lunch, figured you'd be hungry."

"Thanks, James. Always thinking of me. I appreciate it."

I handed him the bag. "Sloppy Joe's. It's not a Fat Freddie, but a close second. Sorry, I forgot the shake." I lied. "But there's water in the front office fridge."

"Don't worry about it." Jack tore into the food like a Labrador retriever. "Water's good. Where's your lunch?" He asked through a mouthful of burger.

"Already ate. Any luck with your data search?" I asked, my tummy growling from hunger.

"Well, Skye's her real name, Skye Meadow Goldberg. Parents are David and Judith. Born in Santa Rosa, listed as a home birth, with no hospital records. She's thirty-eight now. She wasn't issued a Social Security number until she turned twenty. Her driver's license expired eight years ago, non-renewal. No forwarding address with the post office. No recent employment history, and by recent, I mean not in over nine years."

"That would be about when she went missing." I interrupted.

"No unemployment claims either. No active bank account use, no credit card use. Her financial affairs seem to be in limbo, as it seems a death certificate was never issued. It's unknown if anyone has a power of attorney for her. If she did fake her own death, she's been very disciplined about not trying to pick up the pieces of her old life."

"Until now, perhaps," I added. "I wonder what tempted her to come back?"

"Looks like she had an apartment of her own. She wasn't only living with Dan. I'll text you the address if you want to check it out. Can't imagine her stuff is still there after all these years, though."

"Be worth talking to the landlord at least. Find out what happened to her stuff."

"It sounds like an ADU. So, the landlord may live at the same address."

"What about her parents? You said they lived in Santa Rosa."

"They have a post office box in Santa Maria, now. No other known address."

"Hmmm. Maybe Dan knows where to find them." I walked over to the stack of boxes filled with case files from Jon. I pulled a folder out of the top box. Inside was paper-clipped a photo of Skye I hadn't seen before, a Polaroid that had been ripped in half and scotch-taped together again. She was pretty, with long blonde hair, on the short side, maybe five-two, a slight build, and bright eyes with a wide ear-to-ear grin. I must have seen her dozens of times that summer, but strangely, she didn't look all that familiar. Still, there was something emotional about looking at her now, once thought dead and now back to life.

CHAPTER

SIX

Dan only had a vague idea of the parents' whereabouts. He said he thought they lived on a commune in the hills east of town. But he was pretty sure the locals all knew where the commune was and felt I could find it easily enough if I asked around.

I had traded in my old Civic for a shiny new Tesla at the beginning of the year and planned on driving up there in that. My map said it was one hundred and fifty miles one way. Three hundred miles was the limit I could go on a full charge. I sure didn't want to run out of juice on the road in the middle of nowhere, but neither did I want to cool my heels in a farm town for hours charging my car.

The A/C in my old Mercury wasn't that great, and I knew it was going to be hot out there. So, I figured to live life on the edge and chance it with the Tesla.

I had never been to Santa Maria. I pictured it as a sleepy little farm town where the farmers gathered outside the feed store or the country grocers, chewing tobacco and discussing the price of pork bellies. As I drove up the 101, which turned into Broadway in town, I was surprised. The place was far from the quaint and dusty collection of old buildings I'd imagined. It looked like most of it had been all built in the last ten years and resembled nearly every other community in America, the same corner gas stations, the same Starbucks and McDonald's on every block.

The wide streets were lined with the same big box stores and chain retailers, a Tesla car dealer and half a dozen Superchargers, Trader Joe's and wine tasting rooms. Is this what America had become, cookie-cutter towns? The ratio of pick-up trucks to four-door sedans was about the only clue to my location. I despaired of finding any place with old men in rockers eyeing the strangers who'd drifted into town. I drove around, thinking there must be an "old town" or something more like my imagination. I finally spotted a Home Depot and hoped I might find some workers lingering outside who I could question. My Spanish wasn't great, but I figured I could manage a few questions. Unfortunately, it was already nearly noon, and all the day laborers had either found work or given up and left. The parking lot was mostly filled with people in SUVs loading up flowers and plants for their yards.

I continued cruising around, not knowing now what I was even looking for, when I spied a Cannabis dispensary. If anyone would know where to find a hippie commune, it would be these people, I reasoned.

The little bell over the door tinkled as I entered. Inside, everything was clean and boutique-like, with no Zig-zag rolling paper ads nor Dayglo rock art pieces; no Grateful Dead tunes playing in the background. I half expected to see Gucci bongs and Louis Vuitton joint cases. There were assorted buds in jars, labelled by source – Hawaiian, Colombian, Thai, etc. They had more blends than my favorite coffee shop. In another case were edibles, THC, CBD, HHC, and more in various fruit flavors. I was at a loss with all the new varieties, having given up on pot smoking a decade ago. I looked around for a Cheech and Chong or Fabulous Furry Freak Brothers poster, anything that would look familiar.

A tall, thin, middle-aged man looked at me from behind the counter. "May I help you?" He asked.

He didn't have long hair or even a beard, just a well-trimmed mustache. He wore a T-shirt. It wasn't tie-dyed but had an unobtrusive logo for a local winery over the left breast.

"Yes," I said as I approached. "I'm not really looking to buy anything today, but I heard there was a commune not far out of town, and I thought you might know where I could find it."

He gave me a long look. "Seriously? Are you profiling me, man?"

"No." I protested. "Well, yes. I'm sorry. I was just driving around and I saw your shop. It just popped into my head, you know, pot…hippies…"

The man just rolled his eyes and shook his head in disbelief. "Most of my customers are just everyday folk, plumbers, nurses, grocery store clerks. Yeah, I've heard the stories, but I have no idea where it might be. You should try the police. I'm sure they know. I hear they're out there on a regular basis."

"That's a good idea. Look, I'm sorry for the dumb assumptions. I didn't mean anything by it."

"You aren't the first." He replied with a disapproving look. I could feel him staring daggers as I left the store.

I made my way to the police station. It was a pretty modern building, looking more like a big box discount store than anything else. I made my way in and asked the desk sergeant if any detectives were available for a few minutes to talk. Of course, he was immediately suspicious.

"What's this regarding?"

I didn't want to have to explain it all twice, but I could see I wasn't going to get past the gatekeeper without telling my tale. I pulled out my ID.

"I'm a private investigator on a missing person's search. I understand the woman I'm looking for has parents who live in the area, on a commune in the hills. I thought someone here might know about this place."

"Yeah, you must mean that bunch out on Tepusquet Road. Let me see if Detective Ramos is around. He can fill you in."

Detective Ramos was an older man with black hair, and a dark, sun-lined complexion. He reminded me of a cowboy version of my old friend, Lieutenant Mejia. He wore a white business shirt, sleeves rolled up, and a black bolo tie. He leaned forward, hands clasped, resting on his desk blotter.

"What can I do for you, son?"

"I'm following up on a missing person's case, a woman named Skye Goldberg. I am told she has parents who live in this area, David and Judith Goldberg. They keep a post office box in town but are said to live somewhere in the hills east of town, a kind of commune, I guess. I was hoping you might be able to point me in the right direction."

Ramos narrowed his eyes, thinking, and said nothing for at least a minute, though it seemed much longer.

"Yeah, I know those two, and the rest of their clan. Not nice people if you don't mind me saying."

"They've caused you trouble?"

"No, not so much that we can't handle it. They do have a bit of a rap sheet: solicitation, shoplifting, and drug dealing. They are not as self-sufficient as they pretend to be and take to breaking the law to make ends meet. I'm not saying they're another Manson gang or anything, but we keep an eye on them. The older ones, like David and Judith, are the most hostile. Probably a carryover from their "kill the pigs" youth.
The younger ones aren't so bad, just victims of poor upbringing in my opinion."

"Did Skye get arrested for any of those offenses?"

"Oh, yeah. All of the above."

"How many people are out there?"

"Never took a proper head count, maybe twenty, plus people come and go, and they have new babies every so often. They have a couple of small ranch houses, a stable and barn, don't know if anyone uses that for a residence, and a half dozen broken down RVs."

"But you'd have no problem with me going out there to talk to them."

"I wouldn't recommend it. As I said, they are not nice people. They don't like strangers, especially strangers poking around asking questions. But it's a free country."

"I would think David and Judith would be interested in the welfare of their daughter."

Just then, I could see a little lightbulb light up behind Ramos's eyes.

"They had a daughter murdered about ten years ago. I remember L.A. detectives up here interviewing them. This doesn't have anything to do with that now, does it?"

"It seems that maybe that murder was staged, and she didn't die after all. That's what I'm looking into."

"Hmmm." Ramos lifted his clasped hands to his face and pondered this for a moment. "Faking a crime is a crime itself." He announced. "Though, unless there was money to be made, I doubt that her parents had anything to do with it."

"I don't suspect that they did. I'm just checking to see if she fled back here to hide out or has had any contact with them in the last ten years."

"If she's hiding out there, they won't give her up. So, you're wasting your time. But have at it. You got Google Maps in your car? I'll give you the address. It's not hard to find."

I walked a couple of blocks down to a nearby taqueria for a quick lunch of an al pastor burrito and a large horchata while I charged up the Tesla. I always judge a Mexican eatery by their chips and salsa. Here, the chips were fresh and the salsa had a nice bite to it. *Muy bueno!* While eating, I searched Google Earth for a satellite view of the old homestead, then I hit the road.

This part of California, the Central Coast, was mostly miles of gently rolling hills of hay colored grass with a bare sprinkling of green trees, mostly Live Oaks and Buckeye.

Houses were scarcer still. It was beautiful countryside. I could consider living here, but there was not much here to keep me occupied. I'm sure I'd go stir crazy. Ramos was right; the place was not hard to find. Despite the fact that there was no house number in sight, it was the only property anywhere close to the destination flag on my digital car map. The property was fenced with old chain link, and a dirt road ran from the highway down to a gate, which conveniently had been left open. A noisy murder of crows populated the surrounding trees.

I drove in, tires crunching in the gravel and dust. The birds took flight in a raucous din of squawking, like some Hitchcockian alarm system, before settling back to their perches and watching me pull to a stop. The pitted and boulder-strewn dirt road turned into a dirt parking lot, a half-acre of weeds and dust. I watched as a little dirt-devil swirled through the area.

At first, the place looked deserted; no one seemed to be around. Dan had referred to the place as a hippie compound. I didn't know what a hippie compound was supposed to look like, having never been to one. Here, there was a large pile of discarded lumber, bleached from the sun, cement blocks, and other building material stacked haphazardly off to one side, probably home to more than a few rats and snakes and such.

Behind it appeared to be a vehicle junk yard. Some of the rusted heaps looked quite old, pre-war coupes and trucks. I recognized a Dodge, a Chevy and a Ford. Some were missing wheels, another with no hood and no engine. Scattered among the cars were what looked like old washers and dryers, now rusted out, along with dozens of old 50-gallon drums. The most striking thing, directly to the north of me, was a big old barn. The structure itself had seen better days, but the side facing me, and anyone entering the property, was painted with a huge, colorful mural. And by colorful, I mean in a childish sort of tribute to Peter Max. Bright primary colors, boldly outlined coloring book style, depicted a variety of new age symbols, a yin-yang, a star of David, and an Egyptian ankh, and some sort of hand with an eye in its palm, whatever that is, along with many rainbows, palm trees, and crescent moons. I snapped a few pictures of the mural and the old cars. I like taking pictures, even if only for my own amusement.

About then, a couple of preschool-aged kids came running out towards my car, followed shortly by what I could only assume was their older sister. She was quite pretty with dirty blonde hair, dirty bare feet, and wearing only a faded pink and yellow sundress, also dirty.

I stepped out of the car and waited until she had caught up and corralled the two boys. "I'm looking for David and Judith Goldberg. I'm told they live here."

"Bubbah!" Squealed one of the boys.

"Yes, Bobbah. Now hush." She looked at me. "Is she expecting you?"

"No, sorry, I didn't have a phone number, or I would have called ahead."

"We don't have phones here."

"Oh," I said, surprised. "Well, if either or both of them are here, would you let them know I've come up from Los Angeles to discuss some news about their daughter, Skye. I'm James Gardiner, by the way." I offered my hand to shake.

She just looked at mine, but her hands were full with the shirt collars of her two squirming boys. "Summer."

"Excuse me?"

"My name is Summer." She said, looking back up to me. "I'll go see if they want to see you." Then she turned and dragged the kids back into the house.

As I waited, I wandered around a bit, being careful not to stray too far from the car. Ramos's caution about them being not nice people stuck in my head. I didn't want to be looking at the business end of a shotgun. Not far from the house, I could see what looked to be a large vegetable garden. Lots of plots of different plants, some staked, others not. They didn't look to be very healthy. Must be the lack of rain we've experienced, I thought. On the far side of the garden was another house. I caught sight of three or four young women at the window, grimy faces staring back at me through grimy glass. One gal was breastfeeding a newborn; another was very pregnant. I got a very creepy vibe from it all.

At length, a very tiny old woman came out of the house and approached me. She couldn't have been even five feet tall. With gray hair tied up in a snood and a faded, brown and white print peasant dress, she could have stepped out of a Millet painting.

"Can I help you, young man?"

"Are you Judith Goldberg?"

"I am."

"I wanted to ask you a few questions about your daughter, Skye."

"She's dead."

"I know you were told that. Though I have reason to believe she is not dead, and that is what I wanted to talk to you about."

"Are you police?"

"No, I'm a private investigator, and certain facts have come to light that have led us to believe that someone staged her death. That it didn't really happen the way it was reported."

"Doesn't matter. True or not, she's dead to us. She's been dead to us ever since she left here, eighteen years ago."

"So, she hasn't been in contact with you at all, by phone or letter."

"If she had, we would not still be thinking she was dead, now, would we?"

"Of course you're right. That was a stupid question. Does she have any other family that she might contact?"

"None that she knew of."

As we were talking, the young girl named Summer silently joined us.

"Is your husband around? Could I talk to him?"

"He's out back with the men digging a new septic tank. He won't want to take time away from that to talk to you, neither. If you're not police, you should go now."

"Is this about mother?" Summer asked.

"This young man is here just stirring up the past. It's no concern of ours now." The older woman replied. "We'd best be getting back to our chores."

"Can I give you my card?" I asked, fishing some out of my wallet. "If you hear from her, maybe you could give me a call."

The old woman made no effort to take my card. "You'd best be leaving now."

As the old woman turned away and started for the house, I called after her. "Don't you want me to find her?" But the old woman ignored me and kept walking. "Don't tarry now, Summer." She called back.

Summer, though, hesitated. I quickly handed her one of my cards, which she stuffed in a pocket before she hurried to catch up to her grandmother.

I glanced again at the line of women watching me through the streaked windows. Their gazes were still dead, unflinching. I felt like I was in a horror picture with backwoods maniacs. I decided to leave while I still could, Ramos' warning ringing in my ear.

***

It was another long, three-hour drive back to my place in Hollywood, and I was beat, so I went to bed early. I had no sooner dozed off when my phone buzzed. I reached over to glance at the number. It was not one I recognized. Probably spam, I thought. Why would they be calling at this hour of the night? I was about to hang up, but some impulse caused me to answer instead.

"Hello?"

"Is this Mister Gardiner?" A female voice whispered.

"Speaking."

"This is Summer. You gave me your business card earlier today."

I was immediately awake. "I'm surprised, actually, that you called so soon. I didn't think you had phones at your place."

"Danny has a secret phone that he doesn't tell the elders about."

"Well, it was nice of him to let you use it."

"Oh, I had to fuck him for it."

"Oh."

"I get two hundred dollars for that in town. Well, the family keeps the money, but...it was worth it. I had to speak to you."

"What can I do for you, Summer?"

"Did you tell Bubba my mother was alive? Have you seen her?"

"I haven't seen her, and I can't say for sure she is alive. But someone who knows her claims to have seen her recently, so I am investigating. How long has it been since you've seen her?"

"I've never seen her. She ran away after I was born. Bobba raised me."

"I see. Were those two boys I met, your sons?"

"Yes, Abe and Issac. Aren't they handsome?"

"They are. So, I gather you can't tell me much about the circumstances around your mother leaving home."

"No, Bobba and Zayda never speak of her. But others here know, and they have told me a little. She was very pretty."

"Yes, she was, or is, I should say."

"Then you have met her?"

"A long, long time ago."

"If you see my mother again, please tell her to contact me, would you? I really want to see her and have her meet my boys. They're her grandsons!"

"Of course, if I find her, I will definitely put her in touch with you."

"That's all I wanted to ask. Thank you, Mr. Gardiner. Goodbye."

The line went dead. I sat in bed for a while, thinking. This was not the first time Skye had disappeared. I found it funny that in my brief experience searching for missing persons, I ended up spending as much time investigating who they were as where they were. Maybe the two things are intertwined.

CHAPTER

SEVEN

The next morning, I was back in the office. Over coffee, I related to Yana what I had learned about Skye. I wanted to get her take from a female's perspective.

"So, if I met her twelve years ago, I'm guessing she was 26 going on 27 maybe." I rambled along, thinking out loud. "Her birthday was in the summer. I was seventeen, but I thought she was about ten years older than me. She had that older girl aura about her, I guess. So that would have made her nineteen when she ran away from home. So, she must have had Summer when she was eighteen or nineteen. Not sure how long she stuck around after she had the baby. I get the impression, and I could be wrong, that Skye's baby, Summer, and Summer's two boys, Abe and Ike, are accidents. Accidents from prostituting. Summer, I figure, can't be more than twenty, and she has two boys, three and four years old. So, the Goldbergs were selling her underage."

"That's sick. I'm not surprised Skye ran away. If it were me, I couldn't get away fast enough."

"Even leaving your child behind?"

"That would make it tougher. I wouldn't be shocked if it has messed her up because of it."

"I remember her now from that one summer I was hanging out down there. I didn't really know her well. She was Dan's girlfriend. She lived at the house, I think. We only talked a few times, and she was always pushing Tarot card readings or palm readings, or delving into my astrology sign. You know, which stars were with which planets in retrograde or whatever."

"Sounds like her parents weren't traditionally Jewish. Or maybe they were, and this is her way of rejecting them."

"They could be ultra-conservatives. I mean, kibbutzim is just a commune in Hebrew. Although the prostitution and drug dealing don't fit. I'm thinking, maybe she didn't mean to set Dan up for a murder rap. Maybe she was just trying to deter him from trying to look for her when she ran away."

"Pretty heavy-duty deterrence. Plus, it doesn't explain why she left her purse and IDs behind."

"She's pretty resourceful. When she fled her parents, I'm sure she didn't have money or IDs then either. Maybe this is her way of making a clean break of it."

"Hmmm." She said, slowly sipping her Frappuccino while she thought through these possibilities.

"I guess I'm going to hire Vera," I said, changing the subject.

"She seems pretty competent, all-round. I don't think she'll be happy just answering phones, but that's just my take on her."

"No, I'm sure I'll have to include her in some of the sleuthing to keep her happy. But I've got no one else. No one has applied for the job."

"Really? But you're so famous now."

"Ha, ha." I laughed sarcastically. "Do you think she's lesbian?" I mused.

"What?"

"Gay."

"I'm gay. She's not gay." Yana gave me a disbelieving frown.

"You're gay?" I said, surprised.

"How long have you known me?"

"I thought you were just Goth."

"One does not preclude the other. You can be both. Honestly, James, you can be so naïve."

"Do you have a girlfriend?"

"No. I have no time for relationships right now. If I'm not here, I'm in class or studying. I barely have time to sleep these days."

"It'll get better. After you've passed your bar exam."

"You bet it will. I have a lot of catch-up partying to do."

We toasted coffee cups to that.

While waiting for the morning traffic to clear, I put in a call to the prosecutor's office to see if I could get an appointment to talk, explaining who and what I was investigating. I wasn't expecting to get much cooperation for reopening a case that they lost, especially if I were to turn up evidence that the whole thing was one big scam and that they were the mark. They didn't disappoint and put me off with a vague promise to call me back next week.

I then headed back down to Manhattan Beach. Dan hadn't mentioned that Skye had her own apartment, even while living with him. Jack had texted me with the address, also in Manhattan. Her apartment turned out to be a little four-hundred-square-foot studio built over the two-car garage with a private entrance up a wooden stairway from the alley, a few blocks up from the beach. I could see from the outside that it probably had a nice ocean view, so there was that.

It turned out that the same older couple still owned the main house as when Skye was a tenant there. I interviewed them. They were a cute pair of eighty-somethings. He was small and spry, very tanned with little hair and thick over-sized glasses; she was bigger than her husband in every way, with a wide, happy face that hinted at maybe a Pacific-Islander background. They remembered Skye as a quiet, friendly girl who was rarely home, never complained, never had people over, or played loud music, which they liked. They couldn't point me towards any friends or acquaintances since they had never met any. They first learned of the murder when the police came knocking and searched her place. They had to leave the place untouched for the duration of the trial. At that point, since no one had surfaced to claim her belongings, they boxed all her things up and stored them in the garage and re-rented the place. Those boxes languished there, taking up one of the parking spaces for several years before they finally got rid of it all.

Of course, as is always the case, not but a few weeks after they had cleaned out the garage, someone came by inquiring after the stuff. It was a young Hispanic girl who said she was a friend of the family and had a letter authorizing her to take everything. She seemed quite disappointed to hear it was all thrown away.

That last part, the Hispanic girl, intrigued me as I didn't imagine from my brief meeting with the Goldbergs that they had any family that wasn't white and Jewish. I asked about the car, Skye's VW bug. They said it had sat in the alley next to the stairs for weeks, then one day it was gone. They figured the police had come and towed it away.

"So that's it?" I asked finally. "There is nothing of hers left here."

"No." The old man said, shaking his head.

"Except for the hand!" His wife piped in helpfully.

The old man looked at his mate, confused. "Oh, that." He said, remembering. "She had a carving of a wooden hand hanging outside her doorway. We had forgotten about it when we got rid of her stuff.

"But we liked it, so we left it up." The wife chimed in.

"A hand?" I asked.

"Some kind of New Age talisman, I figure. It had an eye in the palm." He held up his hand and demonstrated the location of the eye. "It's still there if you want to see it."

"Sure," I said. I figured I could take a picture and see if it meant anything to anyone. I thought back to the mural on the barn.

They led me out the back door to the alley and around to the stairs that climbed above the garage.

"Oh!" The old woman exclaimed. "I could have sworn I saw it there just last week." She shook her head tsk-tsking. "You just can't have nice things outside these days or someone will steal them."

I looked up at the door to the apartment. I could barely make out a shadow of a spot where the object had shielded the sun's bleaching rays over the years.

***

Since I was already down in the South Bay, I thought I'd try to scare up some old acquaintances of Skye's. the police had already done a pretty thorough job, and I had read all their interview transcripts. But I thought it wouldn't hurt to see some of these people face-to-face.

There was a psychic reader and massage therapist listed in the interviews as a friend of Skye's. Aisha al-Farisi had a small shop on Pier Avenue in Hermosa Beach. That was my first stop.

Her business was in an old bungalow, one of three, squeezed side by side onto a small parcel of land. On one side was a locksmith, and on the other a pet groomer. I was surprised that these old buildings were still standing and hadn't given way long ago to some big new development. The owner must be holding out for top dollar for the land, I thought.

The cottage was painted pink and white, though now peeling. A palmistry hand in bright red neon decorated the front window, and a sign announced "Psychic Readings and Therapeutic Massage".

As I opened the door, I heard the tinkling of wind chimes, but on looking around, I spied none. Must be a digital door chime, I figured. Aisha was apparently in a back room, as the front parlor was deserted. The place smelled pleasantly of incense. I looked around. There was a chakra chart on one wall and a large poster of the Potala Palace and Monastery in Tibet on the other. I didn't know the Buddha was into divination. In the center of the room was a round table surrounded by several comfortable-looking chairs. All that was missing was the crystal ball, I thought.

Aisha entered, barefoot and dressed in a pink and orange sari. She was thin, with sharp features, high cheekbones, and an aquiline nose. She had very long, dark blonde hair with a trace of gray at the crown in her part. She had a tanned face with fine lines around her eyes and mouth, and no make-up.

"How can I help you today?" she cooed.

"I hope you can," I replied a little too eagerly as I pulled out my ID. "I was hoping to take a few minutes of your time to ask a couple of questions. I'm a private detective looking into the disappearance of Skye Goldberg."

"She isn't missing, she's dead," Aisha replied with a concerned and confused look on her face.

"Some new facts have been uncovered that lead us to believe that maybe she is not dead. I understand that you were a friend of hers."

Aisha leaned back, her guard up. "We were friendly, but I wouldn't say we were friends."

"I read in your police interview that you hadn't seen her for more than a week before she disappeared. Did anyone ever contact you on her behalf afterwards, looking for information or to retrieve personal belongings?"

"No, of course not, why would they? As I said, we weren't friends. I had nothing that belonged to her."

"What was the nature of your relationship with her?"

"As you can see, I give psychic readings. Skye had expressed an interest in that. She told me she had purchased a deck of Tarot cards and was teaching herself how to read the cards. She came to me to see about more professional instruction."

"And did you?"

"Sure, why not? She was willing to pay for it."

"No concerns that she would be a competitor?"

"Oh, no. She said she was only interested in doing it for fun and for friends. Those friends often turn into customers for me when they seek a deeper reading."

"I think she read my cards once or twice."

"You knew her?"

"I used to hang out down here as a kid, ten, twelve years ago. We crossed paths, but I wouldn't say I knew her. How long have you had your business here in Hermosa?

"Over twenty years, and before that, a few years in Hollywood."

"How did you end up here?"

"Hollywood was getting too dangerous for me. Sure, that's where the tourists were, but I was afraid of being robbed all the time. Hermosa seemed like a nice beach town with the kind of residents who might be interested in my services. But business was slow, and the rent was high, so I expanded into massage therapy and holistic wellness counseling."

"So, you taught Skye about Tarot?"

"And astrology and palmistry. She had a knack for it even though she was an amateur. She was a cute young girl, and people naturally took to her."

"She wasn't that young; I think she was in her late twenties when I met her."

"I guess, but she had that look. She could be twenty-eight and pass for eighteen. She knew how to talk to the clients. I'm sure she could have made a career of it if she applied herself. I even offered to let her work from here while she studied if she wanted to bring in clients."

"Wouldn't that hurt your business?"

"Not really. I thought she might be able to help with the rent. Rent is so damn expensive down here."

"Yeah, you said that. I gather she didn't take you up on it."

"She did at first, for a while, but not for long enough to be helpful."

"So, she gave up on it, then?"

"Sort of. She wasn't interested in doing it for money, just for fun. She wasn't serious about the art of divination. She was more into mood rings and luck charms, the whole retro 60s scene. Skye was such a sweet girl; she was just born forty years too late. Once she learned the basics enough to entertain her friends, she lost interest in further study. But we continued to see each other now and then. It's a small town."

"Did you ever meet her boyfriend, Dan?"

"No, never did. She never talked about him except in passing when she would talk about their parties."

"No other friends that you knew of?"

"No. Actually, it seemed that whenever I ran into her, she was alone."

"Hmm," I muttered, lost in thought.

"Would you like a reading today? Maybe, together, we can see where your investigation may be heading."

"Another time, perhaps. But thank you for your time."

Stepping outside, I looked back at the large front window and the neon hand.

"Excuse me, Aisha," I called back to her as she was shutting the door. She paused, expectantly. "Does your hand sign ever have an eye in the palm?" I asked, pointing.

She glanced at her sign, momentarily confused, then realized what I was asking. "No, this just advertises my chiromancy practice, palm reading. The hand you are talking about is the Hamsa. In Islam, it is a good luck charm used to ward off evil spirits."

"Islam, not Judaism?"

"It is the same. The Jews call it the Hand of Miriam."

I shook my head as if understanding, but I wasn't. After Aisha closed the door, I glanced around what was sort of downtown, the heart of Hermosa. It was largely the same, but somehow different, a different vibe than what I remembered from a decade ago.

I thought I'd grab lunch before looking up the next person on my list. I was curious if Burger World was still around. I used to love that place. They had nearly a hundred different kinds of burgers, all named after different cities in the world, a Lahaina burger with pineapple, a Seoul burger with kimchi, a Berlin burger with sauerkraut, etc. One of my favorites was the Roma burger - marinara, mozzarella, prosciutto, and black olives.

I found my favorite dive where I'd left it, on Pacific Coast Highway. The joint had been recently remodeled, but the menu was the same. I munched down a Bangkok burger – spicy peanut sauce and bean sprouts, with seasoned curly fries and a Coke, while I jotted down some notes from my talks with the landlords and the fortune teller. I looked over who else I needed to track down.

After lunch, I strolled back down to Pier Avenue, to the heart of Hermosa. It had been many years since I had been here last. They had closed off the street and created a plaza, meaning no cars, and covered the pavement with fancy tiles and potted palms. About half of the bars and souvenir shops that I remembered had since changed hands or changed names in those intervening years. Still, it brought back a lot of memories.

McGrath's was an Irish bar near the pier, right on the Strand, just steps from the sand. Not many bars are open at 10 AM, but beach bars are a whole genre unto themselves. I headed over for a beer and to see if any of Skye's fellow bar girls were still working there.

When the cute blonde brought me my Guinness, I ran through my list of names with her. None of the former waitresses were still around. The bartender, though, was. He now owned the place. She said he was in the back office, but she'd see if he could come out.

Pat, the bartender/owner, looked like a six-foot-two leprechaun. He had a ruddy red face from too much sun, framed by longish white hair and a glorious white beard. The smile lines around his eyes and mouth seemed miles deep.

"I never liked Dan." He expounded. "Skye was sweet and innocent, and he was a pompous blowhard, a self-proclaimed expert on anything and everything, and an opinion to go with it."

"Sounds like an odd couple." I mused.

"Yeah, I didn't get it either. Skye was not well educated, but she had street sense. She was good with people. Mr. Wikipedia couldn't read a room. He was always getting into verbal brawls, a real sarcastic son-of-a-bitch, too. He'd dish out insults that would make Don Rickles cringe."

"But they didn't call on you to testify."

"The prosecution apparently had more than enough character witnesses. Besides, I would have to admit, being an asshole doesn't make you a killer. If Skye faked her own death to get away from him, I wouldn't be surprised."

"Skye always looked younger than she was. I'm assuming she satisfied you with a proper ID that proved she was of age to serve liquor."

"Yeah, she did look underage, but I'm pretty practiced in spotting a fake ID. She must have had a legitimate driver's license or something to get hired."

I ran my list of names by Pat to see if he might know where any of his old waitresses might have gone. Only one came to mind, Sarah. He said she had gone over to work at Bay City Blues, a club about a block away, and took Skye with her. He thought she might still be there.

Bay City Blues was a jazz club, one of several music clubs and comedy clubs along a strip a couple of blocks from the beach. It was also on my list. Skye had worked there up until she disappeared and was friends with the booking manager, a guy named Howard Washington. Maybe I'd get lucky and catch up with them both.

Most of these clubs were only open in the evening, but Bay City had a Happy Hour promotion, so they opened at four. I had a couple of hours to kill, so I went for a walk along the Strand and out to the end of the pier. The Hermosa pier was pretty basic – a wooden walkway surrounded by a steel railing – no shops, no bathroom facilities. It was a place to look out over the ocean or look back at the beach and the town. It was also a place to fish, and the end of the pier was full of fishermen, sitting in their lawn chairs or upended plastic buckets and minding their poles. I tarried for a while, then walked back to the promenade.

Not much had changed here either in the time since I had been here last. The promenade was still a conglomeration of bars, casual restaurants, and tourist shops selling t-shirts, boogie boards and swim goggles. Along the Strand, there were a few new three-story, five-thousand-square-foot beach bungalows in steel and glass, replacing the old clapboard cottages from days gone by. But the people had changed. There were still the cyclists on their beach cruisers, but gone were the roller skaters with their boom boxes on their shoulders and strains of the Eagles pouring out for all to hear. They had been replaced by kids on E-bikes and moms with jogging strollers as far as the eye could see. The weather was still the best in the country.

Things were pretty slow when I entered Bay City Blues at four o'clock. The live music wouldn't start for a few hours. They had some Dave Brubeck piped in in the meantime. I ordered a jalapeno margarita and asked if either Sarah or Howard was in. Sarah wasn't due until six, but Howard was in the back office.

Bay City had one of those decors of exposed brick walls, well-worn wooden floors, and open ceilings with visible air ducts and such. Hirschfield-style ink caricatures of famous jazz greats hung above the booths. The A/C kept it cool, and the lighting was low, in stark contrast to the outside. I had finished my first drink and was starting on another when Howard finally made it out. He was a youngish black dude, tall and thin, clean-shaven and with close-cropped hair and square rimless eyeglasses. He looked more like an accountant than a musician, and I couldn't believe he was old enough to have been working here ten years ago.

He introduced himself, then sat down and said nothing, waiting for me to explain why I was bothering him. I introduced myself and explained again how I was looking into Skye's whereabouts, as there was now suspicion that she might only be missing, not dead. Records showed that she was working here up until the day she disappeared.

"Yeah, I knew Skye. I had only recently been hired on to manage the talent here while I was working on launching my own career." He began. "Skye had apparently worked a few places around town before she ended up here. It's a good gig. Hours aren't bad if you're a night owl, and the tips are good. Rarely any trouble, neither. Jazz fans don't come here to get drunk and start fights. If you know what I mean."

I offered to buy him a drink, but Howard always waited until nearly closing before imbibing. A guy can't drink a lot every night and keep his health, he allowed. We swapped favorite artists and albums, and songs. Howard was a piano man, liked Art Tatum, McCoy Tyner, Oscar, and Herbie. Me - I was a ladies' man, Billie, Ella, Peggy Lee.

"Do you remember the last time you saw her?" I asked, returning to my original line of questioning.

"Man, that was a long time ago. I don't remember one night from another from last week."

"How about her boyfriend, Dan. He ever come around?"

"Oh, yeah. I remember him, alright."

"How so?"

"He only came around on certain nights, depending on who was playing. He would always come early, before the set. He was dropping off a few bags of blow for some of the band."

"He was pushing coke?"

"That's what they call it."

"Management let him get away with that?"

"He was very discreet and only dealt with the talent, never sold to the help or the customers. So, the boss looked the other way."

I let that last bit sink in while I swirled my drink around in the glass. I looked up at Howard. He smiled back, pleasantly, waiting for the next question.

"Excuse me for saying, but you don't look old enough to have been working here twelve years ago."

"I'm thirty-four. I had just graduated from the Colburn Music School and was trying to land gigs for a jazz trio I started. The Lighthouse was one of our first jobs. While we were playing here, the booking manager quit to go work at a club in Vegas. I told the owner I was pretty well connected and could fill in, bring in some good acts. I lied, 'cause the club dates weren't paying the bills and I needed a full-time job. But it worked out. I hustled, worked the few friends I knew, and landed a couple of name groups. In the meantime, my trio kept playing opening sets."

"You still have your trio?"

"Different guys, but yes."

"You'll have to let me know where you're playing. I'd like to come listen."

"Sure, man." He looked up over my shoulder. "There's Sarah, now. She just walked in."

Sarah was not what I would have considered a beach babe. She had no tan; her skin was as white as I'd ever seen. It went well with her fiery red hair. She had a cute face. Her eyebrows were the same light orange as the freckles that dusted her nose and cheeks.

Howard signaled her to come over. "Sarah, you got five minutes to talk to Mr. Gardiner here before you clock in?"

"Sure. What about?" Sarah had a chipper quality to her voice.

Howard and I both rose to our feet. "Sorry, I couldn't have been of more help. But I've got a lot of stuff to get done before the set starts." I shook his hand. "Yeah. Thanks, though. I'll come back some time to sit and listen."

Howard headed to the back room. I turned to look at Sarah. She had her head tilted, patient and expectant as a schoolgirl.

"Hi, Sarah. I'm James. Why don't you sit down? I just had a few questions I wanted to ask you about Skye."

At the mention of her name, Sarah's demeanor changed. "What about her? You know she's dead, right?"

"Maybe, not. I'm a private detective. I've been hired to look into her disappearance."

Sarah put her bag and clothes on the table and slowly sat. "What do you mean, maybe not?"

"There has been a report of her being sighted in the area recently."

Sarah looked very confused.

"I'm investigating whether the murder scene was staged to hide her disappearance, and by whom and why. I wanted to get some background on Skye, and I am told that you were pretty close friends with her at the time."

"You're not suggesting that she would do such a thing. Skye was a very innocent girl. If there is such a thing these days."

"No. It may be that there are several moving pieces to this story. Someone may have used her disappearance to frame Dan for some reason."

"That jerk. I hope he's still in jail."

"He actually was found not guilty at trial."

"Oh, yeah, right."

"Did you know that Skye ran away from home as a young girl? Never looked back. I'm wondering if she might have wanted to run away again; you know, start over. Did she ever talk about wanting to live or visit anywhere in particular?"

"Not that I remember. We mostly just talked about what was happening around town, with mutual friends, other people we knew. That kind of small talk. We weren't really friends, just work friends, you know."

"Did she have any friends from out of the area? Maybe they'd come into the bar, McGraths or here, to visit?"

Sarah thought for a minute. "Well, there was one guy. He used to hang around a lot with his friends. He's from south of the border. I mean, he lived here in So-Cal, but he was from some country down south. Not Mexico. He hated it if you thought he was Mexican. He was from one of those other countries, maybe El Salvador or something."

"Where did he live when he was up here in L.A.?"

"Oh, I don't know. Not many Hispanics in the beach cities, that's for sure. He lived somewhere east of here, is all I know."

"I gather that you didn't care much for Dan, though."

"Oh, he was a jerk. I don't know why she stayed with him. I mean, besides the fact that he was rich and had a cool house right on the Strand. But he was like twice her age. A pretty grumpy old man, in my opinion."

"And he did like the young girls, I'm told."

"He was a horn dog. Always throwing parties at his house for the kids in hopes of banging one. Skye said they had an open relationship, but that just meant cheating without recriminations."

"Did you ever go to any of those parties?"

"Never. They were all full of high school and college kids. I mean, I wasn't that much older, but you never want to be the oldest girl at a party."

"Yeah, I know what you mean. I was there for a few, one summer."

"You were?"

"The summer before my senior year in high school."

"So that's how you know Dan? And he just called you up ten years later?"

"Actually, we just happened to run into each other. But let me ask you, did Dan know about this other guy?"

"Maybe not. If she was cheating on him, she didn't flaunt it like he did. He probably wouldn't have cared, though. Takes the guilt card away. But you can never tell how a guy will react."

"Do you think he was abusive, maybe violent? Did he ever hit her that you know of?"

"You mean Dan? No. He was more of the emotional blackmailer type, if you catch my drift."

"No. How's that?"

"She was a free spirit, as I'm sure others have already told you. But he'd control her by pretending to get depressed and suicidal if she strayed too far. The open relationship only really went one way. Even his cheating became her fault. I don't know why she put up with it, to tell you the truth. Maybe there was something else, maybe he had something on her. Could be that faking her own death was the only way to make a clean break with him."

"I guess he and this other guy never ran into each other here then."

"No, Dan would usually come in with Skye at the start of her shift and sit around and drink for an hour or so, then scoot when the place started to fill up. If her other friend came at all, it was closer to closing time, and she'd leave with him."

"Did this guy have a name?"

Sarah stopped and looked down, then looked up and glanced around the room, twisting up her eyes as if trying to remember.

"Hugo. I think." She said quietly. "Hugo something. I don't know the last name. She never introduced me."

"And on those nights when neither were around, how did she come and go to work?"

"She walked. They only lived fifteen minutes away."

"She didn't have a car?"

"No, cars are a big hassle around here. No place to park. Besides, I don't think she knew how to drive." She laughed. "I remember her making a weird comment one time about stepping on the reverse pedal. She thought the brake pedal was to go backwards, not stop."

I laughed with her. "You know the original Model T did have a reverse pedal. But I'm sure that's not what she was talking about."

"Really? I've never heard of such a thing."

"Yeah, it would be tough to drive one today. The arrangement was not at all like what we were used to. The brake was a hand brake."

Sarah just nodded her head, confounded by the whole notion, then glanced at her watch and stood up. "Look, I've got to start getting prepared."

"Sure. Thanks for talking with me. Oh, one last thing. Has either Dan or Hugo been in here since Skye's disappearance?"

"Nope." She said, shaking her head. "Neither one."

"If I have any more questions, I'll come back, and if you think of anything, here's my card." I handed one to her before she hurried into the back.

As I sat there finishing my drink, the quip about the car started to nag at me. I remember Jack saying she had a driver's license. She could have gotten that later, though I doubted it. She was doing a good job of hiding her trail. She certainly wouldn't go and get a license with a new address. I made a mental note to look at the date on her license. Tomorrow, I would try to track down the MGB. How many could there be? In the meantime, I needed to call Vera and offer her the job. I was going to need help. She seemed competent for her age, and it was not as if I had a line of applicants waiting at the door.

CHAPTER

EIGHT

I put Jack on looking into DMV records for all MGBs in Southern California. It was a long shot, but maybe one was registered to Skye. While he was in the database, I wanted to see if he could track down her old VW. Either way, I was going to play a hunch and visit repair shops that specialized in English or foreign cars. I had an older model Jag in college. The electrical systems on those old English cars had a reputation for being troublesome. I was counting on Skye's MG needing the same repair work. I take my Mercury to a guy who only works on classic cars. He has a bulletin board by the office door that is usually crammed with people wanting to buy or sell this car or that. Oftentimes, they are great bargains, totally restored cars for a fraction of the cost of the restoration. I figured that at some time, Skye must have brought her car to one of these independent mechanics for service work, or maybe she had bought her car in one of these shops. The photo I had of Skye was ten years old, but I imagined that she probably was still looking pretty much the same. Dan had recognized her.

There were British specialty car repair shops in Inglewood, Hawthorne, and Bellflower. I would start with them. I posed as an aficionado, looking to buy something in good condition. My story was that my dad once had one and always spoke fondly of it, kept a framed picture of it on his desk. I was looking for something like his, preferably in red. I eschewed buying from someone online, preferring instead to scout the car shops where I might be able to talk to the mechanic who had worked on it. I would hold off bringing up Skye until I found a similar car. The first couple of shops didn't turn up anything, though I did learn a lot more about British cars than I had planned on. I got a hit in Bellflower.

Bellflower is a city about fifteen or twenty-miles due east of Hermosa. Mike Nguyen was the shop owner and chief mechanic. He was an older guy, maybe sixty, very thin but muscular. He wore an olive-drab sleeveless T-shirt and camo cargo pants, both oil-stained, and an olive-green patrol cap. He wiped his hand clean on a rag before accepting my handshake. His shop was small, with two lifts, and not very clean; there seemed to be a thin film of grease and grime on most surfaces, but very orderly. There were no MGs visible, but a half dozen other cars: Minis, Smarts, two Peugeots, and a Citroen, mostly small sports cars. All were in various stages of repair.

I told Mike I was looking to find an MGB, in good working condition, the cleaner the better, preferably red. I said I had already checked out what was online, and they were either too expensive or needed too much work, so I was looking around at the various shops for a posting.

Mike said he got the occasional MG in now and then, but they were becoming increasingly scarce. I agreed and noted my surprise at the number of French cars in his place. He explained that his father opened the shop after he moved the family here following the war. His dad had gotten his start in the car business by working at a Citroen assembly plant in Saigon. Lacking any other skills, he decided to try his hand at auto repair when he arrived here. Citroens were what he knew best; other European models followed as his business grew, VWs, Beemers, Fiats, etc. As he happily related his history to me, Mike lit up a cigarette. I half expected he'd pull out a Gauloise or something, but his brand was Camel unfiltered.

While he smoked, I told him about my Lola. Mike had an appreciation for classic American cars. He had seen a lot of those older model cars on the streets as a kid in Nam. After we were done swapping stories, I offered him my card and asked him to let me know if any likely prospects came into the shop. Mike remembered that there was one possible candidate, a blonde, white woman who had her MGB in for a new fuel pump. MGs were notorious for their fuel pumps going out. Anyway, he didn't figure that she was all that happy with the car. Women didn't much like stick shifts to begin with, in his opinion. But it was a beauty, a red '77 Mark IV roadster. Needed a new paint job, but ran well when he put in the new pump.

My ears pricked up at the mention of a blonde. I asked if he had a name or an address I could have. I'd try to contact her and make her an offer.

He shook his head. "She paid cash."

"Did you fill out any paperwork, license number, VIN, anything?"

"No. Cash work is mostly under the table, no paperwork, no taxes. You know?"

"How about a photo?" I pressed.

"Nope. I only take pictures if the owner wants to sell, or if it's in great condition and I need to document any nicks or dings beforehand."

"Well, if you see her again, give me a call, or give her my card. I'd much appreciate it." I said as I handed him one of my phony alias business cards and a twenty, then headed out. Mike pocketed both and gave me a nod before ducking back under the hood.

I didn't walk away with anything but optimism. It would have been nice to see a photo; I could have run the plates, but I felt certain that the woman was Skye. MGs are scarce enough; the odds of a blonde woman driving one were even higher. But I couldn't really wait around for her car to break down again. I hoped that Jack would be able to come up with something on his search.

It was late afternoon by the time I got back to my office. No Jack around, and of course, being Saturday, no Yana. I decided to put in a couple of hours going through Jon's files, which included the court transcripts. I wanted to see if Sarah or Howard or Pat, or Aisha were interviewed or testified and if they said anything new or contradictory to what they had told me yesterday.

I had already read the detective interviews with Aisha and Pat, and Sarah. They had also interviewed the old couple who were Skye's landlords, but it seems they didn't talk to Howard. I guess they had barely crossed paths, and Howard probably couldn't add anything to what they already knew.

"Except about the drugs," I said aloud to no one.

None of them had been called to testify. Apparently, the prosecution could find plenty of people who didn't like Dan, but no one who could say that Dan didn't like Skye. By all accounts, he doted on her.

The sky was getting dark and I was getting hungry. I was just about to grab my hat and go out for a bite when my cell rang.

"Mr. Gardiner." It was Mike from the repair shop.

"Mr. Nguyen?"

"I was able to get an address for you. No name or phone number, though. I'm sorry. I remembered that the young lady had to have the car towed in. She paid cash for the tow, but the driver did have an address to pick up the car. It's on Figaroa Place, a cul-de-sac tucked up under the Harbor Freeway. I guess that's Long Beach."

I wrote down the address he gave me. "Thanks. Thank you very much. It's a little late to be dropping in unannounced, but I'll swing by there sometime next week and leave my card if no one's home. Maybe they'll give me a call back."

"Glad to be of help."

As I hung up the phone, I noticed it was getting late. I had a standing date with Rachel every Friday night, and tonight we were going to the Magic Castle. That's a private club in Hollywood, not too far from my office, just behind and up the hill from Grauman's Chinese Theater. It was a members-only club, but I had a friend of a friend who knew a guy and managed to score an invite. I had to get home quickly and get cleaned up. The club had a strict dress code – coat and tie for men, semi-formal dress for women. In the foyer, where you can mingle and enjoy a drink before dinner, there is a piano that takes requests. Just the piano, there is no one sitting at the keys, you make your requests to the piano itself, and it plays any tune! A great way to start your night of mystery.

On our dates, we usually talked about most anything but my work. Rachel had expressed a distinct disinterest in my job when she thought all I did was spy on errant husbands or workers' comp cheats. But ever since I told her the story of my summer down in Hermosa and the subsequent mystery of Professor Dan and Skye, she was hooked like a soap opera TV addict. She couldn't get enough and was always pressing me for the latest updates. Tonight, I would finally have some interesting tales to tell.

That night, I had the prime rib and Rachel had the Condon Bleu. We split a bottle of Bordeaux while I filled her in on my investigation to date. I relayed in ghastly detail my adventurous road trip up to the central coast to see Skye's creepy Manson family relatives, and the unusual late-night phone call from her abandoned daughter.

"This is getting interesting," Rachel admitted.

I related what I had learned from the psychic, the bartender, and the waitress, plus the dirt I picked up on Dan from the musician scheduler at the jazz house.

"Seems like there's more to him you should be checking out, too." She added.

I wrapped it up with the part about my getting a lead on the little red MGB.

"So, after the trial, the Hermosa Police never followed up on a missing person's investigation?" Rachel asked.

"No. I'm guessing they were either too angry or too embarrassed or both that their murder charge didn't stick. Besides, you know how many people go missing every year in this country?"

Off of her blank look, I continued. "Over six hundred thousand. That's like, about two thousand a week. Granted, ninety-nine percent of those get resolved one way or another, but that means at least twenty people a week go missing and are never heard from again."

"I'm impressed that you have all those statistics at hand."

"I've taken on missing person cases before; I looked it up once. Besides, I have a head for random trivia. Not that this information is good for much other than just cocktail chatter. It's probably too gruesome a statistic for Jeopardy!"

Dinner finished, we proceeded to the Palace of Mystery for the big stage show. The Palace was for the bigger acts. The magician would perform his tricks, usually with the aid of an assistant or member of the audience. The

Castle also had a smaller venue for slightly more intimate bits, and then my favorite, the close-up room, where you can actually sit at the table and watch the card tricks right in front of your eyes.

It's a full evening of fun by the time you've watched all three shows. The detective in me wants to figure out how they did it, but the child in me wants to be amazed. Usually, the child wins out.

CHAPTER

NINE

Saturday morning, Rachel had her regular eight a.m. spinning class, so I dropped her off and drove on down to Long Beach. On a weekday, this would be over an hour's drive, but with no traffic, I was there in a little over forty minutes. The address took me to a little neighborhood, a few blocks long, of nearly identical one-thousand-square-foot houses squeezed between the Harbor Freeway and a square mile of oil storage tanks. I exited the freeway and cruised down the street. The houses were older, 1950s era, but neat and well-kept, painted various pastel colors. The yards were cared for with an abundance of flowers and fruit trees. No place to park, though, the streets were lined with cars and pick-up trucks – more trucks than cars it seemed. As it was trash collection day, even the red curbs were blocked with green, blue, and black trash containers. The address I was looking for was at the end, on a big circular cul-de-sac. The little red MG was parked right out front, with the top down. I stopped long enough to get out and snap a picture of the license. I noticed that the tags were out of date. I had to drive two blocks back to find a parking spot, but I could still see the house well enough. I hunkered down and grabbed my now cold cup of coffee and waited. If I were lucky, Skye would walk out.

I texted a picture of the license to Jack to see if he could track down the owner. I knew it was Sunday, but this wouldn't be the first time I called on him over a weekend.

The neighborhood was pretty quiet, even for a Sunday morning, no joggers or dog walkers out. After a few minutes, I heard the distant sound of a lawnmower starting up, then the shriek of little kids running around in their backyard somewhere. The place was waking up.

Lola was not the most inconspicuous of cars, but on this street, it was probably less out of place than my Tesla. I just hoped it didn't draw too many admirers. I already had a story if people got too nosy about what I was doing hanging out here. I would tell them I had a little too much to drink last night and felt too drunk to drive, so I pulled off the freeway and slept here in my car. I pulled my hat down over my eyes, leaving just a gap to watch the house, and pretended to be asleep.

Sitting there, my mind wandered back to a year before, surveilling another house in another neighborhood and getting beaten up and shot at and later arrested for being in the wrong place at the wrong time. After about an hour or so, I noticed an older Hispanic woman exit the front door of the house I was surveilling. I watched as she went and grabbed a garden hose, unfurling it to begin watering various pots and garden areas in front of the house. I hopped out of my car and walked casually up to her house, stopping to admire the MG. It was nice and clean on the outside, no nicks or scratches. But the inside was a bit of a mess, empty coffee cups in the cup holders, candy wrappers, and an empty Amazon box filled with junk mail on the passenger side floor.

"Disculpe!" I turned and called out to the old woman.

She turned her head towards me and squinted, continuing her watering.

My meager grasp of Spanish failed me then. "Is this your car?

Esta...tu auto?"

"*No Ingles.*" She turned away from me.

I walked a few steps toward her. "*El auto rojo.* I would like to buy it. Is it for sale?

"*No Ingles.*" She glared over her shoulder at me.

I had opened up Google Translate on my phone, trying to engage her. "*Es de ... tu Marido?*"

"*Mis hijos.*"

Her son. "*Este tu Hijo en Casa?*"

She shook her head, no.

"*Puedo tener tu numero de telefono?*"

She shook her head again. "*No telefono.*"

I turned back to the car, walked around it, pretending to admire it while I strategized my next move. I didn't want to show her a picture of Skye. I didn't want Skye to know I was looking for her. It might spook her into disappearing again. For now, I was just a random car buyer. I wanted to leave her one of my fake business cards. I couldn't really disclose that I was a private investigator. I didn't have anything else to write my number down. I noticed a scrap of paper among the trash on the floor of the passenger's side and reached down to grab it. I turned back to the old woman to ask if she might have a pencil or pen when I saw a young man step through the front doorway. The screen door slammed behind him. He was in his mid-twenties, wore blue jeans, a white sleeveless tee-shirt, and was barefoot. His arms were completely tattooed, and I could see ink on his chest and throat up to his jawline. He glowered with a sullen expression as he walked down the sidewalk toward me.

"What you doing here?" He challenged.

"Oh, hi. Hola." I answered, wiping the sweat from my palms,

happy at least that he spoke English. "I was looking at the little MG here and was interested in buying it."

"Not for sale."

"I'll pay a good price, better than you'll get for a trade-in." I urged.

"Not for sale."

"Okay. Well, if you ever change your mind, maybe I could leave you my phone number."

"You deaf? Not for sale." He stepped toward me, his fists clenched.

I stared back at him, not sure how far to push it.

"Leave." He said in a low-key but very threatening tone."

"Okay." I started to walk backwards towards my car, palms out, trying to act nonchalant. I had heard and read enough about these gang members not to want to risk any further interaction. Best just to walk away. This was a new complication, but at least I had found the car. I had a lead. Time to regroup.

I settled back into my car, only now looking at the scrap of paper still in my hand. It was a betting slip from the Santa Anita horse track. I looked up. The tattooed man still watched me from a block away. I stared back, then pulled out my phone and called Vera. "How do you take your coffee?"

"Black. Two sugars."

"See you in the morning.

CHAPTER

TEN

This was to be Yana's last week. I had asked Vera to come in at nine so that Yana could start to show her the ropes before she had to head out to class. I had made my usual Starbucks run and brought an extra, black with two sugars, for Vera. If she wasn't punctual, her coffee was going to get cold.

She walked in, right on the dot. She was dressed the same as when she interviewed, blue slacks, a white short-sleeved dress shirt, rolled up at the bicep. I motioned to the coffee and sugar packets on the desk.

"Good morning, Vera."

"Good morning, Mr. Gardiner."

"Call me James. Let's have a brief chat and then I'll let Yana take over and fill you in on how the office is run. Come on into the office."

I leaned back in my chair, sipping my coffee, and watched Vera doctor hers up. As she stirred in the sugar, she glanced up. "So that E and E on the corner selling tourist maps, is he on the payroll or does he just work for coffee?"

From the confused expression on my face Vera guessed I didn't get the acronym.

"Eyes and ears. It's detective lingo."

"Oh, you mean Jimmy? I give him some cash now and then when I ask him to do something for me. I didn't notice you waiting outside when I came in."

"I was in the coffee shop on the other corner."

"That was very observant of you. Of course, I could have just been being friendly. You should never jump to conclusions."

She took a sip of her coffee. "I try not to. Jimmy tells me you've been bringing him coffee for a couple of years now."

I looked up, arching one eyebrow in surprise.

She continued. "You park your '57 Marquis in the outdoor lot down the street, probably because it is too big to make the turn on the ramp down into the parking garage in this building. That gives you a short walk up Cahuenga to work, where you buy a copy of the Times and the Journal. You've been passing Jimmy every day. One day, he probably gave you a tip. Maybe someone was waiting to serve you a summons or something. After that, you decided you could use some eyes and ears on the street. Every detective has them."

I stared at Vera with a newfound appreciation. "So, you've been checking me out?"

"Standard due diligence. I want to know what I'm getting into."

"So, what else have you found out?"

"You live in Beachwood Canyon, bought your house six years ago all cash, your other car is a Tesla, which you recently bought, trading in your Civic. Though a Civic is a much less conspicuous car if you're doing surveillance. You graduated from Stanford, were a pretty good golfer in High School, but I guess you didn't follow that through. You've been arrested twice, but in neither case were charges filed."

"Yeah, that's one of the hazards of being an investigator, the police always think you're getting in the way." I tossed my empty coffee cup in the trash and leaned forward over my desk, trying not to look too impressed. I hadn't done anything to vet her, hadn't even called her references, yet.

"And despite that, you've decided to take the job anyway. I'm glad. You're a pretty good detective already. Let me fill you in on the case I'm currently working."

I started at the beginning and laid out the whole story to date, starting with my chance encounter with Dan at the chili festival, leaving out some of the details of my association with him during my teen years, and everything I'd learned so far about the mysterious Skye.

I reached into my desk drawer and pulled out a notepad and pen, which I gave to Vera, then pulled up a recent text from Jack.

"The MG is registered to a guy named Hugo Martinez, but he hasn't paid the registration fees for a couple of years now. I'll forward you Jack's info from the DMV with the license and VIN. You'll meet Jack sooner or later. He's another member of the team. I suspect that this Hugo is the same one that Sarah mentioned in my interview with her. I want you to find out anything you can about this guy. It's probably a very common name, which will make it more difficult. He may not be a citizen, but I suspect he has a driver's license. Also, let's check the ownership of the house on Figaroa Place."

"In addition to that, I want you to look into Dan's background. He used to have a realty company, which he sold. Also, he owned a number of rental properties, I'm guessing most, if not all, in the South Bay, but see what you can find out. He says he's sold them as well, but maybe he has quietly kept one or two. Let's see if we can get some background on him. Where did he come from? Where did he go to school? Any family in the area? Anything and everything could be helpful."

I indicated a stack of boxes by the file cabinets. "Those are the transcripts of the trial plus his attorney's notes. When you get a chance, you should read through all of that. But first, let me hand you over to Yana, and she will have you fill out some new hire paperwork. In the meantime, she can fill you in on how the office works, the voice mail, bank accounts, bills, et cetera."

I stood up and walked her to the door. "In the meantime, I think I owe my buddy, Dan, another visit."

I told Dan I wanted to drop by and fill him in on what I had uncovered so far. He was only too happy to have me come by the house. It had been a long time since I was last there. I wasn't expecting it to look at all familiar. And I was right. As I drove down PCH-1, Pacific Coast Highway, the main thoroughfare through the beach cities, I spied a lot of new businesses, new fast-food joints, new motels, and new retail. Everything was clean and shiny. A lot of the charm had been lost, especially in Hermosa, which was always the funkiest of the three.

As I hit the red light at Pier and waited for my turn to turn right and head down toward Dan's, I noticed the Trader Joe's across the street. This was the light where Dan must have seen Skye two weeks ago. Why did she take that chance, I wondered. Where was she going? To Long Beach, where I found her car? Where was she coming from? What lies along this street that so enticed her to risk discovery?

I turned, drove down Pier, then turned again and drove up Hermosa Avenue to Dan's place and parked behind his garage. Dan was waiting for me at the front door in his matching grey sweat pants and hoodie. He must have seen me coming on his security cameras. The main floor seemed much bigger than I remembered. Then I noticed that there was hardly any furniture, and definitely no clutter.

"You didn't have to clean up on my account." I joked. Dan snorted a stifled laugh. "Seriously, it looks like you're getting ready to sell the place. Are you?"

Dan led me back toward the kitchen, also ready for the Architectural Digest photographer. "Can I get you a drink?"

"No, I don't drink before four anymore."

"Happy Hour! That's a good habit. Coffee then?"

"Sure."

Dan fussed around preparing some coffee for both of us, first by grinding some fresh beans from the refrigerator. "I'm trying to pare back on material things. Simplify my life, you know. Get rid of my Jacob Marley chain of possessions. As Tyler Durden said, 'The things you own end up owning you.'"

"That's deep. Still the professor, I see."

"It sets you free, James. You should try it."

We settled in on barstools at the kitchen island. Dan poured boiling water into a French press while I ran through the events of the past week. I told him about my visit up north with Skye's family and the weird vibe I got from them.

"Never met them myself," Dan said as he handed me a steaming cup. "Skye never mentioned her folks one way or another."

"Really?" I asked. "She never told stories about her youth in the compound, never waxed nostalgic about her hippie childhood."

"Maybe a little. She could be sentimental at times, but those feelings didn't seem to include her parents. She never spoke of them."

"She has a daughter, it seems. Skye must have left her behind while she was still an infant. Name is Summer. I guess they're sticking with the hippie vibe. Summer would desperately love to meet her mother eventually, if we find her. She also has grandkids, if you can believe it. I don't know how many."

I related what conversations I'd had with her landlord, the fortune teller, Aisha, Pat the bartender, and Sarah the barmaid, omitting the parts where they disparaged him. Most of that he had heard before. Then I came to Howard.

"This is really good coffee," I remarked after taking my first sip. "No, really, what is it?"

"Kopi Luwak. Two hundred dollars a pound."

"I've heard of that. It's that cat shit stuff, right?"

"Something like that."

"Anyway, there's a guy at Bay City Blues who manages the bookings there. He remembers seeing you on a fairly regular basis. You'd come in with Skye at the start of her shift and usually leave before the first set started."

"I'm not much into jazz, more of an old rocker myself. But I liked walking Skye to work."

"So, this guy tells me that you were dealing blow to the artists."

Dan said nothing for a minute. He just stared at me with half-lidded eyes and sipped his coffee. "You think I'm a dealer? You know how it was. There was a lot of pot at those parties…"

"And powder."

"But it was all party drugs. Never any hard stuff. I didn't supply it all, but I confess, I did provide some. I'd go back to the dressing rooms, lay out a few lines, and we'd get high. My treat. In exchange, I got to hang with the band, so to speak. It was my way into the music scene. I'm just as big a starfucker as the next guy, I guess. Word got out that I had access, and people would hit me up to score for them. I was just trying to be a good friend. Those guys at the jazz club heard I could get my hands on some good coke, safe stuff, nothing laced with junk. I would occasionally buy for them. I wasn't dealing."

"I don't care. I'm not here to be judgmental. I'm just surprised it didn't come out at trial. An allegation like that plays for the prosecution on character."

"Maybe there was nothing to allege. I'm sure if the police heard this, they would have talked to the musicians."

"Like I said, I don't care. I had my first taste in this very house. But I'm working for you right now, and it helps to have all the information. Was Skye aware of this?"

"Skye was a pot head. She only smoked weed or hash from a bong and drank that cheap Moscato wine, or sometimes Sangria, very much the hippie flower child in her tastes. She was in many ways like a child. I felt protective of her."

"Let's talk about Skye some more. The barmaids tell me you two had an open relationship."

"That was just talk, gossip, showing off how liberal minded we were. We loved each other, but weren't ready to commit to marriage."

"So, Skye wasn't seeing anyone else, didn't have another boyfriend that you knew of?"

"If she did, it is news to me."

"There was a guy named Hugo who was a regular at Bay City. The other girls seemed to think she was seeing him."

"I'm sure she had friends. Skye was a very pretty young woman. But I had to trust her. I wasn't going to keep her on a leash."

"I don't mean to be insensitive, but if she was cheating on you, well, jealousy is a prime motive for murder. I'm surprised the prosecution didn't raise that if they heard some of the allegations that I have."

"It was a sloppy investigation. I always felt targeted. The prosecutors wanted a quick conviction for the public. They were either duped or in on it."

"Skye kept her own place."

"She had that before we got together. I let her keep it. As you may remember, this place was one party after another. It was hard to find a little quiet space. Hard to find a little privacy. I could appreciate her need for refuge, to have a little sanctuary to retreat to now and then."

"Ten years ago, when this all went down, did you think Skye had actually been murdered? Or did you suspect this was all a scam, an elaborate frame-up?"

"I thought she was dead. It never occurred to me that it was all staged. My lawyer tried to get me to see that, but I was doubtful."

I finished my coffee and leaned forward across the counter. "In order for me to find her, I think I need to understand what happened that night. The way I see it, we are looking at a couple of options. One: Skye faked her own death and framed you. Now I've done my share of divorce cases, but I've never come across someone faking their own death to get out of a relationship, and I've never even heard of someone setting up their S.O. for the crime."

"She wouldn't do that. Obviously."

"Option two is that she was used, unwittingly perhaps, by someone out to get you. So, if we can pinpoint the motive, we can find this other party, and that will lead us to Skye."

I leaned back, finished presenting my case. "So, who did you think would stage killing Skye and pin it on you? Any ideas? Do you have any enemies?"

Dan wiped his hand back across his bald pate. "I racked my brain in those months trying to think of anyone who would do that. I'm sure there are lots of people who don't like me. I come off as a pompous know-it-all; I know that. But who would dislike me enough to kill my girlfriend? And why wouldn't they try to kill me?" He shook his head, eyes downcast.

I pushed my empty coffee cup away. "That's what I have to figure out. But I've saved the best for last."

Dan looked up.

"I found the car."

His eyes instantly lit up.

"I've tracked it to an address in Long Beach. It's registered to this guy, Hugo. Hugo Martinez. Ring a bell?"

"No. I mean, I may have met this, Hugo guy. He could have come to any one of my parties. There were more people there than I would ever remember."

"Maybe she's been hiding out with him all along, or maybe she hooked up with him recently. I haven't tracked him down yet. By the way, whatever happened to her Volkswagen? Her landlord said it was parked in that alley for weeks after she disappeared, and then one day it was gone."

"Oh, that? I couldn't tell you. At that period of my life, the last thing I worried about was that old car."

"Did you buy it for her?"

"Yes. When I first met her, she had no car. She didn't know how to drive. She was a master of the bus schedules. Of course, she had no driver's license, although she did have a non-driver ID. My place was convenient enough; she could walk a short way to work from here. Her place was only a short bike ride down the strand. But I took it upon myself to teach her to drive. This is L.A. How can you function without wheels? I had a Porsche at the time, and I wasn't about to let her learn in that, so I bought a beat-up old Bug for a couple of thousand dollars and took her out to the shopping center parking lot early in the mornings to teach her to drive. She loved that car even though it had seen better days. She plastered it with flower decals to cover up the dings in the bodywork. It looked like one of those hippie cars from the 60s, naturally. It fit her. She never did take a test for her license, though. I think she was afraid of failing. She never could quite get the hang of using the clutch on the hills. If she came to a stop sign on an incline, she's run it." He laughed.

"You saw her driving an old MG. That's a stick."

"It's been ten years. People acquire a lot of skills in ten years." Dan got up and put the coffee cups in the sink. "What do you say we walk down and grab a bit of lunch?"

We walked down to the pier. The block before the pier had long since been closed to traffic, now paved with decorative bricks and adorned with palm trees in planters. It made for a nice plaza. We headed to Fat Freddie's. It was one of only a few places that I recognized from all those years ago. The bars and restaurants were constantly changing, with just two or three legacy establishments left. Freddies was a typical beach bar, serving mostly beer and bar food. I had a hamburger, fries, and a Coke, sticking to my 'no drinking before four' resolution.

As we dove into our sandwiches, I prodded Dan for more personal info. "How long were you and Skye together before she disappeared?"

Dan thought for a while. "Seemed like a long time, but I guess it was only three, maybe four years."

"And before that, you were the Hugh Hefner of Hermosa?" I joked.

"For a short time. Skye was a rebound romance. I had recently been dumped, sort of. A girl broke my heart. Skye mended it."

I was intrigued. "Tell me about her."

Dan carefully studied my face before he spoke. "Michelle. She was a dancer, pretty, great bod, thin, muscular. She sported a bobbed haircut like a brunette Lady Gaga. I first met her a year or so out of UCLA. She worked on TV specials and such. I guess she was good; she worked a lot. I never saw anything she was in, though."

"So, another young gal like Skye."

"They were about the same age, but she was as different from Skye as a person could be. She was wild; she partied hard and fearlessly. She would drag me to places I would have never ventured on my own. Every weekend, I didn't know whether I'd wake up in an A-lister's guest room, in jail, or dead. But being with her was like a drug, and I was addicted. She was my Sally Bowles."

"How long were you two together?"

"Maybe two years. It was a wild ride, I tell you. We were experimenting with drugs, acid, mushrooms, all kinds of pills. But where she really got her claws into me was the sex – not just in the car, but on the balcony in broad daylight, in department store fitting rooms, once in a church, hell, I fucked her once in a graveyard!"

"Wow. So, what happened? Couldn't you keep up? You mentioned she was only twenty-two, twenty-three."

"That's about when I started having the parties at the house, to surround her with younger people. But, no, it was something more mundane. She finally landed a role on Broadway as a lead dancer. She was packed up and gone in a couple of days with an 'It's been fun' farewell. I couldn't believe she'd left me after all I'd done for her, but I guess career comes first for some people. I never heard from her again, not a call, not a letter, not even a postcard. I didn't even have an address to track her down."

"You could have gone to the theater."

"I thought of that, seriously. I was ready to move to New York and track her down, but her show opened and closed in a few weeks. If she had reached out, I would have moved there in a flash to be with her.

She probably took up with someone else by then, anyway." Dan dropped his napkin on the plate and pushed away from the table. "So, that's my sad story. I probably would have played the fool and chased her all over Manhattan, but Skye came along."

The check came. I noticed Dan hesitated to grab it, so I swooped in and picked it up. "It's on me. Don't worry, I won't be expensing it."

"I probably told you, fighting that charge pretty much wiped me out. I still have my Strand house. It's paid for, but insurance and taxes are hard to keep up with."

"I suppose eventually I'll have to sell it and move somewhere less expensive. I'll be alright then, but I hate the idea that this business has defeated me."

We walked back towards his place, stopping at the pier to lean against the rail and stare into the waves.

"I don't recall seeing you the next summer. You said before that you never came back?" Dan said.

"I'm surprised you noticed, what with the number of kids tramping through your house every summer. No, I didn't really apply myself that year at school, so I stayed for the summer session to catch up."

"I remember your buddy, Jack. He was a regular at the poker table. I guess that's why I noticed. Though you did kind of stand out. You were tall and awkward and not like the usual kids I got. You were a golfer, right?"

"In high school. I didn't make the Stanford team. Hey, do you remember a girl named Heather? Her brother, Ike, was a golfer. That's how I knew her. She's the one who invited me to your place the first time."

"Oh, yeah. I remember Heather. She was quite the looker and friendly. If you know what I mean. She came around a lot, made friends with Skye. Skye taught her Tarot cards. I heard she joined the PGA."
"What?"

"Party Girls of America. They're groupies that follow the tour, hoping to land a husband or at least have some fun trying. I hear some of them can actually play the game. Some of them have their own YouTube channels."

"Really. I'd never heard of that."

"Every professional sport has its own version. I heard Heather got lucky, got married, and lives down in Florida now. Did you have a thing for her?"

"No. Well, yes, I guess. But she wasn't interested in me except for maybe playing me along."

"You and every other guy. I never liked that girl. She ran with what I considered a dangerous crowd, but she was friends with Skye."

We walked back to Dan's place, where I had parked the car. I declined an offer of another drink, saying I had lots of things to catch up on. Dan took a moment to admire my car, stroking the fenders appreciatively.

"I keep wondering what she was doing driving down PCH in the middle of the day and risking being discovered."

"Maybe she thought enough time had passed. Ten years is a long time. Maybe she thought I would have left the area by now."

"As she was driving south, she could have been heading to Long Beach, where I found the car. And, she could have been coming from Manhattan. PCH is the most direct route."

"So why would she have gone to Manhattan?" Dan asked.

"I'm thinking she's nostalgic, sentimental. She wants to see her old place, see her old neighborhood."

"Not me. I couldn't care less about the places I've lived. I moved on for a reason."

"Did you ever visit her little apartment over the garage?"

"Sure. Any number of times."

"Do you remember that carved wooden hand she hung next to the door? It's called a Hamsa, or Hand of Miriam. It's a good luck charm. Supposed to keep the evil spirits at bay."

"Can't say that I recall it. She was into all that New Age stuff. The inside of her place was full of crap like that, crystal wind chimes, Navajo dream catchers, the whole lot."

"Anyway. When talking to her landlords, they said that when they got rid of all her stuff, some years later, they forgot about the Hamsa. It remained, hanging on the wall. I'm thinking Skye drove by to see the old place. Saw that the Hamsa was still there and took it."

"So?"

I got in my car and prepared to leave. "So, I think it explains why she came back. She was driven by the urge to reconnect with her past. Maybe we can use that knowledge of her sentiment to find her. If you think of anything…"

"It looks like you're making progress at least." He said as he leaned down toward my open window. "I hope to hear more from you soon." He tapped the roof as I backed out. I watched him briefly in my rear-view mirror as I pulled away. He looked like a Buddha, swaddled in grey.

CHAPTER

ELEVEN

The next morning, I met with Vera at the office to see if she was able to find anything on our friend Hugo.

"Hugo is not an unpopular name for a guy, but Martinez is only the second or third most common Spanish family name out there, so there are a lot of Hugo Martinezes to choose from." She replied. "Not counting the undocumented, there are over two hundred thousand Martinezes in California; half are male, a quarter of those are between the ages of 35 and 55. Of those twenty-five thousand or so, I have found 213 with the first name Hugo. Twenty-one live within a twenty-mile circle of that house on Figaroa Place. I thought we could start there."

"As good a place as any. Sometimes, investigating is just grinding. Anything else?"

"The house on Figaroa Place is owned by Maria Martinez. Don't know if that's a wife, sister of mother, or even unrelated."

"Not likely. Sure, as you said, Martinez is a common enough name, but I don't believe in coincidences. Let's see what else we can find. Next?"

"Well, your client, Dan, was a lot easier to scope out."

"Okay. Shoot."

"Born in Midland, Michigan; youngest of three kids, older brother,

Paul, older sister, Anne; father owned a car dealership. Dan went to the University of Michigan, got a BA in English Lit. Upon graduation moved to Detroit, worked at the Detroit Free Press, one notable piece he authored with three others was about the drug scene there. Left after a few years and moved to the L.A. area. Got a job with the Daily Breeze; worked mostly on the police and city hall beats. Co-wrote another highly lauded piece about the growing cocaine scene in the South Bay. Parents died in a car accident. He and his siblings sold the business. Dan saw a tidy inheritance that he invested in real estate here. Got his Real Estate license and quit the paper. Worked for a few years for Fred Sands Realty before opening his own office."

Vera paused. I was busy googling Midland, Michigan, to see where it was. I looked up when she stopped. "Two articles about drugs?"

"Well, I'm sure he wrote more articles than that. Those types of stories are the ones that tend to get all the accolades."

"Yeah, I guess. Where was this office he opened?"

"Artesia and PCH. I think it's still there, but with new owners, of course. Why are you investigating Mr. LeBeau? I thought he was your client."

"I'm not, really, but I learned the hard way to never assume anything about anyone, especially a prospective client. You never know why they've hired you. Could be for nefarious reasons."

"Noted."

"I've also come to learn that when you're searching for a missing person, you spend more time uncovering who they are than where they are."

"Interesting."

"I need to talk some more with Professor Dan about how he came to meet and hook up with Skye."

Just then, Jack walked in. I made introductions.

"Jack is my friend from high school. We go way back. He helps me out with all things tech as well as doing research now and then."

"I try to keep him grounded so he doesn't start thinking he's Phillip Marlowe or something," Jack added, shaking hands with Vera. "Good to meet you."

"Vera is replacing Yana, except she will be full-time. Besides running the office, I'm going to try to get her out for some field work as much as possible." I continued.

"Which reminds me, I want to get eyes on the MG. It's our best lead. We know she was driving it just a few weeks ago. If my first visit didn't arouse any suspicions, I would expect she would show sooner or later."

"You mean a stakeout?" Jack asked. "That's a lot of hours for the three of us if we're thinking it may be days or weeks before she returns."

"I'm not sure if it's safe for me to go back myself. Both the old woman and the gang-banger have seen me up close, and my car. I'd worry about blowing our cover."

"That's even more hours if it's just me and Vera, here."

"I saw a thing on a detective series a while back," Vera interjected. "The guy slapped a camera to the underside of a mailbox across the street and watched the house remotely. Actually, he didn't even monitor it; he just ran the video back every day on fast forward."

"Is that doable?" I asked Jack.

Jack thought for a moment. "Sure. They make cameras for drone mounts that have a pretty wide signal radius. You could park a few blocks away and monitor everything. They're smaller than your phone, maybe the size of a deck of cards. Easy enough to secure under a mailbox."

"What about recording and doing the playback thing?" Vera suggested.

"Well, you could plug a laptop into James' Tesla and record from there."

"No, we have to be nearby. It's not enough to see who comes out of the house and gets into the car; we have to be able to follow the car and hope it takes us to Skye." I countered. "How long to procure one of those cameras?"

They're not cheap, but I could get one today."

"Then, how do we plant it without being seen?" I was getting excited about our little spy op.

"Just get a bag of flyers like you find in your mailbox every day," Vera explained. "You walk the neighborhood stuffing mailboxes. When you get to the one you want, you quickly duct tape the camera underneath and walk on. No one will ever remember seeing you. Those guys are invisible."

Jack looked at me with raised eyebrows. "She's good."

"Before you go for the camera, I have one other item to discuss."

"Shoot."

"In reading the trial transcripts, I noticed that the prosecution hammered away on the fact that Skye left everything behind, purse, money, IDs, credit cards, everything. Not the actions of someone who is maybe planning on running away and starting over."

"Yeah, that does kind of point to her being killed." Jack agreed.

"But shortly after the trial concluded, her VW bug disappeared. The landlord said one day it was just gone. They assumed it had been towed. Dan says he didn't reclaim it, though technically it was his. He said he had bought it for Skye. I want to find that car. If the police towed it in, there will be a record. If anyone else towed it, there should still be a record. Someone came looking for Skye's belongings months later. Maybe Skye sent someone to retrieve the car as well."

I reached down into a box by my desk and grabbed a thick stack of papers. I shuffled through most until I came to a bunch of photos printed on cheap copy paper. They were mostly crime scene shots, but a second batch was of Skye's apartment. It was sparsely furnished, mostly with inexpensive Ikea things and lots of New Age knick-knacks like Dan had spoken of. The photo I was looking for was the VW, parked out in the alley. It was robin's egg blue with a multitude of yellow and white sunflower decals everywhere. You could barely make out the license plate in front. I handed the photo to Vera.

"I'll get on it." She volunteered.

The three of us looked at each other, with nothing left to say.

"That's it, I guess. Vera, you're going to trace that VW, and don't forget to keep looking for Hugo. Jack, you're going to buy us a camera and set up a program to record remotely." I said in my best pep-talk bravado. "Okay? Let's start digging."

Meeting over, Vera and Jack both left the office. I leaned back in my chair and dug my wallet out of the back pocket. Inside was the scrap of paper I had grabbed from the MG – a horse race betting receipt. I quickly Googled Santa Anita. The first posting was at 1:00. I still had plenty of time. I didn't know who I thought I might see there, Skye, Hugo, maybe even Dan, but I'd never been to a horse track before. I thought I might need to get familiar with the place first. Who knows, I might be spending more than a few days there watching the crowds. Maybe I'd get lucky and win a few dollars. I grabbed my hat and made for the door.

It was an hour drive from the office to the track. I decided to put the top down. The sun was bright, but it wasn't too hot. The racetrack was just east of Pasadena. With rush hour over, I made good time. I got there early. The gates had just opened, and the first race wasn't for two hours. I decided to find a place where I could study the racing form without too many distractions. *Silks* was a restaurant with a view of the track. I had reserved a table ahead of time, but the place was hardly crowded. Maybe it would fill up as the day wore on. I settled in, ordered a shrimp cocktail and a charcuterie plate, figuring I would be more comfortable picking at food while I studied the racing sheet.

It was a lot to take in: horse stables, trainers, track length and conditions – all had a bearing on the odds. I knew, being a novice, that most of this information was over my head. I figured that the odds were weighted by people who knew better. I might have just as much luck voting for the catchiest name as anything. I decided to start with the favorites and see how it went. The first race featured a filly named Saddle Up going off at three to one. I went over to the betting window and put ten dollars to win, then returned to my table and ordered a scotch and waited for the first race to start. It was a nice sunny day, the usual for So-Cal. I thought this could be a fun afternoon. Out of curiosity, I dug into my pocket and pulled out the old voucher I had found in the MG. It was from a month ago. No doubt a losing ticket, thus not redeemed. I looked at the bet, one hundred dollars on a trifecta. This guy or gal was a gambler!

CHAPTER

TWELVE

I arranged to meet Vera at the 101 the next morning for breakfast. The 101 was my regular hangout for breakfast, an old-fashioned 40's diner type restaurant with great tasting, stomach-filling food. It was about midway between my home and the office, so I swung by there often. Usually, Jack would join me. As I was early, I chatted with my favorite server, Norma, about her son, who worked at JPL, that's the Jet Propulsion Laboratory, NASA's research center in nearby Pasadena. Norma was a good-looking black woman who reminded me a lot of Ella Fitzgerald. I teased her that Jack and I could be her Blues Brothers if only we could sing. I already had the hat and glasses.

"What'll it be today, Mister James?" She called out as she walked towards my booth, pulling out her ticket pad and pencil.

"Well, I'm waiting for my new associate, so I'll just start with coffee, but bring a menu for her if you please."

"A new associate, huh. What happened to Jack?"

"Oh, Jack's still with me. The new girl is replacing Yana, my secretary."

"Yana? I don't think I ever met that one."

"Nah. She never had time for breakfast. Always rushing off to school."

Norma stepped away but was back in a minute with a menu and coffee mug in one hand, which she proceeded to fill from her pot in the other.

"Say, how's your son, Martin, doing up at JPL? He ready to become an astronaut yet?"

"Oh, no." Norma laughed. "You won't catch him going up in one of those things. He's deathly claustrophobic. And in those capsules, you can't scratch your nose without poking somebody in the eye with your elbow."

"That's too bad. He could be the first black astronaut." I urged.

"Where you been, son? Ain't you heard of Guion Bluford? He went up in the Space Shuttle back in '83. You need to get yourself some education and stop playing Dick Tracy."

"You're right, my bad. There are a lot of things I should know better about."

"That's all right. I'm just needling you. The pilot program is a whole nother kettle of fish. Junior's with the engineers, the ones doing all the calculations as such. Like Katherine Johnson. She's also black. And a woman!"

"There you go. Sounds like your Martin has got his life in good order."

Norma paused and grew a bit serious. "Well, it ain't all a bed of roses."

"What do you mean?" I had never seen Norma without an ear-to-ear smile on her face.

"Oh, Martin has gone and taken up with a fella that is bad news in my estimation."

"Well, I'm sure he would listen to you if you tried to set him straight."

As we were talking, Vera appeared behind Norma.

"Oh, Miles knows this other boy is trouble, but he can't seem to shake him. The guy clings to him like a leech. I think Martin is afraid of him. You know, he's a bit of a nerd, as the kids used to call him. He tried to avoid trouble whenever he smelled it. Last thing he'd ever do is get in a fight."

Vera stepped around and slid into the booth. "May I have a coffee, too, please? No cream or sugar, just plain."

"Sure thing, hun. There's a menu to look over if you're hungry." Then Norma turned and left to fetch another cup.

"Norma," I called out to her. She stopped and looked back. "What time is your shift up?"

"I always work from opening till two." She replied.

"I'll come by then and we can talk some more. Maybe there's something I can do to help."

Norma seemed unsure. "Okay." She said tentatively, then turned and went to get the coffee.

"Right on time," I said to Vera, looking at the readout on my phone. "I gather you're the very punctual type."

"My father's advice was always, 'If you're on time, you're late. Five minutes early is on time.' I'm not as anal as he is, but I do hate being late for things. It immediately puts you on the defensive."

"Well, some people in this town see it as a power move. But I'm not one of those people." I replied just as Norma reappeared with coffee.

"You two know what you want to have for breakfast?" She asked.

"I'll have the 101 special, over easy, rye toast. You need a minute?" I asked Vera.

"No, I'm ready." She replied, nose buried in the laminated menu. "I'll have the grilled chicken, egg white omelet with grits." She handed the menu back.

"Comin' right up." Norma finished writing as she turned away.

I studied Vera as she tasted her coffee. Her outfit was a precise as all her mannerisms – navy blue slacks, a lighter blue buttoned short-sleeve shirt with the sleeves rolled up over her biceps as usual, and no jewelry. I half expected a name tag to be stitched over her left breast and a smudge of grease on her nose.

"High protein breakfast. You in training for something?" I asked.

"No. But I CrossFit just to keep in shape. How about you?"

"Sadly, no. I walk, jog sometimes, play golf, but I'd have to admit I'm not in as good a shape as I should be. Just can't seem to find the time or persistence."

"You don't have to exercise every day to stay in shape. Two or three times a week will do."

"Yeah, I know. I should try harder. So, what have you found out?"

"As for the VW, the police didn't impound it. And so far, I haven't turned up any other towing service that bagged it. It could have been stolen. Those older cars were pretty easy to hotwire. A good thief could have started that car as fast as you putting in the key."

"Sure. Maybe whoever helped Skye stage her disappearing act might have come back for the car after the heat died down. Someone did come by later looking to pick up her stuff from her apartment."

"The DMV shows it is still registered to Dan, but the registration fees haven't been paid in years. It would have really old tags on the plates in that case."

"Unless they swiped tags from someone else's car. Those things aren't impossible to remove, you know." I noted, taking another sip of coffee. "But I think it's a dead end. If Skye's trying to disappear, she's not going to want to drive around in a car that is known to be hers."

"So, you don't think she had any of her new friends steal it for her then." Vera mused.

"Why would they?"

"It's not going to be reported stolen, at least not for a while. Easy enough to drive it down to Mexico and sell it. Have you been to Mexico these days? Nothing but Beetles down there. They're everywhere."

"Maybe. That theory is as good as any, I guess. Anything on our friend Hugo?"

"A lot more dead ends. People move around a lot in this town and don't leave forwarding addresses. There are two Hugos with police records, I found. One is too young, I think; he's only twenty-five now, which would have put him in high school at the time. The other guy is about the right age, thirty-nine. He was busted for possession with intent to sell, so I'm guessing he's a small-time dealer."

"That sounds promising. We should try to talk to the prosecutor or arresting officer if we can find them. See if they can give us any info."

Vera flipped through her notes. "Prosecutor was John Cohen, and the arresting officer was … Detective Sam Mejia."

"I know that guy. He's L.A.P.D." I sat up suddenly. "I'll talk to him."

Right about then, Norma showed up with our breakfast. She set down our plates and topped up our coffee cups. Right on cue, Jack walked in and headed straight for our booth. I slid myself and my plate around to make room for him.

"Hey, Norma." Jack greeted her as he sat down and dropped his backpack on the seat between us.

I don't think of myself as a creature of habit. I'm not one of those guys who always goes to the same restaurant at the same time and orders the same thing. But, invariably, whenever I'm at the 101, Jack shows up. I once asked Norma if Jack came here a lot, every day even, and so naturally the odds would be with him to run into me. She said she never saw him there at all unless he was eating with me. She figured we had arranged to meet. I suspect Jack just has a heightened sense of ESP, a radar for a free meal if I'm there. Either that or he has been tracking my phone.

"Morning, Jack," I said with a smile.

"Hey Jimbo. Morning Vera. What did I miss?"

"Nothing much," I replied. "Vera thinks the VW might be in Mexico by now, but she has a possible lead on Hugo."

"You want a few minutes to look at a menu, hun?" Norma interrupted.

"Oh, sorry. I'll have the lumberjack special as usual."

"Coming up. I'll bring you a coffee in the meantime." Norma said, turning to return to the counter.

"Yeah, I agree. It's either in Mexico or it's been chopped up for parts. What's it been, ten years?" Jack reached over and dug into his backpack, pulling out a small camera, about the size of a deck of cards.

"Here you go, Jimbo. This baby's good for about 200 to 250 yards transmission."

"Okay, that's a long par three. I could park at the end of the block. Shouldn't draw too much attention. But, Vera, since this was your idea, I'm going to let you plant this under the neighbor's mailbox and take the first shift. I'll relieve you this afternoon."

"Why don't you let me set it up?" Jack interrupted. "That way I can pair it to the laptop and make sure it's working properly."

"Oh, sure. Good idea." I replied. I could sense that Jack wanted in on some action and was getting a little jealous that the new girl was getting all the field work already.

"James," Vera interjected. "If you think Skye would be quick to ditch the VW because it is tied to her, why do you think she wouldn't also ditch the little red sports car now that she's been spotted?"

"I don't think Skye is hiding out at that house in Long Beach. But it's only been two weeks. Somebody is still driving it, at least to the horse track. I want to surveil the car and hope it takes us to where Skye is hiding."

"Long Beach is kind of close to her old stomping grounds." Jack chimed in.

"That's why I don't think she's there. She's going to want to be far enough away that she won't accidentally bump into anyone who knows her."

"Then what was she doing in Hermosa?" Vera asked.

"Good question. Maybe she thought ten years was long enough away. But I'm guessing she went to see someone, an old friend maybe, someone who we haven't uncovered yet."

"Ten years. She took a gamble and lost. What are the odds?" Jack mused.

After breakfast, while Jack headed out to San Pedro to set up surveillance, Vera and I went to the office. I asked her to see if she could get any leads on my old femme fatale, Heather, while I put in a call to Detective Mejia to arrange a meet.

Not an hour had passed when my phone buzzed and I saw Jack's name pop up on the screen.

"What's up, Jack?"

"It's on the move!" I could hear that Jack was on the speaker phone in his car.

"What's on the move?"

"The red MGB. I was driving up Figaroa Place to the target address when it passed me going the other direction."

I put my phone on speaker, set it in the middle of my desk, and motioned for Vera to join me. "Where are you now?" I asked.

"I'm turning around. I'm still on Figaroa."

"Do you have eyes on the car?"

"Not for long. It just pulled onto the on ramp for the South 110!"

"The South 110? Where is it going? Try to catch up with it. It shouldn't be too difficult to find on the freeway. How many red MGs can there be?"

Vera and I waited as we heard various car sounds and traffic noise coming through the phone. After five long minutes, Jack came back on.

"I see it. It's turning toward the 710, going across the Vincent Thomas Bridge."

I flipped open my laptop and pulled up a map of the Los Angeles area. "Okay," I said. "That's going to take you across the harbor to Long Beach, and then it turns north."

We listened to more sounds of traffic. "Don't get too close, you don't want to be spotted."

"Roger that."

Vera and I stared at each other and shrugged as another five minutes passed by.

"He's heading east on the 405 now." Jack's voice popped in suddenly.

I studied the map on my laptop. "He could be heading east or south."

"Heading for Hugo? Heading for Skye?" Vera guessed.

"Now he's on the 605 heading north," Jack announced.

"Where's he going? Has he spotted Jack behind him?"

"Wait! He's getting off at Katella."

I quickly looked at the map again. "He's going to the race track at Los Alamitos."

"I'm always up for a day at the ponies. Can I expense this, Jimbo?"

"Just be careful. You don't want to get made. This guy could be dangerous. But if you get a chance, try to get a picture of him."

"You got it. If you want me to place a bet for you, just text me." Jack said jokingly before he hung up.

I looked to Vera. "Well, it's something. It may lead to a break, who knows."

"Yeah, maybe. Anyway, I got a hit on a Heather that might be the one you're looking for. It's a news article about a young pro golfer playing on the Korn Ferry Tour. Does that sound right?"

"Yeah, the Korn Ferry is like the minor leagues of pro golf. You do well enough, you get promoted up to the Tour, the big Leagues. If you can't cut it there, you get bumped back down."

"Okay, so this young golfer, Tommy Morris, announced his engagement to Heather Davison of Rolling Hills, California. Didn't you say she was from somewhere in the South Bay area?"

"Yeah, that sounds about right. I mean, how many Heather Davisons can there be? But she's got to be in her thirties by now, and most of the Korn Ferry guys are in their twenties. Maybe she's desperate. Let's see if we can find out where he's playing in the next few weeks. Maybe she's travelling with him."

A little before two, I headed back to the diner for a talk with Norma about her son. It was after the lunch crush, so there were several empty tables. I sat in the back and Norma joined me shortly.

"So, what's the trouble with Martin and his friend?" I began.

Norma sat down with two cups of coffee and pushed one over to me.

"Maybe I'm just being overprotective, but I can't help but think that my boy has gotten himself entangled with a really dangerous person."

"Really? Who is this guy?"

"His name is Eldridge. You know, like the Black Panther guy."

"I'm sure you don't mean the movie."

"I know you well enough that I didn't have to clarify that, James. Eldridge hates his name. If you can believe it. So, his friends call him Fly, I guess on account of him being such a sharp dresser or something. Him and Martin went to high school together, and back then they were pretty good friends, not best friends, but they palled around together sometimes.

"I don't think Fly went on to college, so he and Martin drifted apart. To be honest, I don't think my son had seen him for a few years before bumping into him again last year at the Best Buy in Glendale. After that, they started seeing each other again. Or, I should say, Fly started seeing Martin again. I don't think it was equal in enthusiasm, if you know what I mean.

"So, Martin, being the good soul that he is, bought lunch once. He has his own credit card, and I suppose he used it. Next time they grabbed lunch, Fly was expecting Martin to pick up the bill. When Martin hesitated, Fly laid a whole guilt trip on him. "You making white man money now and you can't buy a brother lunch?" He said. Martin figured Fly just assumed that his working at JPL translated into making big bucks."

I nodded, following along. "Some people." I agreed.

"This turned into a regular thing. Instead of feeling a little gratitude, Fly was acting entitled!"

"That wasn't enough to make your son cut the friendship?"

"No! And there's more. When I ask him how long he was going to keep knuckling under to this pressure, Martin says, "Oh, he's got a job now. I don't buy him lunch anymore.""

"Well, that's good. What kind of job?" I asked.

"I don't know. Some kind of side hustle, but I see his money go into the bank like clockwork, two or three times a week." Martin says.

"What you mean you see his money? I said. I was confused."

"Oh, me and him opened a joint business account." He explains. "Now don't fret, none. I am not putting any of my money in this. We are keeping our monies separate. This is just his money."

"I'm confused," I told him. "Why you need to open a joint account in the first place?"

"On account of Fly not ever having had a bank account before. It was easier since I was already a bank customer." Martin is explaining this to me like I am some kind of know-nothing sharecropper."

"I don't like where this is going," I interjected.

"You telling me! I asked Martin, "What kind of money we talking about?" He said it was a few hundred a week to start. He'd put cash in the ATM. But since then, Fly's business has been taking off, and now it's a few thousand every week."

"I think Fly is using Martin to launder some dirty money. Multiple deposits a week? I'd like to see those bank statements."

"I can't ask Martin for that. He'd feel terrible if he thought I was snooping around his business. I don't want you talking to Martin, either. He's got to trust his mom to give him his space, but I just know this is some bad business he's getting himself into."

"I agree. Let me look into it. I promise, Martin will never know I'm poking around. But if you could get your hands on one of those bank statements. Just take a picture and send it to me. I don't need the actual paper. That would be a big help."

"I'll try."

"What is Fly, or rather, Eldridge's last name?"

"I don't think I ever knew. He's just Fly."

"No matter, we can look it up in his high school yearbook. Do you think you could put your hands on Martin's copy?"

"I told Martin not to buy one. Can you believe they wanted a hundred dollars for that thing? I told him he would look at it once and then never look at it again."

"I can find it online. Now don't you worry, Norma. I'll find out what's going on and let you know. Then you can decide what you want to do after that."

"Bless you, James. I sure do appreciate it."

After I left the diner, I gave Vera a call and had her start tracking down a Marshall High yearbook. I figured Martin had to be at least three years out of school, maybe more. I told her to look for anyone named Eldridge, nicknamed Fly. He shouldn't be too hard to find.

CHAPTER

THIRTEEN

I had suggested to Detective Mejia that we could meet at the Founder's Club the next day, but he thought that was too stuffy for his taste and insisted we meet at the Pantry. I had never been there myself, but knew of it. It had a reputation for being a favorite hangout for the boys in blue. It was only a couple of blocks south of the Club, so I could easily park there and walk down in just a few minutes. Now, I have always been a big fan of the classic diner, the 101 in Hollywood being my local haunt, and the Pantry was the OG of diners. A hundred years old, at one time it used to be owned by the mayor. It was also famous for its free coffee, but like all good things, that too came to an end.

The Pantry had the classic greasy spoon good looks and style, not new and fancy, but homey, like your favorite grandma. Red and white striped awnings shielded the front door below a neon sign that advertised breakfast 24 hours a day. Inside the cafe had a long, well-worn Formica counter with metal barstools, similarly inexpensive tables and chairs filled out the rest of the checkerboard tile floor of the restaurant, each with the de rigueur vintage sugar, salt, and pepper shakers. The menu on the wall featured biscuits and gravy, ham steaks, pancakes and eggs, and several kinds of pie – the usual.

We had planned to meet at 10:30 to try and catch the gap between the breakfast and lunch crowds. I thought I was early, but as I pushed through the front door, I immediately spotted Mejia seated and sipping on a cup of coffee.

"Thanks for meeting with me," I said as I pulled out a chair and sat down.

"No problem." He looked up from under those heavy eyebrows of his. "You're looking better than the last time I saw you."

"I should hope so. That was a year ago. I was in the hospital."

"Mmmm." He muttered, taking another sip. "And what kind of trouble are you causing the police department these days?"

"I'll have you know I am making every effort to be a model citizen." I motioned for the waitress to bring me a coffee. "I've given up the divorce work business. Now I mostly investigate insurance fraud, workman's comp disability issues, that sort of thing."

"Good for you."

"The pay is not as good, and it can be rather boring, but on the plus side, I haven't been shot at in the past year."

The waitress brought Sam his meal: chorizo, eggs, beans and tortillas, and salsa. He obviously hadn't waited for me to arrive to place his order.

"I'll have the same," I said, pointing to his plate as she poured my coffee.

"So, what do you want from me?" He said through a mouthful of sausage.

"Well. I have a new case, a missing persons case of sorts."

"That's good, 'cause the police don't have the time and resources to be chasing after all the missing persons reports we get every week."

"This one might interest you, though. Do you remember a rather sensational case ten years ago down in Manhattan Beach? This guy was accused of killing his girlfriend, chopping her up, and disposing of the pieces in the dumpster of his apartment building?"

"Doesn't ring a bell."

"Really? You used to work down in the South Bay before, didn't you?"

"Redondo. And that was ages ago."

"I seem to recall seeing a picture of you in uniform on a bike on the Strand."

"That would have been my rookie year. Now, where did you see that?"

"Oh, I don't remember. Someplace. It's not important."

The detective gave me a stare. He knew where I had seen it. It was a sore spot between us. I was now sorry I mentioned it.

"Anyway, the guy was acquitted because the prosecutors could never produce a body. I was somewhat acquainted with this guy from years ago when I used to hang out down at the beach. I ran into him a couple of weeks ago, and he told me he had seen his girlfriend, alive and well, and driving around town. Now he's hired me to find her."

"Funny story. So, what? This guy wants to get back together with this gal he supposedly popped off?"

"I doubt that. But he probably does want an explanation. The trial and scandal ruined his life."

"So where do I fit in? What do you want from me? If this was ten years ago, I would have long moved over to Metro by then."

"I've been doing a lot of legwork trying to track her down. It's a cold trail. But I did manage to find the car that my client says he saw her driving. I ran down the registration on it, and it seems to belong to a guy named Hugo Martinez."

Mejia paused mid-bite. "So?"

"So, you arrested a kid named Hugo Martinez many years back. I thought you might remember him."

"Hugo Martinez, huh." He pretended to think for a moment. "You know that name is like John Smith in this part of the country."

"I don't expect you to remember him off the top of your head. But I thought you could pull your file and maybe tell me something about him."

"How long ago was this?"

"Fifteen years."

"Yeah, that would have been about when I left Redondo P.D. So, you want what, his address and phone number? Like, those are still valid?"

"No, I'm not expecting that, though I do still have my same phone number from fifteen years ago."

"Your mommy got you a phone when you were in grade school?"

"Fifteen years ago, I was in high school. That's when most kids get their first." Right then, my breakfast appeared in front of me. We stopped talking for a moment while our cups were refilled and the waitress left.

"I thought you might be able to give me some information, known associates, a mug shot, or something that would help me locate him." I dug into my breakfast now that Sam was finished. He leaned back, savoring his coffee and deciding whether he was going to help.

I'm sure Mejia came across to most people as cold and cynical. But I think that was just a shield he erected to prevent himself from becoming too emotionally attached to the people he met every day. Most of us are not having our best days when first we meet a police detective. He and I had had a pretty rocky start to our relationship. I think he arrested me two or three times last summer. In the end, though, I earned a begrudging respect from him for solving the case and not getting myself killed. He later referred people to me, which I took as the highest of compliments, though in reality, he was probably just sloughing off cases he didn't want to work. He still acted as though I was just some punk kid.

The detective set down his cup, wiped his mouth, and pushed back from the table.

"I'll take a look at the file. If I think there's anything in there that would be of use to you, I'll send it over."

He stood up. "Thanks for breakfast."

I headed back to the office to reconvene with Jack and Vera. Jack had spent the day before at the horse track, allegedly surveilling the MG driver, but he managed to make a few hundred playing the ponies while he was there.

He pulled out his phone and began scrolling through all the pictures he took of the driver.

"Yeah, that's the guy who confronted me," I confirmed. "See, he's got tats all up his neck."

"That's not so unusual these days," Vera noted. "Especially with gang members."

"Well, I recognize him anyway. He probably lives a that house with the older woman. Maybe that's his mother."

"Okay, so what's our next move?" Jack asked.

"Pick the best couple of shots of this guy and send them to Vera and me for future reference. I don't suppose you had a chance to plant the camera under the mailbox, yet."

"Is that still necessary? I'm pretty sure he's driving the car now."

"I agree, but we don't care if he goes to the track. We want to follow him to Hugo or, even better, Skye."

"Okay, well, I put an AirTag under his bumper while we were at the track yesterday. See?" He pulled up the app on his phone and showed me that the car was back on Figaroa Place.

"Well, aren't you the smart one?" I laughed.

"Let me share the app with you both and we can all keep an eye on the car."

As Jack downloaded apps to our phones, I turned to Vera.

"Vera, go through the court records and sort out everyone who was called as a character witness for Dan, especially anyone with real estate connections. So far, all the people I've talked to who knew Skye think that Dan's a real shit. We need to get another perspective on their relationship. Try to get their current contact information. It's been about ten years, so some of them may have moved."

"I'm on it." She replied.

"Oh, and about the VW, did you check that it hadn't been salvaged?"

"Wouldn't that have been reported to the DMV?"

"That's the way it is supposed to work, but things slip through. Check again, specifically that it wasn't salvaged and sitting in a junkyard somewhere. If it is, I'd like to have a look if I can."

Jack looked up from fiddling with my phone. "You just got a message from your buddy, Detective Mejia."

I grabbed the phone back and opened the message. It was an attachment with a mug shot of our prime suspect – Hugo Martinez.

CHAPTER

FOURTEEN

So, it turned out Heather's fiancée, Tommy, was playing a tour event in Malibu this week. I lucked out. The Tour could have been in Florida, not that I wouldn't have hopped on a plane to go track her down. But Malibu was just an hour or so away.

The Korn Ferry Tour is in many ways just like the PGA Tour these days – big playing fields of a hundred and fifty or more players, and these guys are good. Some of them have already been to the big Tour and been sent back for lack of points. The most noticeable difference is the lack of mobs of spectators. It's mostly just family and friends. That translates into a lot less money than the main tour. It's tough to make a go of it. Most feel fortunate to break even, what with travel expenses and money for caddies and coaches, etc.

I drove out in the late morning, arriving around eleven. I had looked up Tom's start time, noon, on the internet. I planned to watch from a distance at first and wait until he was out on the course and focused on his game before approaching Heather. I was counting on her being there since they were engaged, but there was no way of knowing for sure without going there and seeing for myself.

I staked out a place by the first tee and watched a few threesomes tee off and start their round. At one time, I had imagined myself out on the course, playing professional golf. I could still visualize that now, pounding a drive deep down the fairway to appreciative oohs and ahhs from the gallery. But these guys were now out of my league. The amount of dedication required to be a professional athlete these days was beyond my commitment to the sport.

The next group up was supposed to include Tom. I didn't know what he looked like, but the starter was announcing each golfer as they stepped into the tee box. Tom was the third in his group.

"And now from Kokomo, Indiana, please welcome Tom Morris."

There followed appropriate clapping. Tom teed up his ball, took a couple of practice swings, stepped back to eye the fairway and visualize his shot, then took his stance. He hit a nice high draw about three hundred yards down the middle of the fairway. He didn't even pause long to admire his shot before he stooped to pick up his tee and marched down the fairway following the other two golfers. His caddie hurried to catch up.

I lingered back for a moment, searching the few spectators for Heather, but she was not to be seen. My only option was to follow Tom and wait for her to make an appearance. If she were here, she certainly wouldn't be watching any other golfers, even if Tiger Woods was playing.

At the first green, I watched Tom tap in a four-footer for an easy par. Across the green I spotted Heather. She was dressed more for tennis than golf, with a very short white skirt, white halter top, and blue and white windbreaker. She clapped enthusiastically for Tom's par, but his eyes were already looking towards the next tee as he strode away.

I hung back and watched her from a distance as she proceeded to the next hole. She, too, stood quite apart from the golfers, appreciating their need to stay focused. She would know a thing or two about that, I noted.

I kept my distance for the next few holes, though her eyes never wandered in my direction. I didn't expect her to recognize me, even if she did look my way, as it has been ages since we last saw each other. She still looked good, though, and for some reason, I was becoming increasingly nervous about approaching her. It was strictly business, I told myself. You're not here asking for a date.

After the third hole, I made my move and caught up with her as we approached the next hole.

"Heather?" I called out, questioningly, as if I had only just now noticed her.

She turned, and I could see in her face that either she didn't recognize me, or did and couldn't remember my name.

"James Gardiner. I played golf against your brother, Ike, in high school. I remember you used to come out to watch us play."

"James! Oh, right. I remember you now. Wow, it's been what, more than ten years! How the hell are you?"

"I'm good. And yourself? You're looking good."

"I'm doing well, thank you."

"Are you here watching Ike?"

"Oh, no. Ike was never this good. I'm here with my fiancée, Tom Norris. He's the one with the beard and the blue and white Polo." She said, indicating with a nod towards the group teeing off.

"Must be good to make the Korn," I commented.

"He had his PGA Tour card two years ago, but he got his hand caught in a car door, truck door rather, and broke two fingers. As a result, he missed too many starts and didn't qualify to keep his card. But he's all healed now and playing well. He's won once this year and had several top fives."

"That's good to hear. I assume the pressure's on as he gets older to move up."

"Oh, he's the same age as you and Ike. You'd be surprised how many of the guys out here are in their thirties. Do you still play?"

"Not competitively. I gave it up after high school. I tried out for the team at Stanford, but didn't make it. Just as well, though. It would have been tough for me to attend class and keep working on my game. How about Ike, did he keep going?"

"Yes. He played at Illinois. He was good enough to get recruited, but he never really stood out against the other guys on the squad."

"Yeah, Illinois always has one of the top teams in the nation."

"So, he packed it in and became a computer programmer. Now he bounces around from company to company, specializing in security software." She made a face like she wasn't really impressed with how her brother's career was going. "How about yourself?"

"I'm similarly employed. I have my own private investigation firm."

"That sounds sexy." She glanced back at me with a look as she turned and started walking after the golfers.

I followed. "I have to confess. My being here is not accidental."

That stopped her in her tracks. She turned to me, her expression guarded.

"Do you remember Skye?"

Heather thought for a moment and then reacted. "Oh, my god! That was horrible what happened to her."

"Yes, it was horrible, but it was not what you may have read or heard. Skye is not dead. I am re-investigating the matter. I was hoping that I could speak to you for a few minutes. Maybe we could go to the clubhouse for coffee and talk."

"Well, uh." Heather glanced around, confused, glanced back towards Tom and the other golfers, then turned to me. "I need to follow Tom."

"It won't take but a few minutes." You can catch up to him on the turn. As focused as he is, he won't even notice before then."

"Well, all right." She agreed reluctantly.

At the clubhouse, over a couple of Arnold Palmers, I recounted for Heather my investigation to date. I began with the alleged crime and the media's portrayal of that, then continued with the nature of the trial, the damning but eventually inconclusive evidence that led the jury to find Dan not guilty. I explained the aftermath for Dan, his financial and social devastation, and then the sudden sighting not two weeks ago, and my hiring to investigate and track down Skye.

"I don't know what you think I can add. I hadn't seen Skye for over a year, at least before that occurred. I only came down to Hermosa for one more summer after you quit coming. I was beginning to feel out of place, you know, old. I'd been there and done that. It was time to move on. I was in school at UCSD, so I started spending my summers in San Diego as well."

"No, no. I'm not thinking that you've seen her lately or even know where she might be. I'm trying to get a handle on what was happening with her before all that happened."

"What do you mean?"

"I get the sense that you were friends, you hung out, girl talking, and so forth. Maybe you had a sense of what her life was like the other five days of the week when there wasn't a party at the house."

"We were friendly, but I wouldn't say we were friends. She and Dan had a strange relationship. He was a little…how shall I put it…controlling."

"You're not the first person to say that."

"Well, then, let me put it another way. Dan was an emotional blackmailer without peer. Skye was not happy, but didn't know how to get out."

"But from what I hear, Skye was a free spirit. She ran away from home. She took charge of her own life."

"It's complicated. Dan had a scary temper. I've seen it. He never hit Skye, but he sure hit anything else he could vent on. I heard from Skye that once he took a meat tenderizer to her crystal ball. Those things are solid glass. He wailed on it in a fit of rage until he finally managed to break it in half."

"That's a lot of rage."

"Then he'd turn around and beg forgiveness, bawling like a baby. He'd spoil her rotten for a few weeks until something triggered him again."

"If he wasn't happy with her, there certainly were plenty of other girls around."

"Oh, believe me, he screwed around. He flaunted it at Skye. He could cheat, but she couldn't. I think secretly she hoped he would find another girl and dump her. Those parties were a buffet of young girls for him. He tried to have me, but I wouldn't touch the pig."

"Yeah, there was a lot of sex going on in that house. You probably figured it out right away, but you were my first. I was still a virgin that night we hooked up."

Heather looked up as if she had just remembered. "Oh my god!" She reached for my hand. "James, I am so sorry I ran out on you like that." Now I was confused. "What?"

Heather proceeded slowly, not sure if we remembered that night the same way. "You came into the room. I could see you were nervous, but I thought that was cute."

"You were half naked, sitting on the bed. And then…I guess I was a little clumsy."

"Clumsy? You nutted on me the second I pulled your shorts down. I had to run out before I burst out laughing. I couldn't believe your face. I didn't want to laugh at you."

It took a long moment for what she just said to sink in. I'm sure Heather didn't know what to make of my reaction either. "That…that's what happened? It's always been a fuzzy blank in my memory. I would have expected to remember it better."

"I'm sorry, James. I swear, I never mentioned it to anyone, ever."

"That's okay. I was a kid. Got to start somewhere."

We sat for a moment, drinking our tea and lemonade.

"And, I'm sorry I couldn't have been more help to you with Skye. You should talk to Sarah. I don't know her last name, but she used to work at McGrath's with Skye."

"Yeah, I know who she is. We already spoke."

"Well, Sarah was Skye's BFF. They were soul mates, inseparable. If anyone has insights into Skye, it would be Sarah."

"Hmm. Did you know Hugo at all?" I asked.

Heather laughed. "I'll have to confess, I'm the one who introduced Skye to him."

"Oh, really?" I replied, my eyebrows arching almost off my head. "And how did you know Hugo?"

"Those were my naughty years. Hugo was my dealer. The funny thing is, though, Skye never did those drugs. But he was hot for her anyway."

It was a long drive home. As I headed back to Hollywood along Interstate 10, I wouldn't stop thinking about how I couldn't remember that last night at Dan's in the bedroom with Heather. Was I really that traumatized that I repressed the memory all these years? Well, that was the past. No sense torturing myself over it any longer.

I turned my attention to the other little bombshell she dropped on me. So, Sarah tried to mislead me about her friendship with Skye. What was she afraid of telling me, and what other information is she holding back?

On an impulse, I swung onto the connecting ramp to the 405 and headed down to Hermosa. No time like the present to confront her about it.

I remembered Sarah didn't start her shift until four, so I had a couple of hours to kill. As I hadn't had lunch yet, I decided to stop in at McGrath's for a burger and a beer. It was good timing, the lunch rush was over and it was too early for Happy Hour, so I had no problem finding a table. I ordered a jalapeno burger and a pale ale. I skipped on the French fries. It's a tough pass, but the carbs really put the pounds on me.

While I was enjoying my burger, Pat, the owner, spotted me from behind the bar and came over.

"You working or vacationing?" He asked with a smile. But I knew he was leery of me being back in his place, poking around.

"I came down to talk to Sarah, but her shift at Bay City doesn't start until four, so I thought I'd come in and have a late lunch. You make a great jalapeno burger here."

"Thanks. We try. I can only pour the beer and offer a wide selection, but the food we make here, so we try to make it the best we can."

I tried to talk with a mouth full of burger. "That's a pretty damn good burger! I give it five stars."

"Glad you like it. How's the investigation going, if you don't mind my asking?"

"Slow," I replied. "So far, none of my leads have panned out. But I'm learning a lot about Skye. She seems to be pretty well-liked by all."

"She was at that. Excuse me for using the past tense. I still can't get my head wrapped around the idea that she's still alive."

"Well, if I find her, maybe I can convince her to come back. Seems a shame that she felt compelled to walk away from such a close network of friends."

"You don't notice it at first glance, but if you live down here, you find out that Hermosa's a pretty tight community."

"I get that sense. I like it down here. I used to come when I was a teen. Of course, being underage, I wasn't frequenting this place. I missed out. You've got a real nice tavern here, Pat."

"It doesn't come easy or cheap. I've put a lot of money into this, trying to keep up with the neighbors."

"Really? I always figured bar owners were just printing money."

"Once you get established, it's okay, but it's a tough market to break into, especially now with all the corporate owners. Like Bay City. Out of town LLC bought out my friend Keith. Of course, he had not been keeping it up the way he should have. But when they came along, they sunk a shit load of dough into the place and now it's raking in the customers."

I nodded, drinking my beer and trying to make nice.

"Well, they can't beat your location, right on the beach. That's priceless."

"Oh, they've put a price on it." Pat laughed. "I get offers every day."

I walked into Bay City about a half hour before I was expecting Sarah to show. I took a table with a good view of the door. It took a few minutes to adjust to the dim lighting, cool air conditioning, and soft jazz playing in the background. I ordered a beer.

Right at four, Selma walked in, carting her waitress dress over one arm. When she saw me, she stopped abruptly and then crossed to my table,

"What do you want?" She whispered angrily.

"I want to know why you told me you and Skye were just work buddies when in fact you were best friends."

She stared at me for what seemed like an eternity. "We had a falling out." She said, finally. "I didn't want to give you any wrong ideas."

"A falling out? What happened?"

Sarah gave me a look. "It's personal."

I didn't respond. I just stared back at her. Sometimes, if you press, a person will get defensive and clam up. But if you wait, as likely as not, they will blurt out what you want to know. They just can't help themselves but fill the silence.

"She started hanging out with bad people. I didn't want anything to do with them, and I told her so, but she wouldn't listen."

"Bad people, like Hugo?"

"Yes. He and his friends."

"Maybe you just don't like Hispanics."

"I'm half Hispanic. They are all a bunch of wanna be gangsters. Pandillistas! Mafiosos! Okay?!"

"How can you tell? Maybe you just don't like them."

"I know. The tats, the way they talk, the way they spend money. They even brag about it."

"And Skye was okay with it?"

"I think she liked the thrill of hanging with bad boys. I don't know."

"So, when did this falling out happen? I mean, when did you see her last?"

"I don't know exactly. Maybe two weeks or so before she went missing."

I watched her, waiting to see if there was anything more she wanted to add.

She looked away from me toward the back of the house. "I have to go to work." She said and turned and walked away.

I looked in that direction and saw Howard standing in the hallway to the rear offices. He was watching us with interest. He gave a little nod to Sarah as she walked by, then proceeded forward to my table.

"Everything all right here?" He asked.

"Oh, yeah. I just had a couple of follow-up questions for Sarah, that's all." I motioned to an empty chair. "Buy you a drink?"

Howard sat down. "No, thanks."

"I guess Sarah and Skye were a lot closer than she let on. News of her death must have hit her pretty hard."

"I'm sure it did." He replied, not giving up much.

"Say, I heard that they did quite the make-over with this place a few years back. I never saw the before version, but this place looks sharp."

"Yes. Ownership changed hands about five years ago. The new people sunk a lot of money into upgrading the look here. Top to bottom redo. The old place had a kind of homey blues vibe, with mismatched furniture, worn and lived-in, a down-at-the-heels feel. That works for a certain clientele, but not here. There's a lot of money in the beach cities, and they like a classier joint."

"So, you probably book more name groups then, too?"

"Yes. I still do the booking. I can get some top names in here now and then."

"Oh, I thought you were the booking manager."

"I manage the whole club now. I got that gig with the new owners. I still do the booking because I like to keep a hand in the business."
"Who's the new owner? Local?"

Howard paused as if debating whether to tell me.

"You ask a lot of questions."

"Sorry if I come off as nosy. I guess it comes with the job. No harm meant, just making friendly conversation."

"It's corporate. SoCal Clubs." He said with a begrudging smile.

I finished my drink and started to pull out a twenty from my wallet. Howard pushed my hand away.

"On the house."

Outside, I decided to try and ring up Dan since I was already down this way. I had a couple of follow-up questions for him as well. Better to do it in person than over the phone, I always thought.

Dan's was an easy ten-minute walk down the Strand. He was lounging outside with a drink in hand, waiting for me. Foot traffic was light as people were probably making dinner plans, but the sun wouldn't be setting for a few more hours, so it was a nice, somewhat quiet time to be out. The beach is in a timeless zone, weekends are seven days long, and the sun seems to be out for twenty hours at a time, and summer nights are longer still.

"Hey, James!" Dan called out. "What are you drinking?"

"I'll have what you're having."

"Gin and tonic?"

"Why not?"

I followed him into the house and back to the kitchen, where he whipped up another couple of drinks.

"I was wondering if you could recall the last couple of days before Skye went missing. I know they were probably mundane and easily forgotten in the tumultuous days that followed, but I'd be interested in just the day-to-day life you were leading up to that point."

Dan continued his drink-making and answered, not turning around. "I remember it pretty well. The cops grilled me about that over and over. You must have read those interviews in the material Jon gave you."

"I did. I just wanted to hear it again. Maybe something new will stand out on re-examining it."

"Saturday was the last time I saw Skye, so Friday…Friday was just another workday. I usually get up at nine. Skye is always out of the house before then. I eat breakfast at home and head into the office by ten." Dan turned around and handed me my drink. "Friday's I usually confer with my associates for our pre-weekend, morning meeting. We have open houses on Sunday's so I need to make sure those are manned, ads and signs are in place, et cetera. After the meeting, I think I called up our escrow company to check in on the few escrows we have open, just to make sure papers are being signed, inspections are happening, no hiccups, you know."

We settled in on the stools at the counter and sipped our drinks.

"I probably ordered lunch in. I usually get Chinese from a nearby place. After lunch, a few more calls. I think I was having an issue with a title report, so I spoke at length with those people. All that I believe the police detectives followed up on and verified. Nothing unusual. I left the office at three so I could get home in time to walk Skye down to Bay City for her four o'clock shift. I stayed and had a beer or a glass of wine. Walked home. Stopped for an early dinner at my favorite sushi place."

"What kind of sushi do you like?"

"I used to always get the Chef's Choice. Kato-san would always try out new things on me. But he has since retired, and the new owners are into all these fancy rolls, like Elvis roll or Vegas roll, or Hollywood roll. A lot of them include cream cheese, which I don't care for, so I don't go there anymore."

"I'm with you. Lox is the only fish that goes well with cream cheese in my opinion."

"Right?" He said, making a face. "After dinner, I went home and watched television until Skye came home around one. Then we went to bed."

"And Saturday? You said Saturday was the last day you saw her."

"Saturday was pretty much the same. Real Estate agents work weekends, you know. I slept in till nine or ten. Skye is an early riser. She gets up and goes for a bike ride on the Strand before it gets crowded. I made a pot of coffee. Scrounged around for something to eat. I hate cooking, so breakfast is a bagel or a Danish, or a donut with coffee. I didn't go into the office that morning, so I was still in my robe when Skye returned. She showered and dressed, and Sarah came by in her car to pick her up. The two of them were going up to Century City to go shopping at the mall."

"Wait. You said Sarah picked her up?"

"Yes. They did lots of things together. Going to a mall on Saturday was one of them."

"Did you see her? Did she come into the house?"

"Yes, sure. I remember because it was slightly awkward. I was still in my house robe, naked underneath, and was self-conscious about it."

"Okay, go on."

"They left, and that was the last I ever saw of her. Until a few weeks ago."

"When did you sense something was amiss?"

"I was out all afternoon, showing property. I didn't get back in time to walk Skye to her job, but I assumed that's where she was. I did notice a plastic bag from some store on the coffee table, so I knew she had been back at least to change clothes and such to get ready for work. Her purse was there, too, but she often didn't take it. Afraid it would get stolen, she said."

"But when she didn't come home that night?"

"I had gone to bed early, alone. Probably had a few drinks and slept soundly. When I woke on Sunday, she wasn't there, but then she's always out and about early. It wasn't until Sunday afternoon that I started to get concerned. I called her cell and heard it ring in her purse on the table."

"But you didn't call the police."

"As I told you before, we had a pretty loose relationship. It wasn't the first time she'd been gone for a few days without saying something. I let it slide. She's always very happy to see me when she's back."

"And then?"

"That evening, Bay City called, looking for Skye. She hadn't shown up for work and wasn't answering her phone. She could be irresponsible, but I was starting to be concerned. On Monday, I went down to the police department to report her missing. And, you know the rest of the story."

"The CCTV footage of that guy dressed as you putting trash bags in the dumpster was time-stamped for late Saturday night or early Sunday morning. So, whoever staged this knew you were home alone, asleep, with no alibi."

"What are you saying?"

"They either knew where Skye was, had eyes on her, or Skye was in on the frame-up."

Dan said nothing while he thought this over.

"Who did you show property to? Do you remember?"

"A young Hispanic couple. They showed up in a Maserati. I usually ask for a financial before wasting my time showing big-ticket homes. They said their parents would be buying it for them and would be able to show proof of funds if I needed it."

"So, you spent all day showing them around and never saw them again, I take it."

"Well, my life did kind of go to hell shortly thereafter. I don't know if they tried to get in touch again or not. Why do you say that?"

"They may have been a diversion. This is sounding like a well-planned operation."

"But why? Why me?"

CHAPTER

FIFTEEN

I decided to take the weekend off. I told Jack and Vera to take a break themselves. Rachel had invited me to her place for a home-cooked supper. She said Italian, so I picked up a couple of bottles of 2015 Brunello on my way. Rachel had a stylish two-bedroom condo in one of the towers in Century City. It was very modern, all white, white tile floor, white walls, white cabinets. The furniture was in shades of grey, silver, and black. The only color in the place were strategically placed flowers, artwork on the walls, or sculptures on the tables. The place looked like it leapt out of the pages of Architectural Digest. Being on the nineteenth floor, it had a nice view of a couple of golf courses.

The minute she opened the door, I was smothered in the heavenly aroma of Oso Buco. Rachel stood there in a smart black cocktail dress, barely covered by her white kitchen apron. And I thought aprons over formal wear went out with the fifties. She had a wooden spoon in her fist on her hip, ready to smack me if I got out of line. I gave her a polite little kiss on the cheek.

"I'm salivating already." I gushed. "And the food smells delicious, too."

She conked me on the head with her spoon. "Did you write that joke yourself, or steal it from some late-night talk show comic?" She said as she turned and walked back to the kitchen.

"I thought it up all by myself." I protested. "It does have a bit of a Rodney Dangerfield vibe, though. Don't you think?"

"Open that wine. I need a drink. Or would you rather have a cocktail first?"

"Let's have the wine. I brought two bottles. We should be able to get drunk on that."

She set two goblets down on the counter while I got busy opening the first bottle with her fancy electric bottle opener.

"Should I decant it?"

"Can't wait for decanting. I need a drink." She complained. "I've been slaving over a hot stove all afternoon for you."

"Okay. One glass of vino coming up. Subito!"

I poured two glasses and we toasted. I swirled the wine in my glass and studied the legs sliding down the sides. I stuck my nose into the glass and took a deep inhale, then savored a small mouthful, all as if I really knew what I was doing.

"Not bad," I pronounced.

"Yes, good juice," Rachel confirmed. She had already finished half her glass. "I don't go in for all that ritual. I'm surprised you didn't smell the cork."

She set he glass down, donned an oven mitt, and pulled a tray of toasted baguette slices from the oven, then proceeded to spoon her tomato mixture on top of each.

"Mmmm. Bruschetta. Nice."

While I sampled, she pulled another pan of fried calamari from her air fryer and shook them onto a plate. She paired this with a small bowl of marinara from the microwave.

"Careful. They're hot."

"You've gone all out. I'm going to be full before we get to the main course."

"So, how's the investigation going?" She stopped serving for a moment to take another sip of wine.

"Well, could be better. I have a couple of leads I'm following up. I have a theory that when someone lies to you, it means you're on the right track."

"Deets, Jimmy. I want the deets."

"Okay." I agreed. "There's this gal, name's Sarah. She's a cocktail waitress at a jazz club in Hermosa Beach called Bay City Blues. So, she was a co-worker of Skye's. They met while working at a beer bar down the street called MacGrath's, and when Sarah quit and moved to Bay City, she brought Skye along. The police interviewed her. I read their notes, and they didn't seem to see anything worth investigating. Sarah wasn't called as a witness at the trial.

"Being the thorough investigator that I am, I looked her up and re-interviewed her. Sarah claimed that they were friendly but not really friends. She recounted seeing Dan come in with her on occasion. She also noted that another guy, friendly to Skye, would also come in, but the two men never crossed paths. I found all that interesting, but not much use to me in tracking down Skye.

"So then yesterday I finally caught up with Heather." I continued.

"Who's Heather, again?"

"I told you about her. She's the sister of the guy I used to play golf against in high school. She flirted with me during a match and caused me to lose, but then I ran into her again down at Dan's parties."

"Oh, right. You're big, summer conquest. Are you still hot for her after all these years?"

"No, of course not. This was strictly business. Heather was a friend of Skye's. One that apparently the police didn't know about, or at least didn't bother to interview. So, I thought it would be worth hearing what she might have to say about Skye and Dan and that whole scene."

"And maybe see if there wasn't still a spark there?" She teased.

"Stop it." I gave Rachel a dirty look. I didn't really want to confess to the embarrassing part of my conversation with Heather. "It turns out that Heather had stopped going down to Hermosa not long after I last saw her. She hadn't seen Skye in many years. She had read about the murder and was shocked when I told her that Skye was still alive. Of course, she hadn't heard from her and why would she? They weren't friends. She then suggested that I get in touch with a waitress at MacGrath's named Sarah. I said that I already had. She said that if anyone would have heard from Skye, it would have been Sarah, as they were the best of friends."

"Best friends, huh?"

"I immediately drove over to Hermosa to confront Sarah about her little misdirection. She confessed that they were once best of friends, but they'd had a falling out. She'd seen her at the club, but they didn't talk much, and she hadn't seen her for a couple of weeks prior because she'd changed her shift hours to avoid the unpleasantness."

"And you bought that?"

"I didn't discount it out of hand, but I was suspicious. After leaving the club, I stopped by Dan's place. I asked him for a detailed chronology of the days leading up to Skye's disappearance. I knew it had been ten years, but Dan recalled it all pretty well as he had had to repeat that story countless times to the police. Among other details, he recalled that Sarah had stopped by to pick up Skye. The two were on their way to the mall to go shopping. Dan noted that that was the last time he saw Skye."

"So not only was Sarah lying about breaking off with Skye, it turns out she may have been the last person to see her before she disappeared. What a little detective story you have going, James."

"I know, right?!"

"So, what's your next step?"

"Well, this morning I dug back into all my case files. I have copies of all the crime scene photographs, and I found pictures of a shopping bag with a halter top and some leggings, and a time-stamped receipt for eleven o'clock that morning, the morning she disappeared. Also, I found pictures of the contents of her purse, which included a lunch receipt for two from that Italian place time, time-stamped for twelve thirty."

"I need to interview Sarah again, but some place besides her work. I think her manager is getting annoyed that I keep coming to the club to talk. Also, I should be able to lean on her a little harder if she can't skip away to another table."

While I filled up our wine glasses, Rachel ladled out a generous portion of veal shank and vegetables onto my plate.

"Ossobuco. For your dining pleasure." She said proudly.

CHAPTER

SIXTEEN

The next morning, Rachel and I were enjoying croissants and cappuccinos on her balcony and watching the golfers tee off on the first hole far below us. We were too far away to hear the thwack of the balls, or to even see the ball for that matter, but we watched nonetheless. The foursome below all seemed like older men. We watched the first three hits and assumed they were satisfied with the results. The fourth gentleman must have shanked his because he immediately teed up another ball and hit that. A mulligan, or breakfast ball, as they call it. They then piled into their carts and drove off down the fairway.

I felt my phone buzz in my pocket and snuck a glance at the screen. It was Jack, probably looking to see if I was at the 101 diner. Rachel got up and took my cup to freshen up our coffees. While she was gone, I stole a look at my screen to see what Jack was up to.

- *I think Hugo is here!* He texted.

I looked through the balcony doors to check on Rachel, then texted him back.

- *Where?*

- *At the track.*

- *What track?*

- *Los Alamitos.*

- *What are you doing there? It's Sunday. You're supposed to be taking the day off.*

- *I am. I came to play the ponies. And I think I see our guy, Hugo.*

- *Are you sure?*

- *Well, the picture you gave me is old, but I'm pretty sure.*

- *Sit tight. I'll meet you there.*

"Are you on the phone?" Rachel reappeared with two cappuccinos in hand.

"It's Jack. Something's come up."

"It's Sunday."

"I know. But this is important. I have to go."

"James, don't you dare run off." She said as she slammed down the cups.

"I wouldn't leave if it wasn't important. You know that." I quickly tossed off my robe. Fortunately, I was already wearing my boxers. I fished my slacks off the floor and hopped into them. "I'll be back before you know it," I said as I grabbed my shirt.

Rachel, her back to the world, opened her robe, revealing to me her amazingly fit and tanned naked body. "How can you walk away from this?" she said with a smile.

Somewhere I had seen this scene before. I decided to forgo socks and slipped into my loafers as I buttoned up my shirt and backed towards the door. Rachel's smile had turned into a death stare. The army should weaponize that look. It was lethal.

"I'll come back as soon as I can. I promise!" I called out as I stepped through the doorway and closed the door before she thought to throw something at me.

My Tesla's navigation map said 45 minutes. I made it in under forty. Lucky for me, it was Sunday. Jack was waiting in the parking lot by the entrance.

"Where are they?" I asked.

"They're in Burgart's. That's where everyone hangs out." He led the way.

"Just a sec." I ran back to my car and retrieved my camera from the trunk. I put on my old fedora for good measure.

"What's that for?" Jack asked.

"I want to get an up-to-date picture. That mug shot Mejia gave me is twenty years old."

"You know, guys who run afoul of the law tend not to like having their pictures taken."

"I can be discreet. It's what I used to do."

"Not if you're wearing The Hat."

"What do you mean, the hat?"

"When Humphrey Bogart wears a hat, he blends in because everyone else is wearing one. But you are going to be the only guy in this place sporting a felt fedora. Everyone is going to look at you. How are you going to be discreet?"

"Maybe you're right." I thought about returning to my car to ditch it, but I was too impatient. "I'll take it off when we get inside."

Burgart's was a big place, huge wrap-around bar, lots of tables to eat at, and a few more to play pool on. There were screens to view the races on every wall. It was still early, so the place was only about half full. We had no trouble finding a table off in a corner. We settled in, I put my hat on the table, and rested the camera in its crown.

"That's them at the far corner of the bar."

I looked up. There were four guys standing around two pretty girls sitting on stools, laughing loudly, drinking shots, and sharing a big plate of nachos.

Jack had taken the seat with his back to them, so I could have a better view.

"There were fewer people here an hour ago. I saw them come in, but didn't pay any attention to them. They took up residence there at the corner and started drinking. They spoke Spanish, so I wasn't really listening to them, even though they were pretty loud. I was busy figuring out my bets for the day.

"At some point, one of them said something that sounded like 'Hugo'. That caught my attention. I started to watch them, trying to figure out which one of them was our guy. The one in the black polo had his back to me, but when he turned around, it looked a little like the picture you sent me. I pulled it up on my phone to double-check. Then I texted you."

As Jack talked, I quietly fiddled with the camera, slightly turning my hat and adjusting the angle so that it pointed toward those guys. I had a 70mm zoom on the camera, which was more than enough to get in close. I also had a remote shutter release so I could snap without touching the camera. The guy in the black polo was now half sitting on another stool, one foot on the floor, holding court with the other three guys and intermittently flirting with the girls. He was showing off and the girls were hanging all over him. He was obviously the alpha of that group. His face was turned three-quarters towards me. He was a good-looking guy, with dark curly hair and dark eyes. I could see the ladies' attraction to him. I started snapping away.

A waitress came by with menus. I wasn't hungry, but I ordered a hamburger anyway to give cover to my being there. Jack, of course, is always hungry. As the waitress walked away, there was an announcement of a race about to start. Everyone's attention turned to the screens as the announcer began the introductions.

"Isn't anyone going to watch the race live?" I asked, noticing that no one was leaving to go outside.

"Oh, this isn't a live race. It's a simulcast. The race is at another track."

"I don't understand."

"The live races here don't start until this evening. Until then, you can watch races from around the state on the big screens and place bets just as if you were there."

"That doesn't seem quite the same to me."

"Yeah, it's a little like going to a sports bar. There just aren't enough races to attract a crowd otherwise. Horse racing is a dying sport, my friend."

Jack turned around to watch the screen over the bar. As the horses took off, the volume in the bar got loud.

"Did you place a bet?" I shouted.

"No Joke to win." He shouted back.

I watched, refraining from joining in on the cheering. No Joke finished second. The noise level in the bar suddenly subsided.

"Do you get anything for second place?"

"No, only if you cover that on your bet."

I glanced over at our surveillance targets. It didn't look like they had a winning ticket either, but they didn't seem to care. Their raucous laughter rang out. I recognized one of the other guys in the foursome; he was the same guy I had confronted over the MG, the one with the tattoos on his neck.

"You didn't happen to see a red MGB in the parking lot, did you?"

"No. I wasn't really looking. I really came here to play the races, not work, but here we are."

"How many races are there today?"

"Well, the simulcasts run up to about four, I think, then the live races start at six and run till ten or thereabouts."

"I don't think our friends are here for the whole day and evening, not the way they're drinking."

"You'd be surprised," Jack commented.

I tried to call Rachel, but she didn't answer. I decided not to leave a voice message and texted her instead.

- *This may take a little longer than I expected. Don't be mad. I'll come over as soon as possible. Where shall we go for dinner?*

Lunch came, so we settled back and ate, and watched the races all the while keeping one eye on our targets.

"Do you have a good shot of Hugo yet?" Jack asked.

"I think so. I caught him looking around the room, so it's almost full face."

"Can you send it to my phone. I can check it out and maybe see if it's him."

"How can you do that?"

"Vera showed me this free facial recognition app you can download. I'll just load the mug shot and your full frontal and see if it's a match."

"A facial recognition app? How did you come to know to ask her for that?"

"We were just talking shop one afternoon while you were off interviewing at the beach. You know, trade craft, swapping info on this and that. What do people do that in the same profession over coffee?"

"You guys kill me. Trade craft? Are you in the CIA now or what?" I laughed, but sent him the pic file anyway.

We sat for a couple of hours, leisurely eating our lunch and watching the races. Jack managed not to win a single time. Around two, we noticed our boys getting ready to leave. Hugo hopped down from his stool, fished out a wad of bills from his pocket, and peeled off a few for a tip. He clapped the neck tattooed guy on the back, and then he, the girls, and the other two guys proceeded to walk out. I guess tattoo boy was the avid gambler of the group and was planning to stay all night.

"I want to follow him home," I said as I got up and grabbed my camera and hat. We lingered back just enough not to draw attention and still not lose sight of the.

"Where are you parked?" I asked as we emerged from the clubhouse.

"Right up front. Here." Jack gestured to a newish dark grey Kia sedan with tinted windows.

"Did you get a new car?"

"Nah, I just had it repainted and had the windows tinted. Pretty sick, eh?"

"I like it," I said even as I scanned the parking lot for Hugo. He was a couple of rows further away and getting into a black Maserati with the other two men. The girls had disappeared while we were not paying attention.

"When I get to my car, I'll call you. Don't lose them, but don't follow too close."

I hurried, trying not to run, to my car, many rows further away. By the time I pulled out of my parking spot, they were already out on the street. I speed-dialed Jack from the car.

"Where are you?"

"We turned right on Katella. My guess is we are heading for the freeway."

"Okay. I'm pulling out now. When you get to the freeway, try to follow from a different lane so he doesn't see you in his rear view. I'll catch up, then we can tag team it."

"Got it. He's taking the 605 North."

A few minutes later, I, too, was on the 605 heading north and soon caught up to them.

"You stay on the outside lane. I'll take the inside."

We followed Hugo's Maserati up the 605, then east onto the 91. The 91 took us to Fullerton, where he exited onto Harbor Boulevard. It was easy to stay in his blind spot on the freeway with its multiple lanes, but now on the city streets, we had to be more careful. I wasn't too concerned. Hugo had no reason to expect anyone to be following, but Jack and I alternated pulling closer or falling back so that the same car wasn't always in his mirror. We followed him deep into a residential neighborhood, the kind with wide curving streets that wrapped in and around a golf course. Jack was the closer car; I was a couple of blocks back when he called me.

"He's pulling into a driveway."

"Drive past. Go a block down, turn around and come back to where you can have eyes on him. I'm going to pull up and approach him on foot."

"Be careful. There are three of them, remember."

I pulled up seconds later. Hugo and his friends had dawdled in the car just long enough that they had only crossed halfway across the lawn to the house when I arrived. Teslas are very quiet and they didn't seem to hear me. I quickly jumped out of my car and called out to him.

"Hugo! Can I talk with you for a minute?" I shouted.

All three of them froze in mid-step and then slowly turned around. I walked around my car and approached them across the grass.

"Do you have a second to answer a couple of questions? I promise not to take up more than a few minutes of your time."

"Who are you?" Hugo asked, staring at my face and trying to remember if he had ever seen me before. He was obviously the kind of guy who did not like people he didn't know, knowing him.

"My name is James Gardiner. I'm a private detective."

"How do you know my name?" He interrupted.

"Like I said, I'm a private detective. It's my business to know people's names. I wanted to ask you about a woman named Skye."

"I don't know any such person."

"Well. I've spoken to several people who tell me that you regularly picked her up from her job at Bay City Blues at closing."

"Oh, is that her name? She's just some chick I dated. That was a long time ago."

"Have you seen her lately?"

"No. she's dead."

"If you didn't remember her, how did you know she was dead?"

"I read it in the newspaper. Chick had a funny name, caught my eye."

"Turns out, she's not dead."

"Is that a question?"

I didn't see him signal, or maybe the other two took the initiative to start to circle around me, cutting off my retreat to the car.

"No, I was just relaying what I've turned up in my investigation."

"You ask a lot of questions."

"That's my job. I'm an investigator."

"You investigating this chick, Skye or whatever she calls herself?"

"Yes, it seems she faked her death, or maybe had someone fake it for her. When's the last time you've seen Skye?"

I heard one of the guys behind me open a switchblade. It was a familiar click. I glanced behind me. The guy was holding it lightly next to his thigh, but the threat was there.

"I didn't come here to cause trouble," I said, turning back to Hugo. "I'm not even armed." I held out my empty hands, palms up.

"That may have been your mistake," Hugo answered menacingly. "Though armed or not, I don't think it will make any difference."

Now I was starting to sweat. I hadn't expected a friendly reaction, but I wasn't anticipating getting myself killed either.

"You want me to leave? I'll leave."

"I think the time for leaving may have passed."

"What? You're going to kill me here on your lawn in front of your neighbors?"

"I don't see any neighbors."

"I didn't come here alone."

Hugo glanced at my car. "I don't see anyone in your car."

"My partner has his own car."

Hugo glanced up and down the street. Jack's grey Kia was parked a few houses down, but with tinted windows, you couldn't see inside. He didn't seem to pay it any attention.

"I think maybe your partner has been delayed."

I tried my best to stay cool. They're just trying to scare me, I tell myself. At that moment, a red laser dot appeared on Hugo's shoulder and slowly slid to the center of his chest and hovered there. I saw it first; the two guys behind me saw it at almost the same time. Hugo only noticed when he saw us looking.

He glanced up and looked back down the street. Jack's car window was now rolled down about a third of the way. You could still not see inside. Jack had been full of surprises lately, but I never thought he would have a sniper rifle with a laser-sighted scope in his bag of tricks.

Hugo looked down again at the jittering red dot. "That's just a laser pointer." He declared with a snort.

"Could be," I answered. I could see that Hugo's assurance was flagging slightly. It probably was just a laser pointer, but I needed to use this moment of uncertainty to get the hell out of there.

"I don't like people poking around in my business." He said, his attitude quickly changing back to threatening.

Behind me, I could hear another car pull up. I glanced back. A white Honda Civic pulled up on the wrong side of the road, bumper to bumper with my car. We all watched as the window rolled down. The driver, a young woman with dark glasses and blond hair pulled back in a tight ponytail, leaned her left arm out over the open doorframe. Her right hand casually placed a 9mm pistol on her left arm.

The appearance of the gun changed the calculation immediately.

"I have no more time for your questions." Hugo snorted. "Vamanos." He called then to the other two, and they turned and walked into the house, slamming the door behind them.

I stood there for a long moment. I could feel myself trembling involuntarily. I hope that Jack and Vera didn't notice. I took a couple of deep breaths. Then, as calmly as I could muster, I turned and walked back to my car.

"Thanks for stopping by." I joked weakly. "It's Sunday. You're supposed to be off."

"And miss all the fun?" She laughed back.

I scheduled a debriefing with my team, Jack and Vera, for Monday morning. I would spend the rest of the night trying to contact Rachel, unsuccessfully. I guess she was still mad at me and giving me the silent treatment. All of my calls went to voicemail until her mailbox was full. Text messages went unanswered as well. Driving home, I was thinking about what a close call that encounter with Hugo had been and wondered if I was really cut out to be a detective. I expected a little danger now and then, but I seemed to have a knack for almost getting myself killed. If I live long enough, maybe I'll learn a thing or two. After some frank soul searching, I had a drink or two and went to bed.

CHAPTER

SEVENTEEN

In the morning, I made my usual stop at Starbucks to pick up coffee for the three of us. Jack brought the donuts, a half dozen assorted. Vera, the only sensible one of the three of us, took a pass on the pastries. More for me, I thought to myself.

"But that's required eating if you're going to be on the force." I teased.

"That joke is so old, but the guys on the force totally own it." She responded. "Besides, it's just all grease and sugar, you know."

"Well, if you don't overdo it, it never hurts to treat yourself now and then."

"Here's my treat." She pulled a protein bar from her jacket pocket.

"You have a permit for that?" I asked.

"For this granola bar?"

"No. For whatever else you're packing." I smiled, having noticed the butt of her firearm peeking out from under her arm when she reached for her snack.

"Of course. I have concealed carry, too."

"So, if you don't mind me asking, why were you armed?"

"The better question is, why weren't you?"

"Seriously, mate." Jack piped in. "Going up against three guys, any one of whom could have easily taken you alone."

"Thanks for the vote of confidence," I said, then turning back to Vera. "So, how did you know where to find us?"

"Well, I must confess, I texted her that we were surveilling Hugo at the track," Jack added.

"But you didn't tell her we were going to Fullerton." I countered. "We didn't know we were going to Fullerton."

"I tracked his phone with the phone tracker app," Vera explained. "You should let us track your phone." She added. "In case of emergencies."

"I'm not sure I want that," I complained as I grabbed a glazed twist and settled back in my chair, annoyed.

My phone rang. I glanced at the screen. It was my old friend Sam Mejia.

"Lieutenant Mejia, so nice to hear from you," I answered, motioning for my team to stay.

"Gardiner. I need you to come down to my office today."

"What's up?"

"You'll find out when you get here. One o'clock."

"Sure. I'll be there."

He hung up. Well, that was short and sweet.

"What's that all about?" Jack asked.

"Beats me. Maybe he has some new info on our pal Hugo. I can't think of any other reason he'd call."

"This is your friend on the force?" Vera asked. "Doesn't sound too friendly."

"You have to get to know him. Anyway, Jack, here's a snap of Hugo's car plates and that address in Fullerton. Let's see what we can find out. Does he own, rent, lease, use his own name or alias, or family member? Anything might be useful. And Vera, let's get you back on checking out that kid, Fly."

"I'm on it. What do you think is going on there?"

"Here, I'm sending you a pic of the bank statement Norma sent me. You'll see there are generally two deposits a week, eight for the month, and then a cashier's check withdrawal at the end of the month. I'm pretty sure he's using Martin as cover in a money laundering operation. He deposits small amounts of cash in the account at different branches. But then he repeats that cycle, same branch on the same day of the week. If anyone asks, he says he runs a cash business, a food truck, or coin laundry, or something like that. Once a month, he transfers just shy of ten thousand to another account."

"Why is that?"

"For ten thousand and more, the bank has to fill out a CTR, basically a report to the government of money transactions. Keeping it under the limit keeps it out of sight of the IRS and other federal agencies."

"The government gets to monitor our finances now?" Jack asked.

"The Money Laundering Control Act of 1986. It pretty much allows the feds to look at all banking transactions."

"Why would you know all about that?"

"I come from a long line of bankers. It's in my DNA." I laughed. "Vera, I'm also sending you a pic I took of this guy, Fly, from his high school yearbook. Don't know if he still looks like this, but let's see if you can spot him making a deposit. I'm betting he sticks to his routine. He's just a runner, a messenger boy. Somebody else is setting the schedule.

They stood up to leave. Jack grabbed the box with the remainder of the donuts.

"Oh, and get your hours and expenses to me for last week."

After an early lunch, I headed downtown to see the detective. Mejia was in the Central Bureau, Homicide Division. I made sure to arrive a few minutes early. An officer met me at the desk and escorted me down a long white hallway to the lieutenant's office, and opened the door for me. I went in. Mejia rose from behind his desk and extended his hand for a shake.

"Lieutenant." I greeted him as I shook his hand and glanced toward the other man in the room. Two chairs were facing the detective's desk. The one on the right had been pulled around so that it faced me more than the desk. In it sat a black man in a grey suit. He had a toffee-colored complexion, and his hair was cut very short, highlighting his receding hairline. I detected a bit of grey on his temples. I guessed him to be about fifty. I waited for an introduction.

"This is Special Agent Walters." Mejia finally said. "He's with the DEA. He has a few questions for you."

"Have a seat, Mr. Gardiner." Agent Walters gestured to the empty chair.

As I sat, I looked to Sam enquiringly, but he avoided my eyes and looked to Walters.

"Where were you yesterday?" He asked.

"I was at the track, watching the horse races." I was confused about why I was being interviewed, but figured it would become clearer as we went along.

"By yourself?"

"I met a friend there."

"You spend the whole day?"

"No, I left mid-afternoon."

"And then where did you go?"

"I went home."

Agent Walters picked up a manila envelope from his lap and pulled a sheet of paper from it. "You live in Hollywood, right?"

"Yes."

"So why did you go to Fullerton?" Walters set down a picture on the desk in front of me. It was a photo of me with my palms up, talking to Hugo. His henchmen were standing behind me. The photo was a bit grainy and soft focus, probably taken by a closed-circuit camera from across the street. I looked at the photo, then up to Sam, then over to Walters.

"If you know where I've been, then why are you asking?"

"First rule of interrogation is to always know the answer before you ask the question."

"Is this an interrogation?" I asked, turning to my old friend Sam.

"You're not in trouble, James. You're not even under arrest. We're just hoping you can help us out." Sam replied.

"You need to be forthright, young man," Walters added. "Hedging your answers and leaving things out is no different than lying. How do you know Hugo Martinez?"

"I don't. That was the first time we'd ever met."

"Then how did you know to track him down at his house?"

I took a deep sigh and leaned forward, elbows resting on my knees. "I'm a private investigator."

"I know that." Walters interrupted.

"I'm investigating a missing persons case. A woman named Skye Goldberg went missing and was presumed murdered. There was a big trial, lots of salacious details for the media, but in the end, a not guilty verdict for lack of a body.

"The boyfriend, and the accused, is someone I knew briefly from my high school days. I hadn't seen him in over a dozen years, but we bumped into each other a few weeks ago. He remembered me from a case I worked on last year that got me a lot of press exposure. I wasn't aware of his trial, but he filled me in and then told me that he recently saw his girlfriend, Skye, driving down the street. He hired me to find her. I'm not really at liberty to disclose my client's identity."

"We know all about your Mr. Daniel LeBeau." Off my surprised reaction, Walters continued. "You mentioned the case to the Lieutenant last Thursday. It doesn't take a genius to look it up. So where does Hugo fit in? His name doesn't appear in any police investigation notes, and he wasn't called as a witness at the trial."

"In my investigation, I have learned that Hugo was seeing Skye on the side. She was cheating on Mr. LeBeau. I wanted to talk to him."

"And what did Hugo have to say about all this?"

"Oh, he denied having seen her in all these years. But he's a bad liar."

"Why do you say that?"

"All of Skye's friends and associates say she just ghosted on her boyfriend because he was becoming emotionally abusive. But she didn't just split. My client was framed. It was an elaborate undertaking that she couldn't have pulled off alone. Her blood was spattered all over a bathroom and then sloppily cleaned up. A man the same height and weight as my client then pretended to dispose of chopped-up body parts in a dumpster in full view of a closed-circuit TV.

"Lieutenant Mejia informed me that Hugo has priors going back twenty years. He seems like a good fit for someone who would help a girl disappear."

"What else do you know about this Martinez fellow?"

"I traced the car Skye was driving to a house in Long Beach that is owned by a Martinez, maybe a coincidence, and I offered to buy it from a man there who refused to sell. I later spotted this same guy at the racetrack, and he was driving the car. Yesterday he was there again, this time with Hugo and some other friends. I think that's a pretty strong connection that Hugo at least knows where Skye is if nothing else."

"I meant, outside of the scope of his involvement with this girl, what do you know about him?"

"Other than he's been arrested for drug possession and some other minor stuff, nothing."

"The drug possession convictions were where he started. Mr. Martinez is a smart and ambitious man. Right now, he runs a pretty small operation for the distribution and sale of controlled substances, but he has big plans and plenty of connections down south."

"He's cartel?" I asked, suddenly worried. I didn't want to get mixed up with those guys.

"He thinks he's too smart for that. He sees the cartels as just gangs in an endless war. And he's right. They are all about dominance. Martinez thinks he can play both sides. Strictly business. If he makes them money, they'll leave him alone. He has eyes on taking over all of this end of the business in L.A. and Orange Counties."

"Sounds like he's more than capable of helping Skye set up her boyfriend. One way to get rid of the competition, I guess."

"Maybe so, but we don't want you to speak to Martinez again."

"What?" I turned to Mejia for verification. He only nodded.

"Martinez is the subject of a major ongoing DEA investigation. I don't need you muddying things up chasing after this girl."

"But he's my main lead. What am I supposed to do?"

"I'm sure you'll think of something. You have other leads to follow up. I'm serious. Do not approach him again."

"What am I supposed to tell my client?"

"This conversation is strictly confidential. You cannot tell anyone what we've discussed here, not your client, not your associates."

"But…" I protested.

"If we bring him in, I will arrange for you to interview him if you still need to, but that may take months, even years. This is a big operation. We intend to roll it all up. That takes time."

Mejia stood up. "Are you clear, James?"

"I guess so." I stood and walked toward the door.

"Guessing so won't cut it. I don't want to have to bring you in for obstruction." Mejia shouted after me as I left the room.

I pondered what to do all the way back to the office.

Vera was at her desk, and Jack had taken up temporary residence on mine. I really needed to get another desk in the office now that Jack was working almost full-time. Space was tight, but I could move the fish tank into my room and maybe squeeze Jack into the front room. I could always look to move to a larger suite, say three offices, but I really liked this one. It was the top floor, all the way in the back, and one of the last offices not remodeled. It still had the look and feel of the original décor, one hundred years old. I made a mental note to myself to check into the office next door.

I signaled for Vera to follow me and I went into my office and plopped down in one of the guest chairs. Vera took the other chair and we both waited for Jack to finish whatever he was in the middle of.

"I just had an interesting conversation with my buddy Lieutenant Mejia and some guy from the DEA." I began after Jack finally looked up. "It seems our friend Hugo is dealing drugs, and in sufficient quantity to have attracted the attention of the feds."

"What does that have to do with us?" Jack asked.

"It means we've been told to back off. No more contact with Hugo. They don't want us messing things up. They have him under surveillance. They were showing me pictures of my little talk with him on the front lawn of his house."

"Really?" Vera spoke up. I wonder where their camera was."

"Probably on the phone lines or atop one of the poles. The government would not have any problem accessing that, and no one probably paid any attention if they were disguised as repairmen."

"Hmmm. So now what?" She asked. "Hugo was our best lead."

"True, but it wasn't like he was quick to offer up her location. We'll have to find another way."

"We could tag his car and see if maybe he leads us to Skye," Jack suggested.

"That could be dangerous. He might see you." I thought aloud.

"I wouldn't tag it at his house. I'd wait till he went back to the track. Totally discreet in that parking lot."

"Okay, let's do that. And tag the MG while you're at it. Let's hope he'll come back there soon. I don't think he's quite the gambler as his guys are, though. Anything on the Maserati or the house? Dan mentioned that on the day Skye disappeared, he was showing property to a young Hispanic couple in a Maserati. It could be a coincidence, or they could have been keeping Dan busy while they staged the crime scene."

"Yes and no on the car and house. They are both owned by an LLC. But it's an anonymous LLC, or a ghost LLC, as they call them. Can't find out who owns the LLC. The nominee for contact is a law firm in Torrance. The house in Long Beach is a different LLC, but with the same law firm designated. The MGB is registered to Hugo."

"Probably not worth protecting. I wonder how many properties he owns?"

"I can do a reverse search on the LLCs and see if they own any more. But if he's using a lot of different shell companies, we're out of luck. I can't reverse search the law firm."

"Let's see what other properties we can find. Maybe Skye is staying in one of them. Vera, anything on Dan's friends and business associates?"

Vera flipped open her laptop and scrolled through her notes.

"The police didn't interview anyone whom they couldn't connect to the case. The defense team, however, did put together a list of character witnesses, friends and business associates. At trial, though, they didn't call on any of them as they opted for a strategy of insisting that the prosecution hadn't proven their case."

"Maybe they were saving them for the penalty phase." I mused.

"Yeah, maybe. But from that list, the defense attorneys only interviewed six people; two were listed as social friends and four as business associates. The business friends are all in the real estate business. Of those six, two I have found to have moved out of state, one to Austin, Texas, and another to Seattle. Two others I haven't been able to locate, and the remaining two I have phone numbers and addresses for, Helen Allswell, a realtor that has done a number of deals with Mr. LeBeau and George Mahoney, who is listed as an old friend."

"That's great," I said. "I can start with those two. Oh, and have you had a chance to look into Fly, yet?"

"Not much, no employment history, but he does have quite a rap sheet: shoplifting, possession of stolen merchandise, burglary. When we're done here, I'll head over to the bank and see if he makes his weekly deposit."

"Sounds like quite a guy."

"Who's Fly?" Jack asked.

"It's a pro bono case I'm working on for a friend. Just a little background check."

"That's not Norma's son Martin's friend Fly, is it?"

"You know him?"

"No, but Norma has complained about him and Martin more than once to me."

"I suppose that's his handle because he's a sharp dresser or something."

"No, man. Nobody says that anymore. That's so 80s. It's 'cause he's bug-eyed, like Marty Feldman. Some kind of thyroid condition. He just wishes it was because he dressed sharp."

"Anyway, I guess her concerns are growing. Okay, gang, let's get going. Vera, text me those contact numbers for Helen and George."

As the meeting adjourned, I took my usual seat from Jack and settled back to check my phone for messages from Rachel. None. She must be really mad.

I spent the rest of the afternoon trying to set up appointments with Helen and George. George was pretty simple. I called, left a message, and then texted him, trying to explain as little as possible without saying too much about why I wanted to see him. I didn't want to spook him.

Helen was an altogether bigger ordeal. I only had her office number. There's nothing like a cold call to a real estate office to spark a feeding frenzy among the agents. I was fresh meat. Heaven forbid that I would have any other business to discuss other than buying or selling a house. Apparently, she was out showing property. I left several messages.

CHAPTER

EIGHTEEN

George Mahoney lived at the north end of Manhattan Beach. He had returned my call in the evening and we arranged to meet at a little coffee shop on Highland Avenue. It was a Cape Cod style building, oyster grey with white trim, not new, but then not so old either. The décor inside was different from the usual So-Cal look, more Pacific Northwest or East Coast, with fishing nets and pictures of sailing ships, etc.

George looked a bit older than Dan, already showing quite a bit of grey on his head and in his short beard and mustache. I wouldn't say he looked grizzled, but if he sported a knit cap, he would have blended right in. I introduced myself, we shook and I went to buy us a couple of black coffees. Here, they served them in large ceramic mugs, just like at home.

After I sat down and sampled a sip of really excellent coffee, I began.

"I should start off by telling you that Dan's girlfriend, Skye, was recently spotted alive and seemingly well, here in southern California."

George's eyebrows arched up. "Well, I'll be. That is a bit of a surprise. Not that I had any doubt about Dan's innocence in the whole affair, mind you, but that she would reappear here. Have you spoken to her?"

"No. That is what I am attempting to do. Actually, it was Dan who spotted her. He then hired me to find her. I'm a private investigator."

"I see. What do you want from me? I certainly haven't seen or heard from her. I haven't even seen or spoken to Dan in almost ten years."

"Did you have a falling out?"

"Not that I could point to." George sighed deeply and toyed with his coffee mug. "Even though he was found innocent, the trial took a terrible toll on Dan. He wasn't the same afterwards. I tried reaching out to him, but he never returned my calls. I get it that he felt betrayed, but all the more reason to lean on those of us who were his true friends."

"Did you know Skye well?"

"No, not really. She was young, much like yourself. I didn't find much in common to talk about with her when the chance arose. She wasn't into sports or politics, or current affairs. She was all about music or astrology, or celebrity gossip. She was nice to look at, but other than that, I didn't know what Dan saw in her."

"How did you come to know Dan in the first place?"

"It's a story I've told a hundred times if I've told it once. New Year's Day, I was sitting in Pancho's, just across the street from here." He gestured toward a two-story establishment on the opposite corner. "Drinking and watching the Rose Bowl game with some friends. It was Michigan versus USC. Of course, I had on my Michigan jersey. Dan spotted it and came over and introduced himself as a fellow Wolverine. We hit it off right away.

"Dan's one of those guys with a wide array of intellectual interests. He knows a little about a lot of things and can talk on any subject. I'm a little guilty of that myself at times. We could sit in a bar for hours and expound on a multitude of topics until we were too drunk to drive home." He laughed. "I miss that."

"Did you know Michele?"

"His previous girlfriend? Yeah. I think she was there that New Year's when I first met Dan. I think she was a Bruin fan, so she was rooting with us on the game."

"Yeah, no love lost between UCLA and SC. That's for sure." I opined. "Dan described her as a wild party girl."

"I don't know that she was all that wild. I think she was still in college at the time. But that was fifteen or twenty years ago or more. I don't really remember. College kids are always going to seem a little wild to someone older. But she was cute, a dancer, thin and fit. Always wore a leotard top and baggy pants. And a floppy hat. That was her signature look. She kind of reminded me of that girl in the movie, Cabaret, Sally Bowles. Lots of eye make-up."

"Dan said when she got her big break and moved to New York, it really tore him up. He considered moving there with her and selling his business."

"Yeah, well, that's not entirely the way it went down. I didn't really know Michele, not any more than I knew Skye. But we had a mutual friend, a gay fellow, name was Gary. I would always hear the gossip from him. Girls all felt comfortable confiding things with Gary that they would never tell a straight guy. Michele was ready to move on and find a younger boyfriend, someone closer to her own age, but Dan was pretty clingy. Maybe clingy is too polite a word. He was possessive. Started making rules for her, checked up on her. It was smothering to her. She'd try to break it off, and he'd get depressed, talk about suicide, really over the top. I thought it was weird. He wasn't like that about anything else, but I guess he was that insecure about her that he'd do anything to keep her."

"You didn't think that maybe she was overreacting. That it wasn't as crazy as she made it out to be."

"Possibly. I did talk to her at one point. She said she felt afraid for her life. She said she thought Dan might kill her rather than let her go. In the end, she lied about having a role on Broadway and she packed up and left in one day."

"She didn't."

"No. She flew out there with no money and no prospects. Stayed with a friend of Gary's until she got on her feet. Left no forwarding address, got a new phone, a clean break with everyone here in L.A. If I didn't know Gary, I wouldn't have heard any of it."

"Wow. I guess for Dan, knowingly believing the lie was easier than accepting the truth."

"That's true for a lot of us."

George didn't have much else to add. He didn't know anything about Dan's real estate business and didn't know any of Skye's friends; he didn't even know of any of Dan's other friends, which I thought was curious. I thanked him for his time and walked back to my car. I tried Helen's office again and got lucky. She was in. Her office was only five minutes away, on Rosecrans and Sepulveda.

Allswell Realty was in a newer outdoor mall, squeezed in between a chain coffee shop and a chain fitness center. Her realty brokerage was not a chain, though, but an independent. Not many of those are left these days. Helen had the big corner office, of course, and greeted me as if she were happy to see me. I declined another cup of coffee as I took a very comfy chair in a seating area away from her desk.

"I'm a private investigator," I said, handing her my card. "I've been retained by Dan LeBeau to look into the disappearance of his S.O., Skye."

"Skye?" Helen was surprised. "I thought she was dead."

"As you were interviewed by his defense team, I'm sure you heard their argument that he couldn't be convicted of her murder because the prosecution hadn't proved she was really dead. And she isn't."

"I'm not following you. Isn't what?"

"She isn't dead. Dan saw her driving down Sepulveda Boulevard in Hermosa Beach not three weeks ago."

"Really?"

"It was all an elaborate set-up. The evidence was manufactured and staged to point to Dan. I think the police and prosecutors might have had their doubts, but they both think all criminals are stupid anyway. But it was a salacious crime, and the media was running with it. There was pressure to take it to trial. I looked at the evidence. It was both clever and sloppy. I think whoever planted these clues didn't really care if Dan went to jail. They knew the trial would ruin him, and it did."

"Oh, my god. I can't believe it."

"Dan wants me to find Skye. He's convinced that she was not a willing participant in the frame-up and worries that she's a victim herself. Seeing her made him think that after ten years, enough time has passed that he might be able to rescue her if I can find her.

"The key to finding her is finding out who was really behind the staged murder scene. I agree with Dan, Skye couldn't have pulled this off herself."

"What do you want from me? At the time I talked to the police, someone from the prosecutor's office and Dan's legal team. I don't think I had anything useful to add to whatever they already knew."

"I'm sure you were as helpful as you could be," I reassure her. "I wanted to ask you, though, about Dan's real estate business."

"His real estate business?"

"Yes. How did you come to know Dan in the first place?

"Oh, we did a few deals together. Then we'd run into each other at open houses and such. It's a small community down here, very insular. If you live here long enough you get to know the locals."

"I understood he was very successful. Yes?"

"Oh, yes. Well, he didn't sell all that many properties as a broker, but he was very astute as an investor."

"So, he'd take his earnings in commissions and plow that back into buying property. Rentals, I assume?"

"Small rentals. Duplexes and the like."

"If he didn't earn that much in commissions, where did he get the funds to invest?" I queried.

"Dan said he inherited quite a sum from his father. His father was a big car dealer back in Michigan, I take it."

"Oh, that's right. He did tell me that, I think. How many properties do you think he owned at the time?"

"I don't know. Maybe a dozen or so. I didn't really pry."

"But still, he should be worth millions. Property down here doesn't come cheap.

"Most of his holdings he said were in Torrance, Carson, and Inglewood. I think the only house he owned around here was his home." She explained. "But then again, I heard his legal bills forced him to sell at an inopportune time. Investment property is a different animal from residential. He was probably forced to take real low-ball offers. The vultures smell blood and take advantage. That's just the way this business works."

"I see. Did he offer to sell you his business?"

"He did, but I wasn't interested in another office. I'm happy staying small. Down here at the beach, I can compete with the bigger chains because the community is small. Besides, as I said, his business was focused more inland. I didn't want to learn new territory."

"Do you still keep in touch?"

"Sadly, no. I did for maybe six months, during the trial, but then Dan stopped returning my calls. I thought he just wanted a clean break from his past and if that meant his old friends, well, that was his choice. I couldn't force him to do otherwise.'

We chatted for a few more minutes about all things real estate and then I thanked her and left. In the car, I called Vera and asked her to look up whatever she could find on that LeBeau car dealership, maybe one or several, in the Midland area. I explained that it was probably sold through probate ten to fifteen years ago, so maybe it no longer exists in that name.

I glanced at the time. It was already two-thirty. Since I was down here, I figured I should stop in and confront Sarah about the lie she told me regarding when she last saw Skye. But her shift didn't start until four. I hadn't eaten, so I figured I could kill the time by having lunch. I drove down to Hermosa.

Fat Freddie's was only two blocks from Bay City Blues, so I stopped in there. I was in the mood for a chili burger anyway. The place was pretty empty, two-thirty being that dead zone between the lunch crowd and happy hour at four. I ordered my burger with a side of kettle chips and a pint of Smog City, a local ale.

After a leisurely lunch, I wandered over to Bay City. I was still early, and the club was pretty empty. The lights were up and some soft Chuck Mangione flugelhorn was being piped in over the sound system. I ordered a scotch and soda at the bar and grabbed an empty table near the front door, the batter to snag Sarah when she came in for her shift.

Right about ten minutes before four, Sarah walked in. She gave a start seeing me at the table and quickly glanced around the room.

"Hi, Sarah," I called out. "I just had a couple of follow-up questions if you don't mind. It won't take long."

She quickly walked over to my table. "I can't talk to you now. You have to stop coming here to question me."

"It's important. I promise I'll be quick."

"Yeah, right. Look, my boss doesn't like you interviewing me here. Some other time, when I'm not working."

"I can come back after your shift is over."

"Really? Is it that urgent?"

"I need to know why you lied to me?"

That got her attention. "I didn't lie to you."

"You did."

"I can meet you when I finish up."

"Is there a coffee shop nearby?"

"No. they roll up the sidewalks here after midnight. There's a Norm's in Torrance on Hawthorn. I'll meet you there at twelve thirty. I've got to go."

I caught her glancing toward the back. Howard was standing in the doorway watching us. I don't know if he had ESP or hidden cameras, or maybe the bartender gave him a buzz. Sarah hustled past him into the back. Howard just continued to stare at me, not glancing at his waitress.

I gave him a friendly nod, finished my drink, and walked out into the sunlight. I now had eight hours to kill. It was either hang out down here at the beach or head back to the office. I checked in with Rachel. She was still ignoring my calls and texts. I felt like calling her out for acting childish, but I knew that wouldn't get me anywhere. Better to let things run their course.

Next, I called Vera.

"I'm going to have another sit-down with Sarah, but I have to wait until she's off work, so that's after midnight," I informed her.

"Well, since you have nothing but time, I located another of Dan's old business associates, Richard Royale, although it looks like he goes by Dick. Dick now has a real estate business of his own, Dick Royale Realty. It's in Wilmington." She read off the address on Pacific Coast Highway. "I've called a few times, but I only get an answering machine, and so far, no return call. Must be a small outfit."

"Well, I've got nothing else to do. I'll run over there and see if anybody's home."

Wilmington was a little neighborhood north of Long Beach. It was only about five miles from Hermosa, but it might as well have been in another state. That portion of PCH that ran through it was choked with trucks and the street was lined with storage facilities, cheap motels, fast food franchises, and auto repair shops. At one time, it must have been lined with cute little cottages in a variety of pastel colors. One of those still remained. That was Royale Realty.

It was a light lavender blue little cottage with stucco walls and a shingled roof, probably two bedrooms and one bath, a kitchen, and a living room in all of eight hundred square feet. Two stately jacaranda trees with their matching blossoms stood guard at the street behind a low block wall topped with an eight-foot gated iron fence, a testament to the safety of the neighborhood, no doubt. At least it was painted white to complement the house.

As there was no parking on PCH, I turned onto the first side street and parked there. Walking back, I spied an older man with a couple of metal 'For Sale' signs under his arm opening the gate. I hurried to catch up to him.

Dick, or Rick, Royale looked to be in his sixties, with graying, thinning hair and a closely trimmed, salt-and-pepper beard that framed a well-worn face. He was short and overweight, attributes only accented by his attire, brown corduroy pants, a tweed jacket with leather elbow patches, and a yellow shirt with a brown print tie. He looked like my idea of a twentieth-century realtor, not one of the young, attractive, and fast-talking agents that work in the business these days.

I caught up to him just as he unlocked the front door.

"Dick Royale?" I called out.

He stopped and looked back at me, perhaps expecting I was a potential client.

"Yes! Good timing! I just came back from a broker's open house. A great little cottage not far from here, in Lakewood, by the park. Do you know the area?"

"Actually, I'm not in the market for a house at the moment. I was wondering if I could have a few minutes of your time to talk about Dan LeBeau." I followed him into the office as he set down his signs. "I understand you two were friends a few years back."

His smiling face immediately turned sour. "You've been misinformed. We were never friends. What is this concerning?" Dick began to busy himself while I fished in my wallet for a business card. He left the signs leaning against the desk and walked around it, setting a briefcase he carried in his other hand on top. From that, he extracted a stack of brochures, apparently from his open house, as well as what looked to me like a sign-in sheet.

I placed my card on top of the sign-in sheet.

"My name is James Gardiner. I am a private investigator looking into the disappearance of Skye Goldberg."

"I thought she was dead. I thought Dan killed her."

"That turns out not to be the case. It seems that Dan was framed. She's been seen recently, and I've been hired to find her."

"Well, I don't know where she is. I don't even know her."

"I'm not suggesting you do. Do you mind if I have a seat?" I asked, gesturing toward one of the chairs.

"Oh, sure. My manners are terrible. Would you like a bottle of water or something?"

"I'm good," I replied, taking a seat. Dick, seemingly aware now that he had consented to the interview by not objecting, also sat.

"I'm trying to figure out who might have wanted to frame him for murder, so I'm looking into his real estate dealings. I saw your name on a list of people that Dan's defense attorney interviewed for character witness support."

"Yeah, well, they never called me to testify because I didn't have anything good to say about him."

"I was told that you worked with Dan years ago."

"That's right. I hired him at my office. I was a broker for one of the Sanderson Realty offices, the Inglewood office, to be exact. Dan had recently gotten his license and corporate was pushing for us to expand. He seemed to have the right attitude for the business."

"I see you're not with Sanderson anymore yourself."

"No, Sanderson is no more. They sold out to a New York firm. When those guys started consolidating offices, I could see the writing on the wall and decided to hang out my own shingle. I started out with my own agency, seems only fitting to finish out that way. I guess I like being my own boss."

"Tell me more about Dan. What was he like as an agent?"

Dick took off his jacket and loosened his tie. There were sweat stains under his arms, but I guess he decided that he was through for the day with work.

"Dan had it rough the first couple of years. Most new agents do. I gave him a farm to work…"

"Farm?" I interjected.

"A neighborhood for him to go door to door soliciting new business. It's how we all start. Anyway, I think he only sold one house his first year, probably some little three-bedroom, two-bath, twelve-hundred-square-foot cottage for under three hundred. His commission on that would have only been six thousand. You can't live on that, even twenty years ago. I suspected he had a side job. Most new guys just starting out do. It's a tough business to break into. More suitable for housewives who don't need the income."

"You don't know what this side gig was?"

"No, never asked, although at one time I think he mentioned that he had savings that he was living off of until he got established."

"I take it he finally got established?"

"In a way. He appeared to have landed himself a sugar daddy, a deep-pocketed investor. One year, his business just took off. He started buying properties for some unnamed client, all cash deals, the buyer's name was hidden behind an LLC. I think he was closing like one a month, turning them into rentals."

"Where were these?"

"All over. Mostly Hawthorn, Inglewood, Carson. And then I heard he bought himself that house on the Strand. I think he paid two and a half million for it. Well, you don't buy a house like that on commissions, even if you do sell a house a month."

"So, where did the money come from, his savings?"

"He said he came into a large inheritance. I guess his father was a big-time auto dealer back east."

"You sound skeptical."

"Of the windfall? No, but I have always been suspicious of his secret client. No one ever met him. I don't think the client even saw the houses Dan was buying for him. He worked with an attorney who was setting up the blind trusts. No bank loans, of course, so inspections, if there were any, were no problem. The deals just sailed through escrow. Anyone in the office who listed a new property called Dan first."

"Sounds lucky for Dan, but entirely plausible. What's your suspicion?"

"I think he was laundering money."

"What? Like drug money?"

"Could be drug money or foreign money. A lot of Asian money was floating around the West Coast back then. They like to invest in real estate, usually a pretty safe bet and good appreciation."

"But the source of money could be illegal, is what you're saying."

"That was my take on it. Couldn't prove it, and wasn't about to go poking around trying to find out. None of my business."

"So, what happened after that?"

"Dan up and quit. I guess he had been taking his broker's exams. He got his license and opened his own agency, just him and a receptionist. After that, I didn't see him anymore except for an occasional open house."

"Not even on a friendly basis?"

"We were never friends. I was his boss. We were friendly. Sometimes we'd go out for a beer after work, but after Dan's business fortunes picked up, he changed. Maybe he became more guarded because he was afraid of losing his golden goose, I don't know. But he changed."

It was after sunset when I finally walked out of Dick Royal Realty. I still had a good four hours to kill before meeting up with Sarah. I figured I might as well grab some supper. I didn't know Long Beach, so I hopped on the 405 Freeway and headed back toward the beach cities. I made a little detour when I got to Hawthorn Boulevard. I figured since I was nearby, it was best to locate the Norms that I would be meeting Sarah at later on.

It was easy to find. Norms is a chain of all-night diners, sort of the McDonald's of the diner genre, if you will. The restaurants are all built in that 1950s Googie style architecture, sharp angles and geometric shapes, garish colors, and hints of space age fantasy in the motifs. The food was good; you could get breakfast twenty-four hours a day. I decided since I was already here, I might as well eat. Even though it was past nine in the evening, the place was still full. I found a booth and ordered the Lumberjack breakfast. My buddy Jack would be proud.

I was on my first cup of coffee when my cell rang. It was Mother.

"Hello, Mother. What's prompting you to call so late at night?"

"I'm so disappointed in you, James. How can you treat Rachel like that? I just got off the phone with her, and she was crying her eyes out about how mean you've been to her this past week. I thought I raised you better than to treat your girlfriend so poorly."

Mother was talking so loudly that I was afraid the whole restaurant could hear her.

"Whoa, whoa, whoa," I whispered back, avoiding any eye contact with the other patrons. "I know Rachel did not call you up in tears and tell you that."

"She said you walked out on a date with her last weekend."

"I did not walk out on a date with her. Our date was over. It was already Sunday morning and we had finished breakfast. I had to tend to some urgent business. She was mad at that and has been avoiding me ever since. I've called and left messages. I've texted her, but I get no answer back. We will work it out without your interference, Mother."

See, I knew it was that silly detective business of yours that was the cause of all this. If you had a real job, things like this wouldn't happen."

"This is a real job to me. And I seem to recall my father missing many an evening and weekend because of work."

"People of our social status do not look kindly on your playing Sherlock Holmes."

"For your information, Holmes, the fictional man, was quite the celebrity among the upper class. All the early detectives were considered gentlemen."

I looked up to see the waitress standing near with my breakfast. I motioned to her to set it down and gave her a thumbs up that it was fine as is, nothing else needed. I feared it would be cold, though, before I got off the phone.

"I don't care about all that rubbish. You need to call her and apologize for the way you've behaved."

"I haven't behaved badly at all. And I already explained that I have called every day. If you're so concerned, why don't you have Rachel call me and apologize? It's you two who have created such a fuss out of nothing."

"I most certainly will not."

"Then let Rachel and me handle it ourselves. Look, I've got to go. Love you. Bye."

I turned off my phone and set it face down on the table. After dealing every day with people who have a lot bigger issues than I have, it's not hard to put my problems into perspective. I'll send Rachel some flowers in the morning and she'll call me. It's worked before.

I dove into my big breakfast. I still have a couple of hours to kill. I sat in my car in the parking lot, watching "The Third Man" on my phone. A similar story about someone who was supposedly dead but wasn't.

But my Harry Lime was not Skye; maybe it was Hugo. Was my pursuit of Hugo going to lead me into the sewers? I was just at that point in the film when I noticed Sarah entering Norms. I waited a few minutes to see if anyone drove up who might be following her. her edginess earlier in the day had made me suspicious that she might be being watched. Confident that she wasn't being tailed, I exited my car and walked into the restaurant to join her.

"Thanks for coming, Sarah," I said as I sat down. The waitress came right over. It was the same gal who had served me a few hours ago. She was an older woman, thinly built, with grey streaks showing in her hair and sporting large cat-eye style glasses

"Back for more?" she asked cheerfully, pulling her notepad from her apron pocket.

"Just a coffee for me," I said and looked over to Sarah. She stared back curiously, probably wondering why I had been here earlier.

"Can I see a menu?" She asked, and then to me, explaining, "I haven't eaten. I usually don't, just grab a light supper after my shift."

The waitress left to get coffee and a menu.

"This has got to be the last time for questions." She demanded softly.

"Are you being followed? Watched?" I asked.

Sarah paused for a moment. I could tell she was torn about what to tell me, and was also afraid.

"Howard."

"Well, Howard's not here. I checked. No one followed you here. I was sitting in the parking lot when you arrived and waited to see that you weren't being tailed." I tried to reassure her. The waitress returned with my coffee and a menu for Sarah.

"Why would Howard be watching you, anyway?" I continued after the waitress had left.

"Because Hugo asked him to." She said, not looking up from the menu.

"And he would do this for Hugo because…"

"They're partners. Partners in the club."

"Oh. When did that happen?"

"Hugo bought the club about five years ago."

"That's when they remodeled."

"Right. He made Howard a manager and partner."

"I see. But what makes you think they're watching you?"

Sarah looked up at me, annoyed. "I wasn't aware of it until you came poking around."

"Okay. But why are they… You'd always known that Skye wasn't dead, hadn't you?"

Sarah didn't answer. Well, she answered by not answering.

"Why do you stay? Certainly, you could have found another job by now if you wanted to."

"They pay me a lot of money. More than I can earn elsewhere."

"What's a lot of money?"

"Two thousand a week, plus tips."

"That's pretty good. Why is that, you think?"

"I'm sure Skye had a hand in it."

"Because she's still with Hugo, and she told Hugo to take good care of you?"

"Something like that. I saw her once. This was after Hugo had bought the club. She came in with him. When Hugo went off to talk to

Howard, she loitered by the door, not wanting to come in any further. She had on a black wig and big black sunglasses. At first, I wasn't sure it was her. She was scanning the place, looking for anyone who might recognize her, I guess, but it was dark, and with the glasses, I figure she couldn't see that well, so she took them off. She'd penciled her eyebrows black and had on a lot of mascara, but I recognized her. I was at the bar setting up drinks. She finally looked my way and we made eye contact. I knew she knew I recognized her, but fled into the kitchen and waited there until she and Hugo left. Never saw her again.

"Two thousand a week plus tips! That's lap dance money."

We both looked up suddenly to see that the waitress had returned and hovered at the table, notepad in hand. "You need more time?"

"I'll have the cob salad, no cheese, dressing on the side. And an iced tea."

Anything for you, sir?"

"No. I'm good with coffee."

We waited until she'd left before returning to our conversation.

"Let me try to maybe address some concerns you may have beforehand. I'm working for Dan. He wants to get in contact with Skye again, if he can. I am not working for the police or the prosecutor's office or anything like that. So, whatever you say to me will remain strictly confidential. No one will even know we talked. But I have to ask, did you help in any way with staging the murder?"

"What?" Sarah looked up, quite surprised. "No, of course not. I would never."

"But you were with her earlier in the day. At the time, you were the last person known to have seen her. She didn't say anything, no clue as to what was about to happen. I mean, you all but admitted you knew she wasn't dead."

It wasn't like that." Sarah protested. "Skye and I had scheduled a trip to the mall for that day. When we got there, she said she wanted to buy me something special. I protested that it wasn't necessary, but I knew she felt she owed me big time, so I let her. While we were shopping, she confided in me that she was leaving Dan. She knew Dan wasn't going to be easy to dump, so she was going to just disappear. She couldn't tell me where, and she was letting me know that I wouldn't be able to contact her either. She promised that when the time was right, she would be back in touch."

"That was quite a disappearing act."

"When I heard that Dan had been arrested and accused of murdering Skye, I knew that this was how she left him, but I was afraid to say anything."

"Afraid of who?"

"Hugo. I figured that he arranged the whole thing, either himself or directed some of his gang to do it."

"You couldn't anonymously go to the police?"

"I was afraid to even chance that. Hugo is a very scary guy. I think he's part of one of those Mexican cartels. Those guys will kill you without a second thought. I don't know why I still stick around. I tell myself it's just for the money, but it's not. It's been ten years. I thought we were best friends, but Skye never called. Now that you've stirred things up again, I don't feel safe anymore. I've saved up quite a bit of money. I'm going to leave this state, maybe go to the East Coast."

The waitress brought Sarah's salad and refilled my cup. I let her eat for a few minutes in silence before I began again.

"Why did Skye feel she owed you something?"

Sarah didn't answer right away. I could sense she was fighting to contain her emotions. I could see the tears welling up in her eyes.

"A few months before she disappeared, Skye asked me if I would go out with her, Hugo, and some of the guys. She said she was tired of having no one to talk to, as the guys generally ignored her, but Hugo insisted she tag along. I was reluctant, but agreed. The night started out fine. We went club hopping. The guys were loud and rowdy, but we ignored them and mostly talked to each other. As the evening wore on, most of the guys left until it was just me and Skye, Hugo, and Jesus. Jesus is like his lieutenant or whatever. Actually, I think Jesus is his younger brother, but I'm not sure. Hugo suggested we go back to his house and watch some movies. So, we did."

By now, tears were dropping into her salad.

"Not even halfway through the movie, Skye and Hugo disappeared into the bedroom, leaving me alone with Jesus. He must have figured this was all previously agreed to, because he immediately started coming onto me, physically. When I protested, he got angry, very angry. I won't bore you with the dirty details, but he raped me on the couch."

"With Skye and Hugo in the next room?"

"I tried to scream, but he put his hand over my mouth. Skys said she didn't know. I expect Hugo figured that was bound to happen. Maybe he planned it all along for his little brother to get some."

"And Skye never got back in touch like she promised."

"No, well, she kind of did. I never saw her again, but I'd get notes delivered to me through Howard. Apologies, mostly; promises to make it up to me. She never said where she was, but I figured she had to be in So-Cal somewhere. I never tried to reply."

I watched as Sarah pushed her salad around on the plate with her fork. She wasn't eating. She probably wasn't going to eat. She would leave here and pull a disappearing act like her friend.

I knew when she left, I would never see her again, but I had nothing more to say.

CHAPTER

NINETEEN

The next morning, my conversation with Sarah was still bothering me. Maybe I was looking at this all wrong. Maybe Skye was also a victim, forced into this ruse by Hugo. Seems like a pretty extreme measure to take to eliminate a rival for a girl's affections. Still, if Hugo is really a stone-cold killer, and I have seen no evidence that he is, why didn't he just kill Dan? Did Skye bargain for his life? Did she agree to the frame-up to keep Hugo from killing him? Maybe she really intended to reconnect with Sarah once Dan was safely in prison, but then, when that didn't happen, she was forced to remain in hiding for a decade and counting. And what is Hugo's motivation? I can't believe this is all about Skye. Was it a drug deal gone bad? Was Dan dealing drugs? Is that his connection to Hugo? Maybe that's how Hugo first met Skye, through his association with Dan. So many questions. No, wait. It was Heather who introduced Hugo to Skye and Dan, or so she says. It seems the more I learn, the more I find out I don't know.

I arrived a bit late to the office, having overslept. I brought my usual tray of three coffees, except my pal Jimmy wasn't at his usual post on the corner to receive his. I wondered about that and worried that something might have happened to him. I'd have to keep an eye out to see when he showed up again. So, now I had one extra coffee. Jack could have it if he showed up; otherwise, I guess I could drink two. Vera was already busy at her desk, searching the internet for a list of things I had tasked her to find out.

"Vera, what are the apropos flowers for an apology these days?" I asked her as I handed her a cup.

"I'm not the best person to ask since I'm not in a relationship, but I imagine roses are always safe for these sorts of things."

"So, maybe a dozen roses, you think?"

"I don't know. How much trouble are you in?"

"I didn't do anything wrong!"

"That much, huh. I'd make it at least two dozen."

"Hell, why don't I make it three?" I set the half-empty coffee tray on the desk, grabbed mine and slumped into the guest chair. I had nothing to do at the moment, so I might as well talk things through with Vera.

I relayed my conversation with Sarah to her, along with my new thoughts about who, why, and what went on back then. Vera nodded along, listening attentively, and agreed with my assessment that this new information raised more questions than it answered.

"I have a couple of tasks to add to your list. One, find out who the prosecutor was in Dan's case and where he's working or what he's doing now. I've been calling the main office and not getting any callbacks. Maybe if I had a name, I could get through. I want to get an appointment for a face-to-face and ask him some questions. Secondly, about fifteen to twenty years ago, Dan wrote for the Daily Breese, which is a South Bay paper. He wrote a series of stories about the cocaine scene that was exploding back then. I am pretty sure there were other reporters in on that story. Their names would be with his on the bi-line. I want you to track them down so I can talk to them, too. Okay?"

"No problem. Speaking of him, Dan called a little earlier. Said he was going to be in the neighborhood and wanted to drop in and get an update. He didn't leave a number."

"I have it. I'll give him a call."

"So, I looked into the LeBeau car dealership. It was a used car dealership. Average yearly gross sales were seven hundred and fifty thousand, and inventory at the time of sale was one point five million. It sold for two million."

"That's all?"

"Well, it was twenty years ago. That would translate into four to five million today. Plus, the sale didn't include the land. The lot was leased."

"Then Dan would have gotten a third of that. Not enough to buy that house on the Strand, or any of the other investments for that matter."

"No. Seven hundred thousand is nothing to sneeze at, but it doesn't make you rich."

"Okay, then he either used that money to turn a quick profit in the stock market, or he had another source of income. Good job on finding that info. I'll have to bring that up with Dan next time I see him."

"That would be tomorrow. He said he wanted to come by, remember."

"Right, I'll give him a call. Maybe we can grab lunch at Musso's."

The nearest flower store was a few blocks away, down Hollywood Boulevard past the Pantages Theater. I decided I could use the steps. I hadn't been getting much exercise lately. Three dozen long-stem roses probably wouldn't come cheap, but I figured it was worth it to put this little spat behind us.

On the way out, I swung by Jimmy's corner spot across from my building. He was back, or rather just back as he was still rolling out his carpet and putting out his sign – "Murder Maps! See the famous crime sites of L.A.!", complete with a picture of Charlie Manson.

"Hey Jimmy, I missed you this morning."

"Oh, hey man. Yeah, I'm running a little late this morning." He turned to me with his red-rimmed, rheumy eyes and proceeded to cough terribly for a minute.

"Wow, you look like shit. Are you sick?"

"Nah, I'll be okay, I just can't seem to shake this cough. I've had it since Friday and it just seems to linger on."

"You should see a doctor."

"Yeah, well, I don't have insurance, bro."

"Go to an Urgent Care then."

"I don't have the coin for that either."

I dug out my wallet and pulled out a hundred-dollar bill, and held it out to him.

"Take this and go get yourself looked at. This could be serious. You can't just expect it to go away on its own."

"Put that away, James. I'll be alright."

"Now's not the time to be proud. You're sick and need to take care of yourself. If I have to, I'll buy up all your maps."

"Thanks, man." He said, finally relenting and taking the money. "I'll pay you back."

"Now roll your rug up and get out of here and go find a doctor to look at yourself. I mean it."

I watched as Jimmy packed up his stuff and headed off down the street. I hoped it wasn't anything too serious. Then I called Dan and arranged to meet at Musso and Franks for lunch tomorrow.

After the call, I wandered back to the office, completely forgetting I had gone out to get flowers. Vera had already completed half of her day's assignment while I'd been out chatting with Jimmy and Dan.

"It was pretty easy tracking down that reporter." She explained. "Alvin Montoya shared a byline with Dan for several of the Daily Breeze stories back then. He's now with the LA Times as senior editor on the City Desk. I've given you his email address and you can also reach him through the Times' main line. I didn't find a personal phone number for him. Also, I forwarded to you the articles if you want to read them."

"Thanks. The main number will be good enough. I'll see if I can reach him. Anything else?"

"The prosecutor's name is Claire Hsu. I will text you her contact info as well. Also, I talked to a friend of mine at the North Hollywood Station and asked about our guy, Fly. He knew of him. Apparently, he hangs around with a really bad crowd. They think he's gotten into fencing stolen merch from these smash-and-grab shoplifting gangs. Then he launders the money through a host of small bank accounts using friends and family to spread it around so nobody will notice."

"So, that's where Norma's boy fits in."

"He's just one of many guys working the back room of this enterprise. They haven't moved on him because they think there's bigger fish to catch up the ladder, so it's a wait-and-watch operation for now."

"I'm going to have to talk to Norma." I headed into my office.

After reading the three-part series on the cocaine trade in the South Bay, I felt like I was going off on a wild tangent with this line of inquiry. People only do extreme acts for love in the movies, I told myself. I called the Times and the automated switchboard put me through to Montoya's extension.

"Alvin, this is James Gardiner. I was hoping to get a few minutes of your time to discuss an old colleague of yours, Dan LeBeau."

"Dan LeBeau. I haven't heard his name in a long time. What's up with Dan these days?"

"Well, you may not recall, but about ten years ago, Dan was tried but found innocent of a first-degree murder charge in a sensational killing in the South Bay."

"Oh, that's right. I had forgotten about that. So, what's prompting you to call me?"

"Dan was not convicted because the alleged victim's body was never found. Recently, she, that being the former girlfriend and would be corpse, has been spotted and Dan's hired me to find her. I'm a private detective if I didn't already mention that."

"You didn't mention it, but I was beginning to suspect. Don't know how I can be helpful, though. I haven't been in touch with Dan since we were both at the Breeze."

"I'm following a thread that starts there. Can I buy you lunch? I know you're busy, but maybe we can talk over sushi? I know a place not far from your office."

"I was going to say no, but you had me at sushi."

I phoned ahead to make a reservation and then met Alvin there at one o'clock. Tako-san Sushi was a little hole-in-the-wall place; the counter sat eight, and there were four tables along the wall and another two by the window. The head chef was an older guy with a young apprentice helping. A young Japanese girl waited on the tables.

I had just sat down when Alvin walked in the door. I knew him from his picture on the Times' web page, so I waved him over.

"Alvin, thanks for making the time to see me."

"Not a problem. I'm easy when good food is involved."

Alvin was a middle-aged man, pushing fifty if I had to guess, with a dark, unruly mop of hair and a day's growth of beard framing his face. He had very bushy eyebrows, which gave him an intense look, even when he was smiling.

"What do you like?" I asked.

"Omakase is good for me. I like everything."

"What about a drink, beer, or sake?"

"No, just tea for me, but you go ahead."

"I thought all of you newspaper men were big lunchtime drinkers."

"That went out with hot lead typesetting. How about you? Aren't all P.I.s gin and rye drinkers?"

"Maybe Philip Marlow. I'm more of a scotch man myself, but I do like a good rye now and then." I signaled to the waitress that we'd take the chef's choice.

"So, I see you're a senior editor now." I continued. "When did you join the Times?"

"I came over about a year after that series ran, that I wrote with Dan. They offered me the South Bay beat, and to tell the truth, the Breeze's future at that time was looking a little shaky. Big media conglomerates were buying up all the smaller press and cutting staff like us to improve the financials. So, when the offer came, I jumped. I think Dan left about the same time, although I heard he went into real estate. Probably a smart move. Journalism is never going to make you rich."

"Were you and Dan writing partners on other stories?"

"No, no. In fact, it was our editor who assigned us together for that piece. I hardly knew Dan before that."

"In reading the articles, I noticed that Dan interviewed all the dealers and you covered the law enforcement angle."

"Yes, we kind of flipped a coin over that. The outlaws were more romantic, if a bit dangerous, although I think you'll find that even criminals like publicity. My side was more plowing through bureaucracy, getting people to speak on record, and sussing out any shenanigans. I was careful not to end up like Gary Webb."

"Who's he?"

"Webb was an investigative journalist for the San Jose Mercury News. He was looking into an alleged plot by the CIA to distribute crack cocaine to the inner cities as a way to fund the counter-insurgencies in Central America. His pieces in '96 raised a lot of eyebrows and got coverage across the US. He committed suicide in '04, but a lot of people think he was killed by the CIA for exposing them."

"Wow, that's heavy."

"Well, our piece was nothing like that. No crooked cops involved as far as we could tell."

Our first item arrived: three pieces of tuna, one lean, one fatty, and one spicy, with a little slice of jalapeno on top.

"So how does our reporting figure into your investigation?" Alvin asked between bites.

"I think Dan got mixed up with a drug dealer somehow. I believe it was this guy who framed Dan for the murder rap. Maybe it was over a girl, or maybe it was about the drugs. I'm trying to find that out, but this dealer seems to be in the background of everything I've turned up so far. When you were writing this piece, did you ever look at Dan's notes?"

"I might have, I don't recall, but we often discussed what we had uncovered before we actually sat down and started writing."

"Do you recall ever hearing the name Hugo Martinez?"

"No. Doesn't ring a bell."

"In the article, Dan used code names or nicknames for all the people he spoke with. None of them sounded quite like this Hugo fellow. I was just wondering if he met him back then in the course of his research."

"You met this guy, then."

"We crossed paths in my search for this woman. I think she's still with him. Hugo was not pleased that I was looking for her."

"Hmmm." Alvin mused. Our next course arrived: halibut and red snapper.

"What was the vibe you got from Dan during your investigation? Was he nervous? Did he ever seem to be afraid for his life talking with these guys?"

"No, on the contrary, he was very jazzed. He thought he was being allowed to pull back the curtain and show the reader that the drug business was just like any other: logistics, accounting, inventory, pricing. The dealers probably appreciated Dan's reluctance to judge the morality of it all."

"He ever bring any samples home?"

"I won't answer that. But, are you looking for this girl or are you investigating Dan's past?"

"Well, both. Dan's my client, but I've found that your client doesn't always give you all the information you need to start out. Sometimes they don't even give you their real motivation for hiring you."

"Oh, I get that. So, I'll tell you this one thing. I like Dan, and this is probably old news; certainly, it's old enough that it won't cause anybody any trouble, but when we were writing together, we were both poor as church mice. I mean, when we went out for a beer together after work, it was for a beer. That's what we could afford. In the year after the story ran, we continued to socialize, but I noticed that Dan started to have more money. He wasn't driving a Lamborghini or anything, but he wasn't scrapping by like before. I thought maybe he was moonlighting at another job to bring home a little extra cash. But later I thought he was probably dealing a little on the side, courtesy of his new friends."

"That's what I was thinking. If he didn't meet Hugo during his research, he may have met him through a friend of a friend. Hugo then met Skye, that's Dan's girlfriend and the woman I'm hunting for. Whether it was a scrap over Skye or a drug deal gone bad, Hugo tried to frame him for murder to get him out of the way. And, Hugo's a player now, so I have to tread carefully."

"Is there a story here for me?" Alvin asked mischievously.

"Well, you can ask around, but don't mention me. I've already been dressed down once by the DEA for stirring things up."

The waitress brought us baked mussels and grilled eel next.

"Say, Alvin, do you know a Ted Carmady? I don't know if he's staff or freelance."

"Sure, I know Ted. He was on my city beat."

"He helped me out on something last year, and I've lost touch with him."

"He quit last year and moved to D.C. to work for one of those internet mags. Hey, I remember you. You were involved in that Councilman Messer fiasco last summer, weren't you?"

"Yeah, that was me."

"Poor Ted got roughed up by some Chinese gangsters and decided that L.A. was too dangerous. At least in D.C., they only kill you metaphorically he said."

"Sorry to hear that."

The rest of our meal consisted of yellowtail, shrimp, scallops, squid, mackerel, monk fish liver, sea urchin, and salmon egg, finishing with a fluffy sweet Japanese egg omelet. It was great.

Since I was already downtown, I thought I'd walk over to the Criminal Justice Center on Temple Street to see if I could collar Claire Hsu, the prosecuting attorney for Dan's case. I had not been having any luck getting a return call from her after repeated tries. The Foltz building is enormous, twenty-storied, and almost a million square feet. It houses over a thousand attorneys, another 800 clerical positions, not to mention a few hundred detectives and other law enforcement personnel. I hoped it wasn't going to take me too long to find my way around.

It turned out Clare was still in the Major Crimes Unit. The receptionist told me that she was in court this afternoon. I explained at length the reason for wanting to speak with her and the difficulty I was having in getting in touch with her. The receptionist said she would pass along a note and try to get back to me by the end of the day. As I made my way out of the building, I thought about how much easier my job would be if I had their resources at hand.

After leaving the Justice Center, I cut across Grand Park heading toward my car in the public parking under the Music Center. My mind was whirling with all the bits and pieces of information I had gathered about Dan and Skye. Though I thought I was making progress in figuring out the who, what, and why of the staged murder, I wasn't any closer to finding Skye. I needed to take some action, any action. I stopped and called Jack.

"Hey. Can you get your hands on another remote camera and some Air Tags today?"

"Sure, what's the plan?"

"I want you to go out to Hugo's place and put a camera where we can see his comings and goings. Be mindful that the Feds already have a camera or two in place there, so you'll have to be pretty discreet."

"Not a problem, bro, I can handle it. What else?"

"Have you been able to tag the MGB and Hugo's car, yet?

"The MG, yes. That dude is at the track all the time. But no telling when Hugo might show up there again."

"I know. That may mean you have to go out there every day until he does. So, keep at it. The sooner we get a tag on him, the better. He might be there right now for all we know."

"You got it. I'm on my way."

"Thanks, pal."

With no reason to rush back to the office, I loitered, grabbed a coffee from the Starbucks by the fountain and found a table outside. It felt good to take action. I needed to be more proactive, as they say. Next up was addressing my problem with Rachel. I should buy her those flowers, the three dozen long stems I had gone out to buy and then promptly forgot. I looked up 'florists near me' on my phone, then it occurred to me that the flower market was not that far away. I was near First, and it was down around Seventh or Eighth Street. I could easily walk there. I wondered what time they closed. It was just after lunch, but I knew they opened before dawn and closed early. I hopped up and began walking.

True, it was only six blocks south, but it turned out it was also six blocks east. Took me a bit longer than I expected. And the market closed at 2:00. I just missed it, but I managed to get in and found a vendor or two who hadn't finished closing up. One in particular was all things roses, red, white, black, or yellow, long-stemmed or short. At this time of the day, though, his stock was pretty picked over. I was looking for something impressive and I wasn't finding it here.

"Come back in the morning." Lorenzo, the owner, suggested. "We'll have whatever you want."

"If I were to buy in bulk, what kind of price could I get?" I asked. In my mind, I was already thinking of going big, no mere three dozen. I would really impress her.

"We only sell in bulk. We're wholesalers."

"But you're open to the public."

"Yes, after the merchants have been through, whatever is left we sell direct to the public, but not at wholesale, but still cheaper than a florist."

"So how much would I have to buy to get the wholesale price?"

"You have to be a registered business and have a badge to get the merchant price."

"Okay, then, what kind of discount could I get for a bulk order as a retail customer?"

"Depends. What are you talking about?"

"Long-stemmed, red roses. I want a lot, but I'm not sure how many I can fit in my car." I tried imagining how much space I had in the back seat.

"We can deliver if that's the problem."

"Oh, that works. What can you give me for a thousand dollars, delivered."

Lorenzo did a quick calculation in his head. "I can give you forty dozen, delivered. Providing it's not too far."

"Century City. How about eighty-three dozen, for two thousand. That's almost a thousand flowers."

"Sure."

"In vases?"

"I only got these plastic ones." He held up a cheap white plastic vase.

"That's fine. Let me write down the address. I'll meet you there. What time would you deliver?" I had keys to Rachel's apartment and I knew she would be at the office.

"Can't get my van out before noon. Say, one o'clock?"

"I'll be there. No, wait. I have a lunch meeting tomorrow. Can we do Friday?"

"You got it."

After he rang up my credit card, I started the long trek back to my car. I was excited. This would really blow her mind, I thought.

Retrieving my car, I headed back to Hollywood. I wanted to catch Norma before her shift ended. She always worked from six in the morning through the lunch crush. It was already past two, but sometimes I knew she'd stay to eat since it was free for her. I was hoping she would still be there having her lunch.

Fortunately, there were parking spots available. I hurried into the diner and looked around. She was in the furthest booth, still eating.

"Norma," I said as I walked up. "You have time for a quick talk?"

"Have a seat, James. Can I get you a coffee?" She started to get up.

"You're off the clock, Norma. Besides, I've already had my limit for the day."

Norma resumed eating her soup, keeping one eye on me.

"I've looked into this friend of Martin's, Fly. He's got a pretty extensive police record."

"Boys these days." She replied. "Wanna be hip with the gangsta life, Straight Outta Compton and all that nonsense."

"I'm sure Martin is not doing anything illegal himself, but that joint bank account is going to get him in trouble."

"I know, I know."

"My associate talked with some of the detectives in North Hollywood. It seems Fly is working with these shoplifting gangs. He's not stealing, but fencing the stolen goods. And he's putting the money in that account he has with Martin."

"Are you sure?"

"No, I don't have proof, but the police are watching, collecting evidence until they can raid their warehouse and bring the whole gang down. At that point, it's going to be too late for Martin to escape some blame. Even if he doesn't get convicted of anything, it's sure to cost him his job at JPL."

"I know, I know." Tears were starting to well up in her eyes. "But, what can I do? I can't talk to him. He'll hate me for interfering in his life. He thinks he's a man, now, not my little boy."

"He is a man. But sometimes there's a big price to be paid if you're a man and you screw up."

"Maybe you can talk to this fella and tell him to leave my boy alone. Tell him he's innocent and gullible and don't want to get mixed up in no shoplifting gang."

"He knows Martin is an innocent. That's why he chose him. Anybody with street smarts would wise up right away and either walk away or want in on the action. And I can't say anything that will blow the cover on the police operation. Plus, he's going to go back to Martin and then he'll know you called me to intervene."

"I'm gonna lose my boy. He's never gonna trust me, he's never gonna want to talk with me again."

"Don't give up hope. Let me think a bit and maybe I can come up with something. It will have to be soon, though. No telling when the police will close in."

I got up to leave. Norma didn't look up or say goodbye; she just stared at her soup, defeated.

CHAPTER

TWENTY

I was up early the next morning, before dawn. I wanted to beat the rush hour to downtown, but even at six in the morning, the freeway was starting to fill up. The eastern sky was a brilliant orange and the rising sun blinded my eyes, making driving difficult for both me and many others who were going way too fast in such limited visibility. Still, I made it, parked and walked across the quadrangle to the Justice Center with time to spare, even stopping off for a coffee along the way.

I had memorized her picture and figured I'd have no problem spotting her as she left her building for the courthouse. She'd be dressed for court with a bulging briefcase in one hand and a no-nonsense pace to her stride. I would get five or ten minutes, however long it took for her to reach her courtroom.

After a short wait, I spotted her scurrying down the steps. She was in a dark blue skirted power suit with a white ruffled blouse underneath. I hurried to intercept her.

"Ms. Hsu!" I called out. "I'm James Gardiner, private investigator. Your assistant said I might get a few minutes to ask some questions before court."

"Yes, I know. I may have to fire that girl if she does it again. What do you want?"

"I wanted to ask you about the Dan LeBeau case you prosecuted about ten years ago. Do you remember it?"

"Of course I do. That disaster set my career back a good five years."

"Why would you prosecute a case like that downtown?"

"It wasn't. I was assigned to the Superior Court in Torrance at that time."

I stopped, but she didn't. "Walk and talk."

"How's that?" I asked, scrambling to catch up.

"Ever watch West Wing?"

"No, what's that?"

"Old TV show. They did a lot of that in that series. Walk and talk. So, walk and talk."

I fell in beside her as she continued her brisk pace down the sidewalk. "You call it a disaster. I'm wondering why you went to trial without more evidence."

"Pressure from higher-ups. This case was front page and on all the nightly news for weeks. Beautiful young girl hacked to death by jealous lover."

"But no evidence."

"We had plenty of evidence, blood, DNA, murder weapon, CCTV footage."

"But no body."

"Don't always need the body. We figured she was chopped up and the pieces went to the county landfill. We knew which one by the truck routes. Had half a dozen cadaver dogs search that place for a week."

"No hits though."

"Too many hits. It's a garbage dump. It's full of garbage and that includes rotting meat. Ever been to a garbage dump? It stinks to high heaven. I felt sorry for those dogs. The assault on their sensitive noses must have been something else. We didn't find the body, but we also couldn't rule out that it wasn't in there somewhere."

"You mentioned a jealous lover. Was that your motive?"

"That was pretty obvious. They fought like cats and dogs. He was cheating on her. She was cheating on him. She wanted to break it off, but he didn't want to let go."

"I assume you had interviews to back that theory up."

"Plenty, friends, neighbors, business associates. It was no secret what went on between them. I figured it wasn't premeditated. Probably an act of passion in the heat of the moment. He killed her and then panicked and tried to hide the body and cover up the evidence."

"But you still charged him with first degree."

"We were prepared to bargain, but his lawyer wanted to go to trial."

"Did the name Hugo Martinez ever come up?"

She stopped at the front door to the courthouse and turned to me. "I don't recall that name, but it's been ten years. Who's he?"

"The other point of the triangle. He's a big-time drug dealer, though perhaps not so big ten years ago. He's also Skye's other lover. Did you ever consider this might have been a drug deal gone bad?"

"We didn't have any reason to think she was into drugs, let alone deep enough to merit execution. LeBeau was known to share and sell to his friends, but no, we never seriously looked in that direction. Usually, the simplest explanation is the best."

"Occam's Razor."

"Right. So, what's this all about? Are you re-investigating this case for someone?"

"Yes. The reported victim has resurfaced. She's been spotted, alive and well."

Hsu raised an eyebrow suspiciously. "By whom?"

"Dan LeBeau, my client. But I have other confirming sources. I'm trying to find her now."

She stood there for a moment holding the door open. "Well, good luck. If you do find her, let me know. There may be charges brought for filing a false police report."

"I don't think she filed a false report."

"Well, somebody did." She passed through the doorway. I let the door close behind her.

I headed back to the office. My brief talk with Ms. Hsu had not netted me any new information. It was pretty much as I had expected, a rush to prosecute, driven by lurid headlines and breathless reporting on the nightly news. If this was Hugo's plan all along, it was pretty slick.

I had a lunch date with Dan at Musso's. He was going to want some kind of report and I hadn't even started one. My notes were few and far between, scribbled on whatever piece of paper was handy. Fortunately, I had a good memory.

Back at the office, I gathered together all my scraps and Post-its and began to hammer out a recap of the investigation to date. I had already told Dan much of it in our occasional meet-ups, but it was good to get it all down in one essay. It would help me, too, to look at everything again to check if I had overlooked some bit of information that wasn't pertinent at the time but might look different now.

I was also trying to frame it so that it didn't look like I was investigating Dan more than looking for Skye. In truth, I was. He had a history, friends and associates to grill. Skye was a cypher, little to no background; her time between leaving Santa Maria and hooking up with Dan was also a blank. She had no friends that I had uncovered, except for Sarah.

I had decided early on, perhaps too early on, that Hugo was the guy and I'd been working that angle at the expense of all else. What if I was wrong? Where else should I have been looking?

I thought, after this meeting, even if it goes well, I should recanvass the few that I had interviewed with an aim to uncover any other friends or close associates.

I wondered if Skye had any family in Southern California. I only knew about her immediate family up north, but could she have had aunts, uncles, or cousins, maybe relatives who were not so cultish.

Writing reports was something I did regularly and was pretty good at. Even so, it was a good three hours before I was finished with something I was satisfied with. I stuffed the report into a standard manila envelope along with an updated invoice. Dan had been good about paying promptly without complaining about the cost. I felt guilty at having so little to show for the time we were spending, so I stopped charging Jack and Vera's hours. As soon as I could find this girl, I would feel better about recouping all the costs.

Now I was in a rush out the door to keep my lunch appointment.

Dan, of course, was there before me and halfway through his first martini as I sat down.

"Sorry, I'm late," I said as I sat down.

"You're not late. I'm early. Bad habit of mine. I find that people are usually just as annoyed about someone who's always early as someone who's always late. My being early makes them feel they're late, which they hate. But I ramble on."

"Did you order?"

"Not yet. Just the drink." Dan replied as the waiter approached with a couple of menus. Dan waved them away. "I'll have the prime rib, medium rare. Extra horseradish, please."

"The fettuccine alfredo for me," I added. "And a glass of the Brunello, thanks."

"Have you tried the fettuccine?" I asked after the waiter had departed. "It's a heart attack on a plate. So much cheese, but it's so good."

"I'm not that partial to cheese, myself," Dan added between sips of his martini.

"I read an interesting tidbit about the dish. Probably on the back of their menu, as I recall. But apparently, Mary Pickford and Douglas Fairbanks first had this dish on their honeymoon in Italy and were so bowled over by it that they coaxed the recipe out of the restaurant owner and brought it to Musso's. It's been a favorite here ever since."

"Is that so? And who did they strong-arm for this martini recipe?"

"Anybody can make a martini. It's only two ingredients. It all depends on how you like it. That and how many olives they can squeeze on a stick." I laughed.

"That may be so. Nevertheless, I gather by your small talk that you have no new news to report."

"It's all in my report." I slid the envelope across the table to him, but he ignored it. "I am convinced that Skye is with the fellow, Hugo Martinez. If not at his house, then he knows where she is. He has two residences that we know of, and they are both under surveillance. Sooner or later, she'll make an appearance, or we will be able to tail him to another location where she's hiding out."

"I have to tell you, I'm about tapped out. I don't know how much longer I can keep paying you to look for her with no results. Especially if now, I'm paying for your men to sit in their cars and watch these houses."

"No, no, they're not. Nobody sits stake-outs in cars these days. It's all modern technology." I pulled out my phone and opened up the app. I showed the camera feed on the screen to Dan. "Here, you can see for yourself. I get a ring whenever anybody comes or goes, including the FedEx or Amazon guys, which can be a little annoying."

Dan stared at the scene on my phone. No emotion crossed his face. "Why do you think she's with him?"

"I asked you about Hugo before. He's a big-time drug dealer now. I'm trying to stay out of the way of the Feds, who also have a big interest in him. Framing you was his play to take you out. I know you said you only scored a little here and there for friends and family, but Hugo still considered you competition. I'm surprised he didn't threaten you, try to scare you away first instead of going nuclear like this right out of the gate."

"He did this, not Skye?"

"This was a well-thought-out operation, planned well in advance. They stockpiled Skye's blood in advance, lined up a body double to pose as you, bought knives and saws from outside the area. Hugo knew a chopped up pretty girl would play big in the media — another Black Dahlia like in the 40's. You were either going to jail or going broke fighting the prosecution. Either way, you were out of the game."

Our conversation fell silent as our lunch arrived. Dan ate for a while in silence, so I did as well. I usually love the alfredo here, but today it was tasting a bit sour. No fault of the chef, though. Dan, too, seemed not to have an appetite. He picked at his meal, finished his drink and ordered another, a double, same as before.

"So, you're saying this was all Hugo and Skye had nothing to do with it?" He asked finally, looking up.

"No, she had to have so-operated. She pinched your jacket or sweatshirt, whatever the guy wore, pretending to be you. She provided the keys to the apartment. She provided her blood."

"But why?"

"The troubles in your relationship were well known. Almost everyone I talked to had a story about one of your very public blow-ups."

"It's true. I have a temper."

"Temper is usually a stress release."

"Yeah, well, now when I'm stressed, I go to the range."

"You hit balls? That's a good idea."

"Hit balls? No, a gun range. I go and shoot off a box of ammo and I feel better."

"Oh. Hitting golf balls on a driving range works, too."

"Anyway, Skye was not one to knuckle under to a raised voice now and then. But all couples have their difficulties; they don't resort to framing their partners for murder."

"You were known to be clingy, possessive even. Maybe she felt that was the only way out of the relationship."

"What do you mean, possessive?"

"Like with Michele. She faked that job dancing on Broadway just to escape you. There was no job waiting for her there. I checked." I was feeling pretty bad for Dan right about now. "Look, man. I hate to be laying this all on you…"

"I know. I always knew." Dan muttered, staring down at his half-eaten meal.

"Look, I really like Skye. I mean, I hardly knew her. That summer, I may have spoken to her a few times; she read my cards and all. She was pretty and personable and cheerful. She had a gift for making you feel better about yourself. I didn't know her, but I felt she knew me. But, now, as I delve into finding her, that Skye was a mask. I don't know how well you really knew her. Her parents are criminals. They tricked her out when she was sixteen. When she wasn't prostituting herself, she and her brothers were shoplifting or begging, stealing cars. That's the life she ran away from. She came here alone, no friends. She wrapped her vulnerability in a hard shell so no one could get to her. After all those years, she still had no friends. Did you never wonder about that?"

"There was Sarah."

"Sarah said she never felt that close. The day it all went down, Skye and Sarah went shopping, remember? Skye wanted to buy her a gift and say goodbye. Sarah was all confused. When the stories hit the paper, she knew Skye wasn't dead, but she had no proof. She was torn about what to do, who to tell. Afraid of Hugo, she thought she was always being watched. She was greatly relieved when you were found not guilty."

"So now she's talking?"

"It wasn't easy getting her to open up. Hugo owns Bay City now. Howard works for him and keeps an eye on her. Actually, I don't know if Hugo even cares anymore if anyone finds out it was all a frame-up. Mission accomplished in his books. But Sarah was terrified. After talking to me, she left town, packed up her things, and fled, didn't give notice, just disappeared. She was that afraid."

Dan's drink arrived. He took a quick swallow, then fished around in his pockets for something. I finished my glass as I watched and ordered another.

Finally, Dan pulled out a small box, the blue velvet kind that usually houses diamond engagement rings. What he pulled out of the box was something else, a large, garish piece of costume jewelry, a ring with a large oval stone, jade maybe, or turquoise about an inch and a half long.

"It's ugly, I know. I would have bought her a diamond, a ruby, an emerald, or anything she wanted. I wanted to give her something she'd be proud to wear, something she'd show off to her girlfriends. It wasn't meant to be an engagement ring, just a friendship ring. But this is what she wanted. She picked it out."

I knew nothing about jewelry. "What is it, jade?"

"It's a mood ring."

"What's that?"

"It was a big fad in the 70s. Some people are still into it, I guess. The stone has liquid crystals inside that change color based on temperature. The story behind the ring is that it is supposed to tell others the mood you're in. If you're not in the mood, it is dark blue or green; if you're excited, it turns purple; angry, it turns red. It's childish, I know, but it's what she wanted."

Dan toyed with it, turning it over in his hand to catch the light from the ceiling lamps. He then handed it to me.

"I brought this for you to give to Skye when you find her. She may not want to see me, I know. And I don't want to force myself onto her. That was the old me, always insistent. I'm over that now. I love her, but if that means I have to let her go, then I will accept that. But give her the ring. She liked it before, but now it may be tainted. If she throws it in the trash, well… don't tell me. I'll pretend she still treasures it."

There wasn't much else to be said. We sat in silence, finishing our drinks. Our meals grew cold on the plate. Finally, the waiter cleared the table. I paid the bill and pocketed the little blue box.

"I'm certain that Hugo has Skye stashed away in one of his many properties. We'll find those properties, and then we will find her. It won't be long now. Look. From here on out, my associates and I are off the clock. And, if we don't find her by this time next week, then you owe me nothing. I'll call you when I have something more to report," I said as I stood to leave.

Dan glanced up and nodded without speaking. I left him, still sitting at the table.

Back at the office, I mulled over my depressing lunch with Dan. I had told him I was certain that Skye was somehow with Hugo. But I had been spinning my wheels, digging into Dan's past, and not really acting on my convictions. I dug the little blue box out of my pocket, opened it, and took out the ring. It was too small to fit, sized for a woman's fingers, but I managed to get it onto the first joint of my little finger. Nothing happened, not that I expected it to. Perhaps my little finger didn't generate enough warmth to activate the liquid crystals inside, or maybe it was all just bogus.

I was determined to make something happen. At this point, I was working for free. I called Jack.

"Hey. Did you ever get that tracker on Hugo's car like I asked?"

"Sure did. I'm at the track right now and looking at the man and his pals whooping it up at their usual spot at the bar. You want me to pass along a message for you."

"Ha. Yeah, right. How long has he been there?"

"Well, I just got here about a half hour ago. He was here when I walked in, so no telling how early he arrived."

"Look, Jack, I'm going to run over to his house in Fullerton. It may take me an hour to get there, depending on traffic. Once inside, I should be able to look around pretty quickly to see if there are any clues to Skye's whereabouts. I need you to give me a heads up the minute Hugo heads out. He's about fifteen or twenty minutes away himself, but the last thing I want is to get caught."

"Wait. You're going to break into his place?"

"I gotta make something happen. It could be months before Hugo goes to visit her personally. We can't just wait that long."

"Let me run back up for you."

"No, you have to keep an eye on Hugo. I'll ask Vera. Don't worry, I'm not going to take any unnecessary chances."

I hung up and turned to Vera. "Ready for a little field work?"

On the drive down, I outlined my plan.

Vera expressed her concern. "I am not breaking and entering. I joined your little agency for experience, not for a police record. You think I would ever get into the Academy with an arrest on my record? That's residential burglary. It's a felony conviction.'

"Relax. I'm not asking you to do anything illegal. I'll go in by myself. I just need you for back-up."

"Back-up? You mean like aiding and abetting?"

"I'm not worried about getting busted by the cops. I'm worried about Hugo or one of his thugs showing up unannounced. Jack has eyes on them right now and will text me the minute one of them starts to move."

"What if they have an alarm?"

"These alarm companies move like snails. And they'll show first before they call the police in."

"I mean, like an alarm that rings on their phone. They could have cameras and ID you the minute you walk in the door."

"Good point. I'll keep an eye out for cameras. And if it rings their phone and they make a dash for the exit, Jack will text me with more than enough time to get out."

About forty-five minutes later, I exited the 91 Freeway onto Harbor Boulevard and headed into the residential area. I had previously saved the address on my navigation app in the car for just this occasion, but I wasn't going to drive up to the front door again. I'd remembered seeing a golf course winding through this neighborhood and had looked up Hugo's house on the map. Sure enough, it backed up to a fairway. Even better, there was a shallow arroyo that separated his backyard from the course itself. It would be easy to access his property from there.

I pulled into a nearby cul-de-sac. "Know how to drive a Tesla?" I asked.

"A car's a car." She answered.

"Pretty much. This lever on the right side is forward and reverse, no gears. That's about all you'll need to know for now." I reached over and opened the glove compartment and retrieved my nine mil.

Vera looked at the gun, then gave me a quizzical side-eyed glance.

"I'll risk going to jail for this case, but I'm not going to risk facing Hugo unarmed."

"Probably best."

"I'm going to go in from the back, through the golf course. Hugo may have cameras there, but I doubt the Feds do." I said as I got out of the car. I loosened my polo shirt so that it hung down outside my pants and stuck the gun between my belt and the small of my back. "You can either wait here or in front. Just be aware that the house is under surveillance. I'll text you when I'm out. You should also see Jack's texts if Hugo is on the move."

Vera got out of the car and walked around to the driver's side. "Okay, but watch yourself and don't dally."

"I won't. I'm probably more nervous than I let on. So, I'm eager to get in and get out."

"Well, except for the flop sweat on our forehead, I'd say you look pretty confident."

"Thanks." I wiped my brow and put on a golf cap and sunglasses, then fetched a five iron and a couple of balls from my bag in the trunk. To Vera's confused expression, I explained. "Cover. Just in case." I turned and hustled down an embankment to a walk path through the arroyo. The path continued on for only a few yards before being replaced by a cement culvert. On the golf course side, they had let the shrubs and grass grow thick. But uphill towards the houses, the embankment was mostly covered with ice plant or other flowering ground cover. I took note of the out-of-bounds stakes along the culvert.

Consulting the map app on my phone, I counted down the houses until I reached Hugo's and scrambled up the hill about twenty feet or so. He had a rear fence, but it was only about three feet tall. I easily hopped over it. His backyard was pretty much all swimming pool with a flagstone patio around it. A couple of pool lounges and an umbrella were all that decorated the area; no towels or toys to be seen. Maybe he was a neat freak.

Before getting any closer, I scoured the eaves for cameras or other alarm systems. Seeing none, I approached the sliding glass doors that opened into the kitchen. I pulled my lock-picking tools from my pocket and set about unlocking the door. Either Hugo had nothing to steal, or he figured that he was such a known bad-ass that no one would ever break in, so the lock was a snap to open. I slid the door open cautiously, listening for any sound of alarm. Hearing nothing, I stepped in, leaving my golf club leaning against the door.

The kitchen was as sterile as the pool area. It looked like the house was staged for sale. A few appliances on the counter, but otherwise no signs of life. I opened a few cabinet doors, finding only a smattering of dishes, glasses, and pots and pans.

The refrigerator was empty except for a case of Modelo and a half-empty tub of salsa. The pantry had a few cans and boxes, but was mostly bags of snack foods. This was looking like a temporary crash pad for Hugo. Then my phone buzzed.

A text from Jack.

- *Dude. You must have set off the alarm.*
- *Hugo took one look at his phone and the whole gang just lit out of here.*
- *Time to abort.*

Then from Vera.

- *Heading to extraction point now.*

Well, hell. I had not looked around at all. I tried to remember how long it took me to drive here from the track last time. I figured I had at least fifteen minutes. I texted them back.

- *Got a good fifteen margin. Be out in ten.*

I set my phone alarm for ten minutes. Now I had to work quickly. I checked the bedrooms first. Fortunately, it was a smallish house, only three bedrooms, a master, and two smaller ones. I figured Hugo would take the main room. It at least looked lived in. The bedsheets and covers were sloppily tossed over the bed. I lifted the mattress, nothing there nor under the bed either. Towels in the bathroom looked used and there were assorted toiletries on the sink counter. I quickly rifled through the drawers, checking in back and under for any taped secrets. I proceeded then to the bureau and inspected the contents of each drawer. The closet had half a dozen things on hangers and a few pairs of shoes on the floor, but the upper shelves were empty and dusty. That was going to be a tell, but I couldn't worry about that now. I felt that since he installed a silent alarm, there must be something here worth hiding.

The other two rooms were totally empty, as well as the second bathroom. My phone timer buzzed that my ten minutes were up. I rushed into the living room.

If Hugo wasn't exactly living here, he was certainly doing business here. Stacked on the coffee table and in several piles along the wall were a couple of dozen post office mailing boxes. All the same size, about the dimensions of a shoe box, they were all labeled and stamped as delivered. A quick look at the address informed me that he had a sizeable post office box where he received all this. I picked one up and shook it, but it was packed solid, no telltale rattles. It could be cash, it could be drugs, who knows? It could even be shoes if he were running a side business to launder all his drug money. Off to one side was a thick stack of envelopes wrapped in a blue rubber band. I flipped through those, mostly junk mail and some notices from the tax assessor's office, all addressed to the same business LLC.

As I was flipping through the mail, I heard the squeal of tires in the distance. Oh shit, I thought. I wanted to grab one of the boxes, but I dared not. I slipped the envelopes down the front of my pants and bolted for the kitchen. I slipped through the sliding glass door and carefully closed it. Now, outside, I could hear the roar of an approaching car. I grabbed my golf club and noticed one of the golf balls had rolled away. No time to look for it. I leaped over the fence. I could feel the cold metal of my gun slip against my back, but it stayed in place. I scrambled down the embankment, across the culvert and through the bushes. Once on the golf course side of the trees, I paused to catch my breath. I dropped a ball in the thick grass and pushed it around with my five iron. I could hear footsteps running up and from the corner of my eye I caught sight of one of Hugo's men running toward me.

I didn't look at him but rather looked out across the fairway. On the other side was a man in a golf cart, two bags strapped on back.

"Found it!" I called out to him and waved. He looked over, confused. I addressed the ball and made a pretty good punch shot, knocking it about a hundred and fifty or so yards down the fairway. Without looking back, I strolled out into the fairway.

Hugo's man apparently bought that I was just another bad golfer hacking it out from the rough. I heard him scrambling up the hill behind me.

It was very difficult to avoid breaking into a run, but I managed to walk across the fairway towards the cart. The other man's partner appeared, sliding his club into a bag and hopping on board.

"Don't mind me," I called out. "If you find a Pro-V1 in the fairway, keep it. It's yours."

They both gave me a strange look but proceeded off towards the green. I checked my phone. There was a text from Vera.

- *Don't come here. Company!*

- *Heading for the clubhouse. Meet me there.* I replied and walked a little faster.

This was not a course I had ever played before, and I had no idea where I was. However, a quick check on my phone's map app quickly oriented me. I was on the sixteenth fairway. It would be a five-minute walk to the parking lot. Vera was already there, leaning against the trunk when I walked up.

"Why don't you drive? I need to get my heart rate down." I smiled and climbed into the passenger side.

"Was it worth it?" Vera asked as she pulled out of the lot and headed back home.

"Don't know yet. No sign of Skye, of course. Hardly any signs of anyone, really. I think Hugo only uses this for moving material around and occasionally as a crash pad. The place is hardly lived in. But I did snag this." I pulled the stack of envelopes out from the front of my pants and pulled off the rubber band.

"Credit card applications, offers of tree trimming services." I continued flipping through the junk mail. "This may be helpful. Notices from the tax assessor."

"You think he didn't pay his taxes?"

"No, probably notices of assessment increases or something like that. But there are one, two… six envelopes, all addressed to the same LLC. These must be all his properties. Maybe one of them is where we will find our girl."

I leaned back and let out a big sigh. "Here's hoping."

Vera drove us back to the office.

CHAPTER

TWENTY-ONE

The next morning, I was over at Rachel's for the flower delivery. I had made a point of telling them not to get there before nine. I knew she left the house around eight, but just to be sure. I was there earlier, of course, to make sure that she left as expected. In a moment of weakness, a few months ago, she had gifted me with a key to her place. Now it was my turn to gift her back. I was excited. This was going to be a mind-blowing experience, I was sure.

I was waiting outside the front entrance when two vans pulled up. I had ordered a hundred dozen roses. I wasn't sure how many that actually was until the delivery guys started unloading. They had twenty-five cardboard boxes containing four glass vases each. They had jerry-rigged cardboard tubes to the corners so that they could stack three boxes high without crushing the flowers. Still, it was going to be eight trips up the elevator to her place. It was late morning, but there were still residents coming and going, mostly older folks who were retired. Our little delivery operation drew numerous stares and muttered comments, but I didn't care.

Up in her place, a different task presented itself – where to put all these flowers. We quickly filled up the kitchen counter, end tables, and coffee table in the living room, also the side tables in her bedroom, and the bathroom sink counter. I started arranging them on the floor after that, outlining a little path from the front door into the living room and then scattering the rest here and there throughout the apartment. About a half hour later, I was satisfied. I tipped the guys, locked up and left, grinning all the way.

Back at the office, Vera was busy looking up the properties from the tax bills I pinched from Hugo's. They were all addressed to the same LLC at the same post office box. The properties were listed by parcel number, but it was a simple enough task to translate that into addresses.

Vera looked up when I entered. "You have company." She said, nodding towards my office, the door ajar.

Inside, Lieutenant Mejia sat, smoking and dropping his ashes into an empty take-out coffee cup from across the street.

"Strolling in a bit late these days, aren't you?" He sneered.

"I do take care of some business on my way in, not that that is important to you." I sensed from his tone that this was not a friendly social call.

"I don't know how I came to be the guy who always has to clean up after your mess. Just lucky, I guess. Somehow, it's gotten around to the higher-ups that you're some sort of friend of mine, a protégé if you will. So, whenever you fuck up, I get a call!" The lieutenant lit a second cigarette from the ash of his first and dropped that one into the coffee cup. "Maybe I wasn't clear enough when I told you to stay away from that Hugo character. That's on me."

"I am staying away from him."

"You broke into his fucking house! How is that staying away?"

"He wasn't there. I didn't run into him; he didn't see me."

"How do you know he didn't see you? He was coming in the front door as you were running out the back!"

"If he saw me, then he'd be sitting in that chair instead of you."

"Don't get smart. For all you know, his boys are waiting for you down in the parking garage right now."

"My client is desperately trying to locate his girlfriend. I know Hugo's got her stashed someplace. I don't want to mix it up with him or his gang, so I'm trying to work around it."

"Well, the Feds don't like it. They're trying to watch him on the down low, and you're busting in through the front door. If they brace you, I won't be there in your corner. You're on your own."

"Give me something and I'll go away. You've got more resources than I do. Someone's got to have seen this woman with him sometime. I'm sure it's written up in a file somewhere. Let me look at the files."

"Can't. That's not my beat. I can kick it over to the DEA, but knowing how much they like you these days, I wouldn't get my hopes up."

We stared at each other in frustration for several minutes.

"Who's the new gal?" He said with a nod towards the door. "Secretary?"

"That's Vera. She does a little bit of everything. Wants to be a cop. Waiting to get into the Academy."

"I like her. I can see she's got her shit together, a straight shooter, got a no-nonsense attitude. You could stand to pick up a few pointers from her."

"Changing the subject." I started. "You know a kid that goes by the name, Fly? I think he's a fence."

"Doesn't ring a bell. Another case of yours?"

"Not really, just doing a favor. The son of a friend of mine got conned into opening a joint checking account. Now his buddy Fly is moving a lot of cash in and out of the account. I'm sure he's laundering it for somebody. Seems to know how to avoid MLCA triggers."

"What do you know about that?"

"I come from a long line of bankers. Majored in banking in school."

"He's not working for your friend, Hugo?"

"Pretty sure not. There's more than one criminal gang in this town, don't you think? Maybe you could pay him a visit. You know, put the fear of God into him."

"We don't do that shit. If there's evidence to back an arrest, we'll take him in."

"Just a thought."

"I'll ask around. If I hear anything, I'll let you know." Mejia stood up to leave. "Please keep your now clean. I've run out of clean handkerchiefs."

After Mejia left, I sat there for a while pondering Martin's problem friend. Norma had tied my hands by making me handle this all confidentially. I really liked the idea of trying to scare him away from her boy, but how to do it? I decided to take the lieutenant's advice and called Vera in to brainstorm ideas.

"How do you feel about impersonating a police officer?" I asked as soon as she sat down, skipping the consulting part and going with my instincts.

"Well, aside from it being a criminal offense punishable by a jail sentence and or a fine, it would totally torpedo any chance of me getting into the Academy. So, no, I won't be doing that, Mr. Gardiner."

"I don't mean a uniform. I'm thinking like a government agent, a Fed, plain clothes, like that."

"Same shit, different shirt."

"Now, now, don't be too quick to say no. You won't have to flash a badge or any kind of fake ID. You won't have to say anything. I'll do all the talking. I just need you for backup and looking the part. Do you have a dark grey or black suit? If not, I can buy you one. You have a concealed carry permit, right? I just need you to stand behind me with your dark glasses and telltale bulge under your coat and look all Sarah Conner-like. Terminator 2 Sarah, not the first one."

"What the hell are you talking about?"

I leaned back in my chair. "I've got to find a way to separate Martin from Fly without letting Martin know that his mother asked me to intervene."

Vera just sat quietly, waiting for me to get to the point.

"I figured if I could rattle Fly's cage a little and tell him to never see Martin again, that would do the trick. Martin would think he'd been ghosted and go on with his life. But the only way to ensure that would be to convince Fly that he's about to get busted for some serious shit, so he'll disappear."

Vera stared at me, expressionless except to say, 'You're kidding me, right? '

"That would work, wouldn't it?"

"Maybe in the movies. Maybe in a bad movie with terrible actors and a second-rate screenwriter." She answered.

"Do you have any better ideas?"

"We could collect our evidence and turn it over to the proper authorities and let them handle it."

"We could, but Martin would be implicated. His name is on the account. He opened it with this guy voluntarily. Naively, but voluntarily. He could lose his job at JPL."

"So, what are you going to do?"

"I'm thinking, I'm thinking." I started flipping through the mail I had heisted from Hugo's house. It was mostly junk mail, ads, and such, but then I came across a series of envelopes from the Tax Assessor's office. I opened one. It was the yearly property tax bill. I flipped through the envelopes. There were six in all.

"Vera. Go online and run the APNs and get the street addresses for these properties. I think they must all be Hugo's houses. There should be two or three here that we didn't know about. Maybe our friend Skye is at one of them."

I handed her the stack of envelopes.

After Vera returned to her desk, I leaned back in my chair, puzzling over how to solve Martin's problem without him knowing. As I sat there, at a loss for ideas, my phone rang. My ringtone was the theme from Peter Gunn. Anyway, one glance told me it was Rachel. I was glad Vera was out of the room because I just knew I had the biggest shit eating grin stretched ear to ear over my face.

"Hey, Rach!"

"WHAT THE FUCK, JAMES!" she shouted, almost breaking my eardrum.

"Wha..?" I was startled."

"Have you lost your goddamned mind?" She raged on. "Why on earth would you pull a prank like that?"

"It wasn't meant to be a prank." I protested meekly. "I..."

"I can't even stand to spend five minutes in my place before the stench of those flowers makes me puke."

"But, but…"

"Get those damn roses out of my flat today, James Gardiner! Today!" With that, she hung up.

I couldn't tell you how that phone call left me. I was alternately depressed, flummoxed, angry, anxious, and frustrated. Vera bailed me out. She found a nursing home that was happy to take the donation of the many dozens of roses that I had adorned Rachel's apartment with. I managed to hire a couple of guys that evening to go over to her place and load up all the flowers to deliver to the home. Rachel was nowhere to be seen, probably avoiding me, but she left a note – "Leave your key!"

I guess I mucked that up pretty badly.

CHAPTER

TWENTY-TWO

The next morning, things went from bad to worse. Lieutenant Mejia woke me up with a phone call instructing me to meet him at the DEA offices at eight o'clock. I had to scramble. Even at seven in the morning, rush hour traffic is in full swing and the drive to downtown would take an hour. The Federal Building is adjacent to Little Tokyo.

I took a five-minute shower, skipped a shave, and threw on my only suit that didn't need ironing and was in the car by five to seven.

It never fails that traffic backs up at the Western and Santa Monica onramps. It was a slow crawl to downtown, and by the time I parked and found my way to the office, Sam gave me I was ten minutes late.

"Sorry, I'm late. Traffic, you know. I tried to get here as quickly as I could."

"Sit down." Said the man behind the desk.
This was my first time in this building, let alone this office. The building was very new, and the office looked like it had never been used, with clean white walls, blue and grey carpeting with that new carpet smell. The desks were unscratched and the blue vinyl-covered chairs were without cracks. There were no pictures on the walls except for one photo of the building

itself, no books on the shelves, and I would wager that the file cabinet was also empty. The desk was clean except for one lone file folder. The lieutenant sat in a guest chair to one side, looking like he really wanted a cigarette. The man behind the desk introduced himself as Special Agent Wilson. He was youngish, I would guess not yet forty, with movie star good looks, a square dimpled chin, a jaw line you could cut paper with, piercing blue eyes, and a nice wave to his black hair. He looked like Clark Kent without his glasses. He was about as handsome as Mejia was ugly. But I had grown to be fond of the lieutenant, so I immediately didn't like this pretty guy.

Special Agent Wilson pulled the folder in front of him, opened it, and pretended to read it. I waited patiently for him to finish his little bit of theatre. A quick glance at the lieutenant revealed he was also impatient but resigned.

"I see here that previously you had been formally warned to avoid any contact with Hugo Martinez." Wilson began.

"Yes," I replied. "And I have followed those orders and have avoided all contact with him."

"How is breaking into his house avoidance?" He questioned angrily. "We have your face in our database. We knew it was you before you got through the back door."

"I had eyes on him. I knew he was not at home. He happened to be at the Santa Anita Track that day."

"But the minute you entered his house, you tripped a silent alarm, alerting him and he raced home."

"I was prepared for that. I knew exactly how long it would take him to get from the track to the house, even driving above the speed limit. I was gone before he arrived."

"By mere seconds!" He exclaimed. "He was coming in the front door as you were going out the back."

"He didn't see me. At least not so that he would know who I was."

"That is beside the point! What the hell were you doing in his house anyway?"

Mejia interjected here. "James has a client, a Mr. Daniel LeBeau, who was brought up on first-degree murder charges with special circumstances about ten years ago. He was found innocent, mostly because the body of his girlfriend was never found. His client hired James here to find his girlfriend after he spotted her these many years later, driving her car through Hermosa Beach. James has come to learn that Mr. Lebeau and Mr. Martinez were involved in a lovers' triangle with this woman. His interest in Mr. Martinez is unrelated to the government's investigation and Mr. Martinez is unlikely to make any connection between the two."

"Actually, I think Dan also had a little 'family and friends' coke business going back then and Hugo wanted him out," I added.

"Nevertheless," Wilson replied, annoyed that Mejia seemed to be defending me. "You risk blowing an operation involving scores of investigators and years of work. What did you take from his house?"

"I didn't take anything. I went in, searched the house for any signs that Skye, the girlfriend, was living there or had ever been there. I found none, so I left. Oh, I did notice a pile of boxes in the living room. UPS, FedEx, that sort. None seemed to be Post Office. I figure they were either drugs or cash, but I didn't touch them. I got a text that they were in the neighborhood, so I split."

"You left with something in your hand. Some papers. We picked that up with the backyard camera."

"I grabbed some junk mail. I noticed that it was a different address, so I wanted to follow that up. Maybe Hugo had another safe house somewhere."

"Why would he bring junk mail from another address to his home?" Wilson asked skeptically.

"I don't know. Maybe one of his men collects the mail for him. He doesn't want to screw up, so he grabs everything and lets Hugo throw it away."

"What was this other address?"

"Look, I haven't had a chance to even look it up. I'll tell you what. The minute I get back to my office, I will text you the address. How's that?"

"Make sure that you do." He slid a business card across the desk to me.

"Look." I began arguing. "Hugo's a pretty small fish in the grand scheme of things. He's got a crew of what, maybe half a dozen guys. But you have him covered with surveillance like he was the head of a cartel!"

"That's how it works." Wilson interrupted. "We work our way up the ladder one rung at a time. The worker bees at the bottom are the easiest to see, the easiest to pin a rap on. Then we move up to their bosses. The guys at the top don't get their hands dirty. It's all behind closed doors. They only give orders to ones that they trust. So, we have to lean on the little guys to turn on their jefes. And if we blow it on one rung of the ladder, we have to start all over again at the bottom."

"I get it. I really do. I will not be going to his house again."

"Or this other one," Wilson warned.

"Or the other one. I'm sending you that address right away. Are we done here?"

Wilson stared at me for a long while. "I'm not arresting you, now. That's for my boss to decide. But you certainly have been obstructing a federal investigation. So don't be surprised if you get a knock on your door."

I stood up. "I won't be the first time."

As I turned to leave, Mejia stood up and followed me out. We walked down the long hallway in silence, stopping at the elevator. The lieutenant pushed the button, then turned to me.

"Don't screw this up, kid. These are Feds. I have no pull with them. If you mess with their investigation and they come after you, you're on your own."

"I know. I get it. I'm not trying to be an annoyance. I'm just trying to find this woman."

"But you're reckless. Not a good trait in this business, despite what you see in the movies."

The elevator was taking a long time.

"Did you happen to get any info on my friend, Fly?" I asked.

"Nothing. He's got a record, but not on anyone's radar. No one's going to go rattle his cage for no reason. We've all got real jobs to take care of."

"Fine. Whatever."

The elevator finally arrived.

"And don't you go getting any ideas about playing dress up. Impersonating an officer is an offence I won't get you out of." He said to my back as I stepped into the empty car. I turned around, gesturing palms up, feigning offense.

"Do you think I'm really that stupid?"

The door closed on Sam's baleful stare.

I fretted over what to do about Martin and Fly all the way back to the office. Vera was busy on her laptop when I walked in.

"Did you get addresses for any of those tax bills?" I asked.

She handed me the bills with pink Post-its slapped on each with an address in pencil. I flipped through the short stack, glancing quickly at each.

"Well, here are three that we didn't know about before." I fished Wilson's business card out of my pocket and handed it along with one of the bills back to Vera. "Send this address to this guy at the DEA. I'll check out these other two later." I dropped the rest of the stack on her desk, pocketing two of the bills.

"You have someone waiting for you in your office."

I glanced at my door; it was ajar, but not so that I could see anything but my desk.

"She looked homeless, but she had your card."

"What do you mean, looked homeless?"

"Dirty blonde hair, dirty yellow dress, dirty feet in worn-out sandals."

"Other than dirty, can you describe her?"

"She's young, no more than twenty, I'd guess. Pretty. Carries a Target bag with her clothes in it."

"Did you talk to her, get a name, what she wants? I hate being ambushed."

"Her name is Summer, Miss Summer."

"Like Elke Sommer?"

"I think it's her first name."

The name rang a bell. A bell like a fire alarm.

"If I had to guess, I'd guess she's the daughter of our missing murder victim, Skye, that you told us about," Vera added.

"Oh, Jeez." I rushed into my office.

"Summer!" I cried to the young girl sitting so primly in my guest chair, the Target bag on her lap. Vera had described her perfectly, a beauty in yellow and dirt. She could have walked out of any Quentin Tarantino movie. "What are you doing here?"

"You gave me your card. I thought that meant you wanted me to help. I came to help you find my mother."

"Oh!" I replied, a bit taken aback. "Have you heard from her?"

"No. I just wanted to help."

"You know you didn't have to come all this way. If you had new information, you could have called."

"Oh, I don't have any new information. I don't have any information at all, but I can help you look." She smiled appealingly. "I want to help."

There was that word again.

"Um. I see." I settled into my own chair. "Have you ever been in L.A. before?"

"No, never. This is my first time." She grinned again.

"How did you get down here, if I may ask?"

"I took the bus. It dropped me off just a couple of blocks away, right here in Hollywood. The nice bus driver was kind enough to point me in the right direction. I must say that Hollywood people appear rather strange to me."

"Strange isn't the half of it. Did Vera offer you something to drink?" I started to get up.

"Oh, yes. I finished it. I threw the bottle in your trash can. That was okay, wasn't it?"

"Yeah, sure. That's what it's for." I replied, sitting down again. I looked to her, still mystified. "Did you just get it? You must be tired. I'm sure that's a long bus ride. Where are you staying?"

"I haven't found a place, yet. I'll do that later."

Now I was suspicious. "Do you have any money?"

"Of course I do. Don't worry about me. So, when do we get started?"

"Do you even know what your mother looks like?" I questioned.

"No, I was just a baby when she left."

"And she probably didn't send any pictures back of herself frolicking on the beach, did she?"

She shook her head, her lower lip starting to quiver. "But you must have pictures."

I reached into my drawer and pulled out the file. Inside was one of the pictures Dan had given me. I pushed it across the desk to Summer. "I'm afraid it's more than ten years old. But that's the most recent one I have. Seriously, how are you going to help?"

As she took the photo, I could see the tears forming in her eyes. "I'm sure I would recognize her if I saw her. She is my mother." She looked up at me. "Can I keep this?"

"Yeah, I suppose. I can always get another. Look, I have some other stuff to deal with at the moment. Why don't you go and find a nice motel; there are plenty around here to choose from, very affordable. You can freshen up. I'm sure you'll want to wash some of the road off. Later, you can give me a call and we can talk further. I'll buy you dinner. How's that?"

"I don't have a phone."

I reached into the bottom drawer of my desk and grabbed a burner, still in the blister pack. I pulled it out and pushed it across the desk to her.

"Take this. My number is number one on the speed dial. Okay?"

She took the phone and stood up; head bowed like a punished child being sent to her room. She turned and quietly left.

I leaned back in my chair, closed my eyes and slowly shook my head. I didn't need this complication now.

But I had things to do. I flipped open my laptop and looked up the two new addresses we'd discovered among the tax bills. One was in Pico Rivera, the other down south in San Diego. Looks like Hugo was spread out pretty evenly. I speculated that each house was a territorial headquarters of sorts.

I walked back into the front office. Vera was still busy with something on her laptop.

"You still here? It's Saturday, go home. And don't come in tomorrow. Monday, I want you to check out this house in Pico Rivera. Don't break in or anything, but see if it's in use or just vacant, any info you can gather." I handed her one of the addresses she had given me. "Before that, I want to tackle this Fly problem. Can I count on you for that?"

"You could lose your license for impersonating a police officer."

"I'm not going to do that."

"Federal officer counts the same."

"I won't be flashing a badge or identifying myself as an agent. I'll just dress and act the part and let him make assumptions. That's all I'm asking of you; show up, look like you mean business and say nothing. Okay?"

Vera thought it over for a long minute. "Yeah. I can do that."

"Do you have a suit?"

"No, why would I?"

I pulled out my phone and shared an address from my contacts. "Here. Go see this guy. He's my tailor. I'll let him know you're coming. He won't be able to make you something on short notice, but he will have something on the rack he can alter quickly. You'll look good. We can pay Fly a visit on his usual Monday route."

Vera was looking at the contact I sent her. "Beverly Hills? That won't come cheap."

"Business expense. You have a concealed carry permit, right? Get yourself a regulation shoulder holster if you don't already. I'll reimburse you. It doesn't have to be loaded; it's just for effect."

"Never carry an unloaded gun."

"Right. We can touch base Monday morning and meet here. I'll drive."

"Sounds like a plan."

"Great. Now git. Enjoy what's left of your weekend."

I walked back into my office, satisfied that I was going to at least get that business off my plate. I looked at the phone in my hand and decided that I needed to call Rachel and check that box on my to-do list. I plopped down in my chair and prepared for a long, difficult conversation. After a few rings, I knew she wasn't going to pick up. Either she was busy, or saw that it was me and didn't want to talk to me, or was waiting to see if I would leave a message. My call went to voicemail.

"Rachel. Hi, it's me. Look, I'm sorry about the roses. Really, I am. I thought it would be something special and cool. I guess I didn't think it through. Hope you're back in your place now without too much inconvenience. I also need to apologize for taking off the other morning.

I confess I get caught up in the romance of the job and think every other moment is life or death drama. I need to work on my work/life balance, and I hope the 'life' part still includes you. I don't blame you for being mad; I am just hoping that you won't punish me for too long. When you're ready, if you can put this in the past, please give me a call. We can go to dinner or something..."

The phone went dead as my allotted three minutes for a message elapsed. Now I would just have to wait and see if she would call.

I heard the front door close as Vera finally left for the day. I looked around the room, thinking, what else did I need to take care of that I had been putting off? Rachel wasn't the only business I let lapse in my eagerness to track down Skye.

I decided to prepare an invoice for Dan. He wouldn't be happy with seeing a huge bill, especially since I had little to show for it. But I did drop off all the time I'd spent since our lunch, like I said I would. I also wouldn't charge for any of Jack or Vera's time since I had not disclosed that I would be using them on this case. Even so, I had logged the better part of three weeks, including weekends now. I picked up the tax bill for the house in San Diego. This and the one I gave to Vera to check out were the only clues I had left.

I spent the rest of the afternoon calling the tailor for Vera's suit, doing paperwork, paying bills, goofing off playing sudoku on my laptop, and stealing glances at my phone to see if Rachel might have texted me. She hadn't. I got up and went to the file cabinet and grabbed a bottle of scotch and my favorite Flintstones jelly jar glass. Plopping back down in my chair, I gave myself a good, healthy pour, thinking at the time that healthy was probably not the right adjective. Anyway, it would be a good start to getting drunk. But as I stared at the glass on my desk, I couldn't take that first swallow. The amber liquid sparkled with many colors as it caught the setting sun, but all its allure was not enough. I was depressed, but not that depressed.

Feeling hungry, I decided to call it a day and grab a bite to eat somewhere. I grabbed my hat, grabbed my phone, and headed for the door, leaving the untouched glass on my desk.

CHAPTER
TWENTY-THREE

Sunday morning, I got up early and headed to the club to play a little golf and try to get my mind off things. I didn't have a tee time reservation, but being a single, it was usually easy to get slotted in with others who were short of a foursome. I checked in, ate a quick breakfast, then hit the range and the putting green for some warm-up. After an hour or so, a spot opened up.

I got paired up with a father-son twosome whom I didn't recognize. The dad was about twenty years my senior, and his son was still in college. I tried to be sociable, but my mind was still on Rachel and the nagging questions about what was happening to us. I hesitated putting my phone on silent in case she called.

Pops was a bogie golfer, but junior was pretty good, played for his college team, didn't have my length but hit it straight — fairways, greens in regulation, two-putt pars. I wasn't keeping score, but in my mind, I was competing with him. I needed something to focus on. In the end, I think the kid probably beat me.

Sunday golf is always slow. It was early afternoon before we finished. I checked my phone afterwards, still no message from Rachel. I stuck around for lunch, chatted with a few acquaintances at the club, then figured I had killed most of the day and went home.

Tomorrow morning, I would be meeting Vera for our little 'Scared Straight' operation with Fly, so I figured I'd swing by the office and pick up my holster and piece so I could dress properly and not be fumbling with it in the office.

She was waiting for me in the hallway, sitting on the floor, her back to the wall.

"Summer! What are you doing here?"

"Hi, Mr. Gardiner." She said softly.

Mr. Gardiner. I still couldn't get used to anyone calling me that. Mr. Gardiner was my father.

"What happened? Didn't you find a motel room?" She was still in the same dirty dress from this morning, with the same grocery bag of belongings clutched to her chest.

"They wouldn't take my money. Said I needed a credit card for security." Her voice was so quiet I could barely hear her.

"Oh. Yeah. I suppose they would. Why didn't you call? I could have helped you out."

She looked down at the floor. "I lost your phone. I was having lunch and I set it down next to my bag, but when I looked to pick it up, it was gone."

"Yeah, you have to be extra careful in Hollywood; there are thieves everywhere. How long have you been sitting here?"

"Not long, I don't think. Maybe an hour. I don't have a watch. It's kind of hard to tell how long time lasts."

"Come on. I'll help you find a place." I reached down to help her to her feet. "You know, why don't you come with me to my place. You can shower and change clothes. We can throw this dress into the washer and then go have dinner. We need to talk, anyway."

"Okay." She whispered.

I had driven the Merc this morning, so of course it wouldn't be in the garage below, so I parked it a couple blocks south on Cahuenga in a lot. It was still light out as we walked there to pick up the car, so the evening crazies hadn't appeared yet. My place was a three-bedroom, two-bath house in the Beachwood Canyon neighborhood. That's about halfway between Hollywood and the Hollywood Sign. It's a cute little house, mid-century, art moderne style. I like it. While she showered, I tossed her sundress into the washer and made myself a drink.

I needed to get her on a bus back to her family. The last thing I needed was to be dealing with her hanging around the office every day. I checked the bus schedule on my phone. There was one bus tomorrow, Sunday, but it was sold out. Plenty of buses on Monday, but Vera and I had to deal with Fly in the morning, and then I wanted to go to San Diego to check out that house of Hugo's. Maybe I could get Jack to put her on the bus, or I could wait till Tuesday.

Summer appeared from the bathroom, clean and looking much more presentable, but her backup outfit was a floral print shift that didn't look any better than the sundress in the wash. I had no clothes to lend her except a cardigan sweater to wear over her dress. I offered her that as it was getting cooler now that evening had set in. We could walk a few blocks to the café, the only place to eat in the canyon. I suggested she could stay the night at my house until we could get her situated. I had a comfortable guest room. One that nobody ever used. The other bedroom was more of a den for me, just a desk, a reading chair and some bookshelves. I decided not to mention it yet, putting her on a bus home as soon as possible. I needed to talk her into it first.

Being Sunday evening, things were pretty quiet in the neighborhood, with few cars and almost no late walkers. We got a table by the window. The café was also half empty. The menu was typical California fare, healthy, inventive fusion-type dishes. I could tell from her questions that most of this was new to Summer. I had the sea bass with quinoa and kale. She ordered two meals, spaghetti and a burger, stuff she was used to; plus, she was very hungry. I gathered she hadn't eaten much all day.

I kept the conversation light, trying not to pry too much into her home life. I had seen it first hand and could only guess what went on there, but Summer was unembarrassed by it all. She pressed me for details on her mother, Skye. I had little that I could or would divulge to her, feeding summer with the innocent stuff like her tarot card reading and cocktail waitressing.

Having been abandoned as a baby, of course, Summer had no firsthand knowledge of her mother's life at the commune, but she'd heard the gossip.

It was worse than I had anticipated. Skye had been regularly raped by her own father, but what was worse, her mother blamed her for being so seductive. Eventually, Skye could take it no longer and fled, but not before stealing a few thousand dollars from the family stash.

That explained a lot: the lack of contact over the years, the wherewithal to start a new life from scratch, and the enmity of her mother when I showed up to investigate. I asked Summer about the circumstances of her leaving and where she got her money. It was from the same man who lent her the phone, and the same exchange of favors. It was the life Summer knew. There was no shame.

I tried to explain to Summer that she needed to go home. She could be of no use to me in finding her mother. She didn't know her mother or know anything about her. She didn't even know what she looked like, as there were no pictures of her back at the commune. She knew no one in Los Angeles. She had never been here before. The longer she stayed and took up my time, the less time I would have to search for her mother.

Summer said she understood, but I knew in her mind she was resisting. I mentioned that I was going to be busy all day tomorrow and suggested she play tourist and enjoy her stay. I would give her some money to spend. But on Tuesday, I was going to put her on a bus back home.

Dessert came, a seven-layer cake a la mode. I watched in silence as she devoured it.

CHAPTER

TWENTY-FOUR

I got up early to make breakfast. I didn't have much in the fridge to work with, but I was able to slap together a Spanish omelet and some toast. I was still in my bathrobe, chopping peppers and onions, when Rachel walked through the door carrying two large coffees from the local café.

"Making breakfast for me? You shouldn't have." She joked.

I looked up. Rachel looked great. She was dressed for work, a sharp business suit with a conservative length skirt, hair up, business-level make-up, like she just stepped off a magazine cover. I was really glad to see her.

"I'm really glad to see you," I said.

"I thought you usually had breakfast at the diner."

"I usually do," I answered, leaning forward to give her a little peck on the cheek. "But today I have a little special op scheduled, so no time for that. You remember Norma, don't you? She works at the 101."

Rachel set our coffees on the kitchen island and pulled up a barstool.

"She has a son, Martin, whom she's very proud of. He works at JPL. Anyway, he's gotten mixed up with this sketchy guy, and I told Norma I'd find a way to break them up. So, Vera and I are going to have a little talk with the guy and tell him it's over between him and Martin and to get lost."

"And, he'll listen to you, why?" Rachel asked, bemused.

"Vera and I are going to go dressed as federal agents and play good cop/bad cop.

"Isn't that against the law?"

"Well, the plan is to tiptoe up to the line but not cross it by not actually claiming to be agents."

"I see."

I wasn't really aware that the shower was running until it turned off. Rachel noticed it, too, and gave me a little frown.

I barreled on. "I figure we can pull it off if we dress the part, discreetly show our sidearms under our jackets, and give a lot of attitude."

"Mmm." Rachel sipped her coffee. "You always were rather too casual about taking risks." She then looked at me, one brow arched questioningly. "Is there someone else in the house?"

"Oh." I must have looked like a deer in headlights. "Yeah, it's just…"

"James." Summer called out. She stepped out of the bathroom, her hair wrapped up in a towel; her long, youthful legs, bare shoulders, and arms sticking out of another towel that just barely covered enough top and bottom to avoid being indecent. "Do you have a hair dryer?"

I glanced back at Summer, who was now tugging at the top of her towel to prevent it from slipping down. I looked to Rachel. Her face was frozen in a dispassionate stare.

"Now, Rachel, it's not what you think. This is Summer. She's the daughter of the woman I've been trying to track down. She showed up at the office yesterday in the hope that I had found her, but with no money and no place to stay. I'm letting her stay here until I can put her on a bus home tomorrow."

Rachel didn't move, didn't blink, didn't look at me, only stared at the half-naked young girl in the doorway.

"It's not what it looks like. Seriously, Rachel. Do you not trust me? Do you really think I would?"

Her lower lip started to tremble as she set her coffee cup on the counter and stood up. "James, I can't... I can't deal..."

I started to approach her, to take her hand, but she pulled away, tears forming in her eyes.

"I just can't." She turned and ran out the front door, not even closing it behind her.

I followed her to the doorway and watched as she quickly got in her car and drove away, bouncing her front wheels over the curb.

"Did I do something wrong?" came a voice from behind me.

"No. It wasn't you. It was me."

We ate our Spanish omelets in silence. I left Summer some money and a list of things to see and do to keep her busy all day. As I dressed, putting on my shoulder holster, she asked, "Are you going to find my mother today?"

"What, this?" I answered, referring to the gun. "No, I have another case this morning that I need to wrap up." I'll be back later today. If there's time, we can go out for dinner." She stood, watching from the doorway as I drove away.

I had rented a suitable car, a dark grey Ford sedan with tinted windows, to further the ruse. I swung by the office to pick up Vera. She looked much older, in her thirties if I didn't know better, wearing a grey pantsuit and white dress shirt with no tie. With her hair pulled back and dark shades, she looked totally badass.

"Monday is Toluca Lake, right?" I asked as she slid into the passenger seat.

"Right. There's a parking lot in the back with a rear entrance to the bank. That's his usual M.O."

I pulled away from the curb and headed up Cahuenga to the freeway onramp that would take us to the Valley.

"So, how do you want to do this?" She asked. "Good cop, bad cop; Friday, Gannon?"

"Oh, you know Dragnet, do you? I thought I would do all the talking. You just stand in the background looking menacing."

"Works for me."

Toluca Lake is a tony little neighborhood nestled between Universal Studios and Warner Bros. Studios. In years past, it was the home of the likes of Bob Hope and Bing Crosby. These days, movie stars tend to live away from Los Angeles. It is also the place where Heather caused me to lose that golf match to her little brother, Ike. It's not a place that has a lot of crime, so I guess it's a good spot to do a little criming as long as no one gets hurt. To some, money laundering for a fence would fall into that category.

I parked in the handicap spot next to the door. We waited about twenty minutes before Vera spotted Fly pulling into the parking lot in his older model white Corolla. The car had one tire in the junkyard, so to speak, but as he stepped out, I could see why they called him Fly. His outfit was probably more expensive than his ride. It wasn't flashy, gaudy, hip -hop expensive, but much more subtle and stylish. It looked like tailored dark grey slacks and a black and grey patterned sports coat over a black cashmere tee bookended by expensive Versace shades and red Nike shoes. He carried a fancy black leather bag, which probably contained a few thousand in cash.

Vera and I hopped out and headed for the bank entrance. Fly didn't seem to pay us any mind. A few yards from the door, I turned around and faced him.

"Eldredge. We need to talk."

He pulled up short and gave me a strange look.

I opened my jacket to show him a badge hanging from my belt and to also allow him to steal a glance at the nine-mil tucked under my arm.

"What? You FBI or something? I ain't done nothing."

"No. Not FBI."

"What then?" He now noticed Vera had circled behind him and stood in a ready position, blocking any escape.

"Doesn't matter. You wouldn't know what agency we were with if I told you. Why don't you come over to my car and we can talk. Won't be but a few minutes."

"You arresting me?"

"No, I'm not arresting you. Though I do know that you are laundering money for a few local fences. You have several thousand dollars in cash in that bag you're carrying. You come here every Monday to make a deposit. On Wednesdays and Fridays, you make deposits at other branches of this bank. Once a month, you wire money to a bank in Texas. But that is for other officers to enforce. I'm here to talk to you about something different. Let's go over to my car."

"You ain't a cop and you ain't arresting me, why should I talk to you?"

"Would you rather be arrested? I'll leave. Someone will be by to pick you up on Wednesday or Friday, or maybe tonight at your home. We can talk at the station. I just thought this might be a little more comfortable for you."

"All right, but I ain't giving you any information about any of my associates if that's what you're after. You will not be getting anything from me, so don't waste your breath."

There was a security guard/parking attendant at the far end of the lot. An older man in uniform, probably retired and doing this part-time to supplement his social security, had been sitting on a metal chair watching us. As we walked to our car, he got up and began to approach. Vera turned to him and raised her hand just slightly. He stopped and then returned to his chair.

We got into our car, I in the driver's seat, Fly in the other front passenger seat, and Vera directly behind him.

"So, what's so all important that you need to pull me off the street to talk to me?"

"You opened this bank account with your friend, Martin. Or rather, Martin opened it and gave you complete access to it. But Martin is not your friend. Martin is just some kid you went to high school with and bumped into much later on the street. You figured he was naïve enough to let you use him to set up this account. You probably told him some lame story about not having a job and not being able to get one because you didn't have a bank account and not being able to get a bank account because you didn't have a job. I'm sure he felt sorry for you and thought he was trying to help an old friend."

"You got that wrong. Me and Marty are tight."

"Marty might be innocent to your way of life and business, but he's a smart guy. He's a scientist. Works for the Jet Propulsion Laboratory. That's a private company, but they do very important work for the US Government, including NASA and the Defense Department."

"So."

"So, we would be concerned if he were to run afoul of the law, even innocently. A person in his position could be subjected to threats of blackmail, extortion, or pressure to compromise his work or security clearance. We wouldn't want that to happen."

"I'm not interested in that shit."

"I believe you. But information has a way of getting out. Your boss or co-worker might hear about Marty and think that's an opportunity to be exploited."

"I can't help that."

"Yes, you can. And here's how. You're going to go into the bank and close the account. You can open up a new one in your own name. I'm sure the bank people know you pretty well by now; they would look the other way if you didn't have all the usual personal information they usually require."

"My boss won't like me doing stuff like that without asking."

"You can tell him that Martin has become unreliable. Maybe too curious. You thought it best to nip it in the bud and cut him loose. Your boss would like it if you could think on your own and head off potential problems."

"Yeah, yeah, you got it all figured out, don't you. But maybe I'm not interested in helping you. Are you the good cop and she's the bad cop?

She gonna break my fingers if I don't cooperate? She looks like Black Widow, I give you that."

"No, we're both the good cops. If we have to resort to bad cops, they won't come to persuade you. They'll just take you out of circulation and let the account close from inactivity."

"What do you mean, out of circulation?"

"Whatever you think it means. Use your imagination. You can go now. I'll know if you followed my instructions and closed the account. You won't be seeing me again."

Vera had gotten out of the car and opened the door for Fly. As he got out, I called out one last directive. "And don't call Martin. Not about this, not about anything. You ghost him, completely. I'll know if you don't."

Fly stared at me for a minute, deciding, then turned and walked into the bank. Vera got back into the car.

"What do you think?" I asked.

"I don't know. He didn't seem particularly rattled, but maybe with the people he hangs around with, he's good at keeping himself under control."

"Hope it works. Don't know what more I can do without involving Martin."

I started the car and drove back to the office, giving a little wave to the attendant as we passed.

CHAPTER
TWENTY-FIVE

I didn't know what to do about Rachel. Probably, there was nothing I could do. I could only apologize so much before it fell on deaf ears. Besides, I hadn't actually done anything wrong. Maybe it was time to face the fact that we were too different to go the distance. There would always be something in the way I lived that clashed with the way she wanted her life to be arranged. She liked things a certain way, orderly and predictable. I was her 'bad boy' fling. Not that I ever saw myself as one of those types of guys. I'm sure I would hear about it from my mother soon enough, but then again, maybe this was a break too dramatic for Rachel to reach out to her. It was better to make a clean break. I felt bad.

I decided to change out of my suit and into something more comfortable, like shorts, sandals, and a wild Hawaiian shirt. Summer was gone. She'd left the front door unlocked, but at this point, I didn't care. I hoped she was having a good time.

It was a long drive down to San Diego, even longer to the address that I had on Seacoast Drive in Imperial Beach. That was a mere five iron from the border. Well, maybe a five wood, okay, a Rory McIlroy five wood.

But I digress. It was going to be a long three-hour drive if I was lucky, but I was taking the Merc, with the top down, and I was determined to enjoy it. It would be night by the time I got home, even if there was nobody there.

But the sun was shining, it was not too hot, and I was prepared for anything. I had a gun in the glove compartment in case there was somebody there, a couple of remote cameras to plant in case there wasn't, and I even remembered to bring the mood ring Dan had given me a couple of days ago in case I got lucky and ran into Skye. I was beginning to feel guilty about how long this case had dragged on with no results. It was going into the fourth week now, and I knew I had been running up a big tab for Dan. Protestations to the contrary, I knew he was no longer flush, but he seemed determined to find her no matter the cost.

I had a good gut feeling about this place. It felt more like a hideout than a command center, like Hugo's other houses. Close to the border, he could make a quick getaway into Mexico if necessary. He probably didn't traffic anything through here either; too many eyes around. This stretch of border with Tijuana was the most heavily patrolled in the whole of the U.S. Skye would probably like it here, too. Of all Hugo's places, this was the only one on the beach; at least the only one that I knew of so far. I had gotten the sense that she really enjoyed her life on the beach, until she didn't. It was already the middle of the afternoon when I exited the 5 Freeway onto Coronado Boulevard and headed west towards Imperial Beach. I was starting to grow a little nervous. Once again, I was off, plunging into an unknown situation with no backup. This far south, I couldn't count on anyone coming to my aid for hours. But I pushed on.

The houses along Seacoast Drive were your typical California beach houses, mostly new or remodeled recently, spacious, luxurious, not unlike the houses in Manhattan or Hermosa Beach, a far cry from the old apartment buildings that lined the boardwalk in Tijuana. I crept along the street, looking at house numbers until I found the one I wanted. It was a two-story East Coast-style house with four carports facing the street under the second story. Three were empty, in the fourth was a newish yellow VW bug convertible with flower decals on the fenders. Above, on the wall, was the hand, a blue-painted carving of a hand with an eye in the palm.

My heart rate jumped a few percentage points. I parked behind the bug and got out. I took a few quick pictures of the car and the license plate. Then, as a last-minute precaution, I retrieved my gun and slipped it into my pocket. It felt heavy and awkward.

Opting not to knock on the door, I walked a few houses down and crossed on a beach access walkway to the ocean side of the houses and walked back. I took off my sandals and walked barefoot through the sand. I spotted her immediately. She was tending a little flower garden of yellow poppies and purple phlox that she had planted in the sand berm that fronted her house. She wore a pink and orange sun dress and a large straw hat on her long black hair. Dark sunglasses framed her tan face. Even tanner arms and bare feet and legs poked out from the thin dress that she wore.

"Maria Garcia?" I called out.

She stood up slowly, turned to me and stared for a long time without speaking. It became strangely quiet, just the crash of the surf and an occasional squawk from a passing seagull. Even the warm breeze seemed tranquillizing at that moment.

"Skye?" I called again, less loudly, taking a few steps forward.

Still no answer from her. I waited, not wanting to approach too quickly, unbidden. I felt like I was approaching a skittish doe.

"I've been expecting you." She finally replied. "Well, not you, but someone like you."

"My name is James Gardiner. I'm a private investigator. I've been hired to find you…"

"I know." She cut me off. We stared at each other for another moment or two.

"Can we talk?" I asked.

She smiled, tightly, with no friendliness. "Let's go inside. No need for the neighbors to watch."

I followed her into the house. Large sliding glass doors opened onto a family room and beyond that a big open kitchen with barstools surrounding an island counter. I took a seat as Skye crossed to the refrigerator and pulled out a pitcher of what turned out to be pre-made margaritas. Grabbing a pair of glasses, she poured us each a drink.

'Hugo may show up here at any time. He won't like seeing you."

"I won't be long. Believe me, I don't want to tangle with him. We've met a few times, and I've already been reprimanded several times by the Feds for squirreling their investigations of him. They'll probably throw the book at me if they find out I've been here."

"So why are you here?"

"I'm sure you must know. You said you were expecting me. After Dan saw you in the little red MGB, he hired me to find you."

"What does he want with me?"

"Seriously? He didn't say explicitly, but I'm sure he wants to see you. He's glad you're still alive. He probably also wants some answers."

"Actually, I was expecting Dan himself. I didn't think he'd hire a P.I. I mean, the clues were easy enough to follow. But then again, Dan was always the kind of guy who would hire someone long before thinking of doing it himself."

I almost spit out my drink. "Wait. Are you saying you planted clues for Dan to find you?"

"Did he really think that was just some lucky coincidence, me driving down the street a few blocks from his house? Dan is a creature of habit. He goes shopping at the same store at the same time on the same days of the week for as long as I've known him. I was parked on that street waiting for him to walk home. I drove up and stopped right in front of him for Christ's sake."

"Hmm. I had figured you'd just gone back to retrieve your Hand of Miriam from your old place, and that was the fastest route home. Well, I had to do some legwork, tracking down your car to the mechanic." I complained.

"An old car like that is always in the shop, and how many shops work on old English cars? Besides, Dan knew that shop. He'd taken my old bug there before when it broke down. Did Mike give me up? No. After you left, he called, and I told him to give you the address. At first, I thought it was Dan tracking me down, but when Hector said that some young guy had come nosing around the car, I realized he might have hired someone."

"Hector's the guy with the neck tattoos?"

"He's Hugo's younger brother, still lives with his mother. Neither of them knew what I was up to; they just didn't like unwanted attention. Anyway, I left an empty Amazon box in the car with this address on it. It's taken you two weeks to follow up?"

"I didn't get that. Hector was out busting my chops before I had a chance. I did manage to pick up a betting slip which led me to Hugo's house in Fullerton, though."

"Yeah. He was not happy about that. He thought Dan was ancient history."

"Not finding the easy clue, I had to interview anyone I could find that knew you, the palm reader, Pat the bartender, Howard, Sarah…"

"Yeah, I knew you'd talked to Sarah. We'd stayed in touch. I convinced Hugo to keep her after he bought the place. I owed her."

"She told me that story."

"But she was afraid of Hugo…and Howard. Wouldn't cooperate with my plan."

"So, what changed her mind?"

"I paid her a ten thou and told her to quit and leave California and never come back."

We sat for a few minutes in silence. The sliders were open, and a soft breeze ruffled the curtains. I could hear the surf crashing, rhythmically, punctuated by the occasional screech of a seagull. I watched her carefully as I drained my drink. She was nothing like I expected. She was calm, calculating. Maybe she wasn't expecting me, but she was expecting this meeting, just with Dan. She'd probably rehearsed the tale of the bread crumbs of clues she planted to lure him here. But for what reason? And what was next in her plan?

"Oh!" I remembered, digging around in my pants pocket, I pulled out the mood ring. "Dan wanted me to give you this." I set it on the counter.

"What's that?"

"Your ring. Dan said he had it made especially for you. A mood ring, I think he called it. He said it meant a lot to you, once."

"Cheap costume jewelry. It didn't even work." She picked up the ring briefly, looked it over, and then set it back on the counter. "Dan liked to encourage all that New Age crap with me. He thought it made me more childlike. It was my fault for playing along, but I hated that ring. It bugged me that he kept pushing it on me. Never wore it."

We settled into another silence.

"You know, we've met before," I commented at last.
Her eyebrows raised. "Really?"

"Eleven or twelve years ago. I used to come down to the beach to Dan's weekend soirees. I was still in high school at the time."

Skye got up to grab the pitcher and refilled our glasses. "I don't remember you. But then again, there were a lot of kids at those parties."

"I came down most every weekend with my friend, Jack. I was hot for this girl, Heather, who hung out there. That was my main motivation for coming."

"And how did that work out for you?"

"I thought it was going pretty well, up until the last weekend before Labor Day. Then it all came crashing down. Let's just say it was the most embarrassing day of my life."

Skye looked at my face seriously for a long moment, and then I saw the light come on.

"I remember you now."

I said nothing. I let the memory come back to her.

"I saw Heather come rushing out of the bedroom. Her top in one hand and the other covering her mouth as she was trying not to laugh. I had to see what was so funny, so I poked my head into the room. I saw you there, sitting on the bed, your shorts down around your ankles. You looked so devastated, like you were about to cry."

"I told myself later that that didn't count. That I was still a virgin." She smiled despite herself.

"But you made it all better," I added.

"I tried." She answered. "So, I was your first. Sex can be a two-edged sword. We all think it will be wonderful, always. But sometimes it can be a vicious weapon. I should know."

"But you survived."

Skye gave me a look. She wasn't sure she understood what I meant by that.

"Your daughter is in town. She came down to help look for you. Of course, she doesn't know what you look like, or has any information that would be at all useful."

"How did she know who you were or where to find you?" Skye interrupted.

"When I first took on this job, I went up to Santa Rosa to get a little background on you from your parents. Your mom wasn't very cooperative, but your daughter seemed to want to help if she could. I slipped her my card after your mother left."

"What's her name?"

"Summer."

"Another damn hippie name."

"She managed to scrounge together just enough money for a bus ticket and a few meals and showed up at my office with a grocery sack for a suitcase. I felt guilty that I somehow lured her down to LA, so I put her up in a hotel. In return, she regaled me with tales of the commune, including the story of how your father … well, and how your mother blamed you instead of him. I'm guessing that's what drove you away finally."

"I don't want to see her."

"Who?"

"Summer. Promise me that you will not tell her you found me. Tell her I'm dead or something. I am not her mother; I am just a story. She deserves better, not that she'll find it up there. I mean it, James, promise me you won't tell her."

"Okay. I promise."

I was so engrossed in my conversation with Skye that I didn't even see Hugo standing in the hallway.

Skye glanced back at him, not with alarm, but with a casual nonchalance of any woman when their man comes home for dinner.

"Well, we've talked to long and now it's too late to leave." She said. "It's Hugo's call what happens next."

She turned to him and slid off her barstool. "He has a gun in his pocket, mi querido."

Hugo didn't seem too concerned. His gun was in his hand.

"Hugo!" I said, forcing a smile. "Didn't expect to see you here."

He stared at me for the longest time. "Nice car."

"Yeah, I like it."

"Not very smart for a private investigator to drive, though. Stands out, easy to remember."

"True, true."

"Maybe when I'm done with you, I'll keep it."

"No need for that. If you really like it, I can sell it to you for a good price."

He fished in his pocket and pulled out my Titleist. "You left your golf ball at my house."

"You can keep that, too. I have plenty."

"What were you doing at my house? What did you steal from me?"

"I was there looking for the address for this house. I only took a piece of paper, your tax bill. I can send it back, but you don't need it, you can pay online."

As I talked, everything began moving in slow motion. I could hear my own heartbeat. My voice sounded like it was coming from the bottom of a well. Skye was putting the pitcher back in the fridge and washing up the glasses at the sink like I was just another neighbor who dropped in for a chat. I don't need to say that I was terrified. Why couldn't I be as calm as Robert Mitchum or Humphrey Bogart? Of course, those guys were on stages, surrounded by a film crew and facing guns with blanks.

My eyes drifted down to the mood ring on the counter. What was wrong with this scene? Why did Dan tell me that she loved the ring when she didn't? Something didn't add up. If it was just a cheap ring, why did it bug Skye so?

Hugo continued to stare, silently. He was not even pointing his gun at me - yet. My gun was still in my pocket, but it might as well have been at home for all the good it was doing me. I watched Skye turn on the radio and dial up the volume of the Mariachi music. I guess to drown out the sound of a gunshot. It was probably loud, but to my ears it didn't even drown out the throb of my own pulse.

Hugo started to raise his gun, level with my face.

"Punks like you never learn, do you?" He said calmly. His words were also slowed down and in a deep register, like a record or a tape played at the wrong speed.

I watched the gun settle, waited for the flash of fire from the muzzle, for the sound of the gunpowder bursting in the chamber. Can you even hear the shot of the bullet that kills you? I wondered.

It seemed like an eternity. I focused on his trigger finger, waiting for it to pull.

I didn't hear the shot. I noticed Hugo's head tilt up suddenly, and then a little burst of blood quirted from his temple. His head rocked slightly away and then settled back.

I snapped to at the sound of Skye's scream. I watch Hugo crumple to the ground, still holding the nine-millimeter in his hand. I turned around, looking behind me at the open sliding door. The curtains blew gently in, and the sound of the crashing waves and the noisy seagulls mingled with the blaring up-tempo music coming from the radio in the room.

Dan stepped in through the curtains, his forty-five held out before him. Satisfied that Hugo was dead, he lowered the gun to his side.

Skye's scream wasn't one of terror, but of surprise. In a moment, she had collected herself and resumed her calm but cold demeanor. She stood in the kitchen behind the island, watching Dan intently. She turned off the radio.

"You found me." She said. "Took you long enough."

"To be honest, James found you. I just followed him."

"Does my car really stand out that much?" I complained. "Where were you a half hour or more ago when I got here? Unless..." My gaze drifted back to the counter.

"You put a tracer in the ring."

"Where's Hector?" Skye interjected.

"He's in his car, but he's also dead."

Skye did not seem surprised. "That was a mistake. The Feds have this house under surveillance. At least on the outside. They'll have seen you kill Hector. They are probably on their way now."

"Look," I said. "You two probably have a lot to talk about. I'll just be going."

"You can't leave," Dan warned, waving his gun at me. "You're at the scene of a double homicide. They've got your car, if not you, on camera. You'll lose your license."

"I'm for sure going to lose it either way. I was warned not to come here."

"So now what? You plan to shoot your way out?"

"No. I knew this would be how things ended up when I came here. That's why I'm here. Skye wanted me to kill Hugo. I wasn't sure how exactly she was planning to arrange that, but it was what she wanted. She's probably also planning to take over Hugo's little business. Isn't that right, dear?" Dan turned to Skye, who hadn't moved. "But why did you have to do that to me?"

"You were never good to me, Dan. It was the only way I could get away from you. I knew they would never execute you, even if you were found guilty. You're a rich white man, that's about as privileged as they come."

"I could have spent the rest of my life in prison, though."

"I hated you, Dan. I thought you had it coming."

"I would have let you go. If your boyfriend wanted me out of the coke business, I would have let that go, too. I loved you, Skye."

"You don't love women. You just love to fuck them."

They said nothing to each other for a few minutes. My head was reeling.

"And now? Why this?"

"You're right. I needed Hugo out of the way. He was too stupid to run this business profitably, and too full of machismo to let me. This was the only way. Too bad about Hector. I liked him."

"You always were a cunning one."

"Well, if you're done killing people." I interrupted. "Maybe you should give me the gun." I stepped toward Dan.

Skye had been waiting for this distraction and pulled out a thirty -eight from behind the counter. Dan was too fast. He must have been practicing all these years. He turned like an old Western gunslinger and put a bullet between her eyes. Skye's gun went off, with the bullet crashing into the ceiling somewhere.

I was frozen in mid-step. Skye had dropped behind the counter where I couldn't see her body. But I believe that Dan could. He stared in that direction for a long time. I dared not move or say anything. Finally, he turned to me and handed me his gun. I hesitated taking it, quickly looked around, and finding a paper napkin, grabbed the gun by the barrel and set it on the counter.

In the distance, I could hear police sirens. As a precaution, I removed the gun from my pocket and set it on the counter as well. Dan went and sat in a large rattan chair and stared out at the ocean, watching the sun set and waiting for the law.

CHAPTER

TWENTY-SIX

It was a beautiful sunset. The orange-red sun dipping into the ocean mirrored the many police lights flashing around the house, inside and out. Before they arrived, I had managed to text Jack to go by the house and check in on Summer to let her know that I wouldn't be home for supper, and probably not for breakfast either. Dan had retreated into his own thoughts, resigned, I suppose, to the idea that the rest of his life was no longer his to control. The first to arrive were the local police. I hadn't heard the gunshot when Dan had killed Hector behind the house, but apparently, the neighbors did and called it in. I'm sure subsequent calls, after Hugo and Skye were dispatched, elevated the calls to a Code 3. In a short amount of time, the house was swarming with officers.

I tried to remain as calm and unthreatening as possible to avoid getting shot; still, I shortly ended up on my face, my hands cuffed behind me. I was okay with that. At least in that position, I wasn't going to be killed by a panicky rookie. As expected, I was grilled for hours, retelling my story to a number of different officers and detectives. Wilson showed up around ten that evening, and I got to do it all over again. Needless to say, he was not happy. True, three key players of one branch of his drug cartel were now off the streets, but he had been denied the accolades of bringing them in, as well as anyone else in the gang who would now scatter. My pal Lieutenant Mejia left a firehose stream of expletives on my phone, but I didn't get the pleasure of listening to them until much later.

Well past midnight, both Dan and I were bundled off to the station for further interviews. I don't know what Dan might have told them; we were kept apart. Around sunup, I was released with the proviso that I show up at Wilson's office the next day to write a full report of my entire investigation. He also promised me that my license would be suspended pending a hearing into my actions.

I caught an Uber back to Skye's house to collect my car, but decided that, having had no sleep, I was in no condition to drive the three hours back home. I checked into a motel and drove back in the afternoon.

I kept my promise to Skye. I told a long story about a fictitious case that kept me out all night. I told her that I was off the case now and no longer hunting for her mother. I confessed it had been three weeks of no results, and my client had decided that was enough. We ate dinner again at the neighborhood bistro. Summer was withdrawn, and I was tired, so the meal passed in silence for the most part.

The next morning, we drove to the office and I walked her down to the bus stop. I had snagged a photo from my files, the one of Skye with the straw hat on the beach, and gave it to Summer before she boarded the bus. It was a particularly attractive picture, one that showed Skye in her happier days. I knew that Summer would look lovingly at it all the bus ride home.

Coming in 2026!

Another James Gardiner

Mystery!

<u>LAKE</u>

<u>HOLLYWOOD</u>

With his license suspended, James fills his days training to run the L.A. Marathon. His favorite running course is around the reservoir near his home, Lake Hollywood. His daily workouts attract the attention of an aging movie star who now lives in seclusion in a mansion high above the lake. She reaches out, and thus begins a weekly afternoon tea. His budding friendship soon takes a turn when James begins to sense that all is not as it seems in the Land of Make-Believe.

www.ingramcontent.com/pod-product-compliance
Lightning Source LLC
Chambersburg PA
CBHW061947170626
46813CB00006B/2564